On the Inside

a novel

by Kim Cano

For my sister-in-law in prison.
You have not been forgotten, and you are loved.
I'll see you again someday... on the outside

Chapter 1

Reaching for a stack of incoming mail, Lakeisha spotted a greeting card, obvious because of its telltale shape and colorful envelope. She opened it and the song "Happy Birthday" began playing. A brief smile formed on her face, and then she let out a sigh. She picked up her letter opener, and with the skill of an artisan, pried the musical device out of the back of the card without ruining its cheerful appearance. After a quick scan of the card's seams for drugs, Lakeisha put it back in its envelope and sealed it with a single piece of tape.

She felt awful defacing the gift, but it was procedure. Inmates with nothing but time on their hands were notorious for taking little things like batteries and wiring and turning them into something dangerous. Musical cards simply weren't allowed.

Lakeisha had been in a hurry to make it to work, so she skipped breakfast. Luckily, Megan, the new prison psychologist, was just passing by with a box of donuts.

"Girl, how'd you know I'd be hungry?" Lakeisha asked.

"Because we're on the same page. Pretty much need to be jacked up on sugar to make it through a day here, right?"

Lakeisha smiled in agreement at the tall brunette. "Ain't that the truth."

Megan popped the lid open so Lakeisha could make a selection. After pulling out a chocolate glazed, Lakeisha thanked her, then took an ample-sized bite of her donut. As she savored her meal, she watched Megan walk away. She was a sweet kid, and she kind of felt bad for her. Gossip was this was the only mental health position she was offered after her recent graduation.

"Guess we all gotta start somewhere," she said out loud. She stared at her desk and had a sobering thought: the problem was sometimes you never left.

Before moving onto the next piece of mail, Lakeisha removed a napkin from her top drawer and carefully wiped her hands. As she pulled the letter out, a photograph spilled onto her desk, a glossy shot of an out-of-shape, heavily tattooed naked white man.

Lakeisha shook her head in disgust, then mumbled, "I didn't need to see that while I was eating."

Not only was it gross, X-rated photos weren't allowed. Now she had to set it aside and fill out an "unauthorized" form. "Always something," she muttered. After completing the form, Lakeisha proceeded to scan every fold and seam for drugs. Seeing none, she put the letter back in its envelope and set it aside.

Prisoners knew she had the right to read everything they wrote. Sometimes folks on the outside were aware of this too, but Lakeisha didn't have time to read all the mail. Her job was to process it and make sure it was free of contraband. With five hundred pieces going through her hands each day, and a thousand during the holidays, she didn't have time to read every word.

But there was some correspondence Lakeisha never missed, a few prisoners whose stories she followed closely. As she learned the details of their lives through the incoming and outgoing mail, it was like a soap opera. With each letter, she was always left wondering what would happen next.

Long ago, Lakeisha had learned not to get close to any of the inmates, to keep her distance. She wasn't allowed to show any form of favoritism. That was against the rules, so she kept her little mail soap operas a secret. The inmates' stories were just a little indulgence to make her job more bearable. Plus, even though she knew they were criminals, some having committed truly despicable acts, they were still people. They had dreams once. And as she delivered the mail to them each day, she often wondered what those dreams looked like. How different were those dreams today?

After a short bathroom break, Lakeisha moved onto the second pile of incoming mail. The return address on one envelope in particular caught her attention.

It was from Kristen's husband Jeremy, the one who hadn't written or visited in three long years, even though she wrote him every week without fail. Lakeisha always read Kristen's correspondence. Anxious to see what he had to say, she ripped open the envelope.

Kristen,
    I've been getting your letters. I haven't written back

because every time I try it always comes out the same way, with me cursing at you, so I give up and toss the pen and paper aside.

My sister suggested I just write what I feel, no matter what it is. That some communication is better than nothing. So, based on her advice, I'm going to say what I've been dying to say for a long time.

You've ruined my life, Kristen, in every way a life can be ruined. And worse, you've hurt the kids. They're suffering without their mother. All because for you it was never enough. You always had to have more. Even if it meant stealing to get it.

I've lost a lot of friends because of what happened, and some good clients will no longer work with me. Because of that and a bad economy and trying to survive on a single income, now the house is gone. I had to rent a small, two-bedroom apartment and am sleeping on an airbed in the family room that I blow up each night and deflate each morning. I do that so the kids can each have their own bedroom, so they won't feel like anything in their lives has changed.

But who am I kidding? Your goddamn mugshot was in the newspaper. People contacted me and asked, "Is that your wife?"

Ryan and Toby were bullied at school once the story spread too. They still struggle to sleep at night, and their grades have suffered.

As if that weren't enough, finding that shit on the computer after you were arrested, when I stood by your side after you got fired. That hurt the most. I

hung in there through the drinking, then came to grips
that you committed white collar crime. But I drew the
line when I discovered you cheating behind my back.
Seriously, why the fuck do you continue to write
me?

Jeremy

Lakeisha slowly refolded the letter and put it back in
its envelope. She felt bad for Jeremy and the kids. Their
side of the story was heartbreaking. But she also had a
soft spot for Kristen, a model prisoner who seemed to be
a genuinely nice human being.

Delivering the mail was usually something that made
Lakeisha happy, as she knew it often was the only bright
spot in a prisoner's day. She dreaded today's trip.

When quitting time came, and Megan stopped by to
say goodnight, Lakeisha was relieved. Maybe Kristen had
taken the news better than expected. She assumed Megan
would've had to make room in her schedule to handle an
inmate's nervous breakdown.

*****

Kristen was thrilled to receive a letter from Jeremy. Once
she tore it open and read it, her spirit deflated.

She had put him through a lot. He had stayed by her
side, dealing with her constant drama. Like the night
Toby and Ryan had noticed her stumbling out the front
door holding car keys in one hand and a bottle of wine in
the other. Fearful she might drive off and kill someone or

hurt herself, Ryan ran out and tried to take the keys from her, but she pushed him to the ground. When he landed, he'd smacked his hand hard on a stone garden gnome and cried out in pain.

Toby saw blood on his older brother's hand and grabbed the phone to call 911. He'd tried his best to speak to the operator, but his mom was making such a ruckus in the background he could barely hear. Instead of helping her son up, she was screaming expletives at the top of her lungs. She whipped the bottle of wine at the side of the house, staining the white stucco red and sending glass shards flying everywhere. The grand finale was when the cops showed up, and she began mouthing off to them just as Jeremy pulled in from a long day at work.

Of course, she didn't remember any of this at all. But her family sure did. And they never let her forget it.

They'd been keen to bring up the pasta incident too. Jeremy kept texting her, asking where she was, and saying the kids were hungry and wanted to eat. He'd worked all day and made dinner, but everyone was waiting for her to return before eating. When Kristen eventually showed up, she was wasted. She stumbled into the house and to the kitchen table. After she sat down, her face fell into her dinner plate.

With unusual calm, Ryan rose and wiped spaghetti noodles and sauce off his mom's cheeks as Jeremy held her limp body. Then they carried her off to bed and made sure to position her on her side in case she vomited in her sleep.

There had been many nights like that one. Most of which Kristen only learned about in embarrassed retrospect. When she first started stealing, she hadn't been drinking much, but then the stress of keeping secrets and telling lies led her to drink more and more each day. That's how she finally got caught. She took it too far, lost focus in her alcoholic haze, and her scheme unraveled.

Even then, Jeremy had stayed. He said they'd figure out how to fix things. He thought they could find a way to raise money to pay back what she'd stolen. He'd been under the impression it was eighty thousand dollars, a large sum but not impossible to obtain. Maybe they could sell the house and use the equity. Maybe it didn't have to go to court.

The truth came out after the arrest. Kristen had stolen almost half a million dollars from her employer, a family-run construction company, over the course of five years. She'd been their controller.

Jeremy and his sons had watched as the police arrested Kristen. The neighbors had seen it too but turned their eyes away, not wanting to get involved. After Jeremy had come to grips with losing his wife of twenty years and the betrayal of being lied to about the actual dollar amount taken, he found the emails.

"Where you been, baby?" the man had written. "I miss you."

Kristen responded, "I'm stuck here with you know who. Wish I could be in your arms. I'll see you soon."

Tears filled Jeremy's eyes as he read the emails. It was

clear he'd been a greater fool than he first thought.

After taking a long walk around the block, Jeremy decided to contact the police. Maybe this boyfriend knew where the majority of the money was because he couldn't figure out where a sum that large could have gone.

And he didn't want to think about it anymore. All he wanted was for her to be out of his mind and heart forever.

Kristen sat on her bunk, thinking of all she'd done and felt sick.

She was forty-five-years-old and had been sentenced to seventeen years in prison. She'd chosen "no restitution" because there was no money left to pay back. All that remained was a mountain of evidence in the form of a second set of books they'd found hidden in the ceiling tiles, and Italian owners who'd felt angered and betrayed by someone they'd once considered family.

She was lucky they hadn't killed her.

The more she thought of it, the more she wished they had. She'd been in prison for three years already and couldn't figure out how she'd make it through. She would have been better off as alligator food in the Everglades. What was there left to live for?

After lights out, the sound of Kristen's anguished cries filled the quiet prison, a deep, guttural wail from the depths of her very being.

Chapter 2

The sound of hurried footsteps echoed and became louder as two prison guards approached Kristen's cell. When the door swung open, she cried out, "Nooooo! Leave me alone!"

"We can't have you screaming at the top of your lungs," one of the guards said. "You wanna cause a riot?"

"I want to be left alone!" Kristen shouted. "Go away!"

Clearly tired of her antics, the larger of the two corrections officers lurched forward and grabbed hold of her. Kristen thrashed around and wouldn't cooperate, so the second guard wrestled her to the ground and cuffed her.

"Let me go!" Kristen screamed. "I want to go home!"

"That ain't gonna happen anytime soon. Get up. Let's go!" the guard said as she yanked her.

Kristen was small but stubborn as a bull when she wanted to be, and she continued fighting them. She had to be dragged against her will.

Once at the infirmary, the nurse on duty stuck a needle into Kristen's arm, and soon her deep sobs and shudders were quieted. After she fell asleep, the guards removed her cuffs and dimmed the lights.

Kristen's dreams were montage-like that evening, a jumble of childhood memories popping up in no particular order.

One was of the time she was a tree in the school play, doing her part to stand very still as the other cast members danced around her. Holiday music filled the air, and her eyes searched the audience for her parents but didn't find them.

Another was of the day she came home from school with an "A" on her book report, anxious to share the news. When she walked in, she found her parents fighting; her mom screaming with slurred words and her dad storming off, slamming the bedroom door behind him.

The dreams were a subconscious trip down memory lane, where Kristen was reminded of how she wanted nothing more than to be noticed by her parents—to be loved by them—and having grown up never hearing the words spoken to her.

She woke to the sound of paper shuffling. She rolled onto her side and saw Megan.

Kristen rubbed her eyes. Her head throbbed like a jackhammer was pounding it from the inside. "Hi," she said in a groggy tone.

"Good morning," Megan replied. "I took the liberty of bringing breakfast in case you're hungry."

Kristen sat up, noticing her body felt sore all over. "Thank you."

Kristen felt oddly comfortable around Megan. Maybe because she treated her like a human being, or like a patient at a high-priced therapist's office. In Megan's care, things seemed civilized, unlike the rest of the place.

"Heard you had a rough night," Megan said.

Kristen stared at the floor, wanting to do anything but talk about what had happened. She took a bite of food. "You could say that," she replied while rubbing her head.

"Do you have a headache right now?"

"Do I ever."

"Let me get you something to help take care of it." Megan rose and reached into a nearby cabinet, and handed Kristen two aspirin. "Probably best to eat a bit more first. They can be hard on the stomach."

Kristen made eye contact with Megan. "Thanks."

As Kristen munched on her tasteless prison breakfast and took a sip of black coffee, Megan busied herself with paperwork. Kristen knew her routine. She waited for you to speak first. Megan never pushed the conversation.

Exhausted, Kristen laid back down. "I got a letter from Jeremy," she eventually said.

Megan nodded, a pragmatic expression on her face. "I see. That must have been a surprise. I know how much you hoped to hear from him."

Kristen sighed. "Be careful what you wish for, right? Isn't that the saying?"

"It is. So why don't you tell me about the letter."

Kristen crossed her hands on top of her abdomen and stared at the ceiling tile. "He read me the riot act. He didn't hold back on anything he was feeling. For a guy who's bad at writing letters, he hit a home run on this one."

"He's finally talking to you. That was what you said you wanted."

"Yeah. But not like this. He told me how angry he still is, even after all these years, and that I ruined their lives."

Megan nodded and looked to be waiting for Kristen to continue.

Kristen spoke the words she already knew were true. "I mean, I know I ruined their lives. I know I screwed up bad, but I had hoped with time they might come around."

"They meaning Jeremy?"

"Jeremy or the kids, somebody. I haven't had a visitor since I've been here. Crack dealer low-lifes and prostitutes get visitors here, but I don't. No one writes, either."

"What about Jeremy's sister-in-law Olivia? I thought she wrote you?" Megan asked.

Kristen sighed. "Yes, she writes. And for that, I'm grateful, of course, but I mean my family. I don't get birthday cards, Christmas cards, nothing. It's like I don't exist."

Megan leaned forward and held Kristen's gaze. "People deal with things that are painful in different ways. Some have odd coping mechanisms. I know it's hard."

"Jeremy asked why I write him. Doesn't he get that I love him? Why else would I write? He's my husband."

Megan opened her mouth to speak, but Kristen spoke first. "And am I supposed to stop writing my kids just because he's angry? They're my kids too!"

Nodding, Megan said, "That's true. They are your kids, and it doesn't sound like he asked you to stop writing them. I guess all you can do is continue to reach out to them and hope they respond one day."

Feeling defeated, Kristen repeated the words. "One day," then went silent. She had already been here for years and was required to do at least eighty-five percent of her sentence. She should've listened to the public defender when he told her she needed a better lawyer to take on the hotshot attorneys he was up against. He suggested she call her parents and ask them for help. They had money, but she'd rather die than rely on them.

Grand theft in the first degree. She'd been given more time than some murderers. And there was nothing she could do about it. She was guilty. Sure, some time could be knocked off here and there for good behavior, but when it came down to it, she'd have to survive another decade in prison.

An eternity.

When Kristen looked up, she noticed Megan seemed concerned. That was her job, wasn't it?

"I guess I'll keep writing. I have nothing left to lose."

"Sounds like a plan. And in the meantime, I'll see you again soon."

*****

Kristen slept the rest of the day. She was thankful to be alone for once, as her cellie had recently been released, and she hadn't yet been assigned a new one. Most of the women liked having a friend to chat with, someone to share their time with, but Kristen preferred solitude. In her life before, when friends and family gathered around, talking and telling stories, she would often disappear into herself. She would laugh and smile along with them, but it often seemed she was hovering around the edges of the conversation rather than interacting.

Olivia had rightly noted that they'd grown closer through their letters than they were in the almost two decades before her incarceration. Kristen was hard to get to know. It's not that she had lived a boring life. There were lots of interesting things about Kristen worthy of conversation. Like having lived in another country as a child. But Kristen acted as if these things were no big deal, playing down the events most people would have enjoyed hearing about.

Not only did she prefer to not talk about herself, she didn't often look others in the eye. Kristen had a tendency to look away while chatting, focusing her attention elsewhere. It happened enough to be noticeable. No one spoke to her about it, of course, but it contributed to the general sense of disconnection. She kept people at bay, and they weren't able to truly get close to her.

She hadn't even been close to the man she'd had an affair with. He just was someone who gave her attention when her world was crumbling and made her feel nice for a little while. A brief escape from the unforgiving reality she knew was on its way.

He never knew she stole money. She told him she had her own business. And at the rate she dropped cash, it must have looked to be a successful one. He also never knew she had a family that cared about her. She'd given him the impression she and her husband didn't sleep in the same room anymore, that they only stayed together for the kids. Since he was much younger than Kristen, and she was insistent about her desire for him, he fell for it. He was naïve and liked to party. He enjoyed drinking and didn't get on her case about doing it. And he complimented her all the time.

It was true her marriage to Jeremy was strained. But that was mostly on her. Her boozing and lies pressed a wedge between them that ate away at any romance. She'd only had the affair to feel loved again, to be touched before they locked her away for God knew how long.

The worst part was he wasn't very good in bed. She'd risked it all for a roll in the hay, and this was the thing Jeremy couldn't get over. Because of her affair, he wouldn't have anything more to do with her.

Kristen wished she could go back in time and at least undo that last mistake. Would she still have her family in her life if she hadn't done that? Would they at least be visiting her? She didn't know. She just knew her life sucked, and she had no one to blame but herself.

That evening, Kristen chose to skip dinner and eat in her cell, making a meal out of her meager stash from Canteen. She munched on Doritos and warm Sprite. The soda would've tasted better cold. Once again, she was amazed at how much she had taken for granted.

Life was like that, she decided. You never knew what you had until it was gone.

Chapter 3

The next day at rec time, Kristen sat alone on a bench. The women who usually hung out with her kept their distance. When someone freaked out and had to be hauled off to see Megan, it was like they had the plague for a while. No one wanted to go near that person for fear they'd catch the disease.

Kristen didn't mind. She enjoyed the solitude outside, too, inhaling the fresh air, feeling the warmth of the sun on her skin. It reminded her of family trips to the beach, Ryan and Toby collecting shells and building sandcastles, and the sound of pelicans chirping in the distance. She loved listening to the ocean surf while watching the white, puffy clouds drift overhead on their slow-motion journey through the heavens.

"Bitch, I said don't touch me," Lupe yelled.

Kristen squinted to see what was going on, lifting her hand to her forehead to block the sun.

Jess mouthed back. "I ain't touchin' you. I'm picking up my basketball and accidentally bumped you."

Lupe, a young, attractive Mexican girl, wasn't to be messed with. Not because she was the toughest, but because she had clout. Her body was tattooed with gang symbols, and her locker was filled with goodies from

Canteen. She was a drug dealer on the outside and had no patience for Jess' personality quirks.

"I'll let you bump into me on accident, but you best be keeping your lesbian hands to yourself," Lupe added.

Jess picked up her ball and gave Lupe a hard look, then spit on the ground before walking away. She looked pissed but probably knew there was nothing she could do about it. She might be a tough girl who looked like a guy, but her only crime on the outside was beating another woman within an inch of her life because she found her in bed with her girlfriend. A domestic dispute gone bad.

Compared to Lupe, she was peanuts. And she knew it.

"Ladies. I think you better take it easy," one of the officers said.

The physical distance between Jess and Lupe grew as they dispersed, but the air between them remained thick with dislike. It surprised Kristen they'd never actually gotten into a fight because she had gotten into one with Jess shortly after her arrival. She remembered it all too well.

After being sentenced and transferred, Kristen was petrified. Her time in the local jail was scary enough. That had been a musty place with cockroaches the size of salt shakers. To make matters worse, they flew! The walls had shit smeared on them. For the life of her, Kristen couldn't figure out how that had happened. All she wanted was to go home. She had a beautiful three-bedroom townhome with a screened-in porch and an in-ground swimming pool. She'd cried to Jeremy on the phone to help her, but he couldn't. She found it ironic that despite all the money she'd stolen, they didn't have enough money to hire a decent attorney. Her parents, who had the means, didn't offer to help.

Kristen quickly learned to exercise and build the muscles on her one hundred and ten pound frame. Looking like a model was great in the real world, not so good behind bars. She'd heard the phrase "gay for the stay" and made a decision that was not happening to her. She'd die first. The first year of pushups, running, and sit-ups paid off. When she arrived at the women's prison to serve the rest of her sentence, trouble was waiting for her.

Right off the bat, Jess had gotten the idea Kristen was going to be hers. She'd even beaten the crap out of another girl who thought she had dibs. But to Jess' surprise, Kristen wasn't having any of it. Her repeated flirtations had fallen on deaf ears, until one day, Jess decided to get aggressive and just take what she wanted.

Jess jumped Kristen from behind and, in an instant, was on top of her. She held her arms down and began salaciously licking her neck. "That's what you been missing, baby," Jess whispered in her ear.

A surge of adrenaline coursed through Kristen, and like a Barbie doll with superpowers, she threw Jess off her and leapt back to her feet. "Don't you ever fucking touch me! Do you understand? I will kill you."

Jess stood with her jaw hanging open. Kristen figured because she'd only committed a white-collar crime, Jess had pegged her as a pushover. Instead, she learned that Kristen had spunk. Jess looked more than a little self-conscious after she'd been so dramatically rejected.

"Why you gotta be so serious? I was just playing," she said.

Terrified, but not letting it show, Kristen continued to stare her down in silence. Her resolution was made firm as Jess turned and finally walked away. The others regarded the newcomer, and Kristen could see something change in their eyes. It was like she'd attained a new level of respect.

She was one of them now.

*****

Kristen watched the current episode with interest. She didn't particularly advocate violence or enjoy fighting, but if she was honest with herself, she'd have liked nothing more than to see Lupe knock Jess flat on her ass.

It wouldn't happen like that, though. Lupe didn't like to get her hands dirty. She didn't have to. There were plenty of inmates who didn't have much, who enjoyed the "gifts" she'd bestow on them from Canteen. Big, strong, hungry women could be a wonderful asset. They'd strangle someone for a candy bar or can of soda.

Kristen liked Lupe. They hadn't spoken much, but she had a way about her. She wouldn't mind having someone like her as a friend and on her side.

A buzzer rang, signaling it was time to go back in. Perhaps she'd get to watch them brawl another time.

That night, Kristen thought about the past. The first time she stole was just to cover a late car payment. She told herself she would pay it back. But she never did.

Then it was Christmas, and she hadn't saved enough for gifts, so she took a little more. No one noticed, but she still convinced herself she'd pay everything back once she got caught up on bills.

During the holidays, the owners weren't as generous as they had been the prior year, but they still managed to take their annual vacation to Hawaii. Kristen was irked. They could easily afford to give her a larger bonus, but they didn't. After that, she decided she wouldn't pay them back, and she continued to take more.

The rush of getting away with it made her feel alive. She'd been added to VIP lists at all her favorite stores at the mall and was treated with respect when she went shopping. The wine of the month club and trips to the spa for facials, Botox injections, and constant pampering were quickly adding up, and she had to create a second set of books to keep track of things.

She'd always enjoyed drinking, but now she was a connoisseur who ordered specialty wines and offered what she believed was particularly valuable feedback in return. Jeremy had expressed concern over how much she was consuming, but she assured him she had it under control. His concern conveniently abated after they bought the big-screen TV he'd always wanted. How lucky she got a bonus and worked for such great employers, he'd said.

Jeremy owned his own car detailing business and did the majority of the physical labor himself. Whenever he tried to hire someone to expand, customers would complain that they preferred his work to theirs. He was, after all, a perfectionist. So he kept his business small. When he came home, he was exhausted. He was thankful that Kristen was so good with paperwork and bills and willing to handle the finances because he didn't like dealing with that stuff.

Kristen sat on her bunk and sighed. Jeremy was a good man. Not perfect. No one was, but he was good. He deserved to have been treated better.

After reaching for a sheet of notebook paper and a pen, she began writing him a letter.

Jeremy,

I wish I could go back in time knowing what I know now and change things. I would have done everything differently. I never meant to hurt you or the kids. You're my life. But I know that's what I've done. I can never fully express how sorry I am.

You were a good husband. I hope one day you will forgive me. I pray when I get out, you will give me another chance. Even if it's just to be your friend. We'll be old then. I'll be almost sixty, and you'll be sixty-five. The kids will be adults.

I'm sad I am missing out on their lives. Will you please ask them to write me? I'm still their mother.

Kristen

*****

The next afternoon, Lakeisha was going through the outgoing mail and saw the letter. After reading it and getting it ready for delivery, she wondered what would happen. It seemed unlikely she'd end up getting her wish, but when a person was locked up for as long as she was, it was good to have something to hope for.

This got her thinking about her own life. She'd majored in English and hoped to get a job in book publishing as an editor or proofreader. She had been willing to start at the bottom as an intern and work her way up, do whatever it took, but after graduation, she didn't have any luck. She was passed over for every position she applied to. Reading prison mail wasn't exactly what she'd had in mind when she envisioned a literary career, but the pay was decent, and the benefits were good. And since she and her husband were trying to get pregnant, she figured it was as good a day job as any.

But there was one thing Lakeisha didn't like about her job: when women who'd been released committed another crime and got sent back to prison. A surprising number, fifty percent of offenders, ended up back in the slammer. The lure of the old lifestyle, combined with the very unlikely chance of getting a job, prompted many convicted felons to do something illegal in order to survive. It was a vicious cycle that no one seemed to know how to fix.

And there was always the issue of not being comfortable back on the outside. For better or worse, fellow inmates became a prisoner's new family after their original one moved on. They felt safer in the presence of other inmates, where they knew their place in the small, tight-knit society. Lakeisha had heard more than a few stories about women purposely doing something wrong after release so they would be sent back. So they could go "home."

She hated when that was the case. Lakeisha wished each one would leave empowered and start life anew, finding whatever it was they wanted to do or become and forging a path in that direction.

She hoped to never see any of them again.

Chapter 4

Jess arrived right on time for her appointment with Megan. No one dragged her there against her will, but it wasn't something she looked forward to either. The only reason she kept going was because she knew someone who had luck with counseling, and she hoped to get fixed too. Lord knew she had enough on her mind.

Seated in her chair instead of lying down, Jess hunched forward, with her hands balled together in her lap. She tried to relax, but it was difficult. She didn't care for authority figures much.

"So why don't you tell me what's been going on? How are you feeling?" Megan asked.

Jess tsked and said, "I'm angry as usual."

Megan paused. "Would you like to tell me why? What's on your mind?"

Jess leaned back and crossed her arms in front of her chest. "It's Rachel. She's still with that woman."

"You mean the woman you found her with?"

"Yeah."

Jess gazed off into the distance, thinking about the day it happened. She'd come home early from work and found Rachel in bed with another woman. She saw red and grabbed the stranger by the hair. "You think you can touch my girlfriend and live!" she'd yelled.

Rachel stood naked, screaming in the background as the sound of Jess' fists repeatedly slammed into the young lady's face. Blood frothed from her mouth and began spilling on the carpet, along with several of her front teeth, until she was knocked unconscious.

"It's still causing you to feel anger?" Megan asked cautiously.

Jess returned to the present. "Uh-huh," she said. "I know I should let it go. Beating her up only guaranteed they'd end up staying together. It's just at that moment. I couldn't think straight, you know."

Megan nodded, then cleared her throat. "I think the focus here is to learn how to control your anger before it turns to rage. I know that's a challenge, but if we can figure that out, your life will improve a lot."

Jess uncrossed her arms and propped them on her knees, resting her head in her hands. Looking at the ground, she said, "Rachel is gone, and I'm here. How's my life gonna get better?"

"Well, if you can learn to control your emotions better, your interactions with others will improve. You may or may not get Rachel back, but when you get out, you'll be prepared to have a healthy relationship."

Jess let out a deep sigh and ran her fingers through her short brown hair. She wasn't ready to accept that she and Rachel might never have another chance. Already exhausted by their short visit, she glanced at Megan. "I guess you're right. I just don't know how to do that. I thought Rachel and I were good, you know. I never saw it coming."

"She should have broken it off with you first. That's true. But sometimes, people don't behave as they should, and we have to be prepared to deal with it in a manner that doesn't negatively affect us. If, for instance, you had handled the situation by having an argument and storming off, which would be expected, it might be possible you could have worked things out later on. Or you might have thought about it some more and decided you didn't really want to. But you don't have that luxury now."

"No shit. Tell me something I don't know."

There was a pause, and Megan started again. "How about this? Let me ask you a question. What attracts you to a person? How should they treat you?"

Jess shrugged. "Nice, I guess."

"Be more specific. Describe nice."

Jess concentrated and said, "I'd want to know they love me, and not just with their words. I'd want their actions to show it too."

"What actions would you like to see?" Megan asked.

"Well, I'd like to have them do little things to make me happy and make me feel special. And I don't want to have to chase after them."

"And why do you feel you have to chase them?" Megan asked.

"I don't know. It's just how it's always been. I want them so bad, and I don't have patience."

Megan paused. "And what do you think would happen

if you didn't chase the next person, if you let things unfold at a natural pace? What if you treated them the way you want to be treated? Do you think they would like that?"

Jess smiled, exposing her crooked teeth, and her face lit up. "Yeah. I think they would."

"And what happens if they make you upset?" Megan asked.

Jess grinned. She knew the answer to this one. They'd been discussing it the last few visits. "I take a deep breath and count to ten."

"Right on," Megan said, then high-fived her.

Jess kept smiling. These psych visits weren't so terrible after all, she thought.

*****

Dinner was another forgettable meal. As Kristen accepted her "mystery meat," mashed potatoes, and soggy green beans, she thought about all the nice dinners she'd eaten before. Jeremy had been a great cook, the "grill master" as he liked to be called, but they'd eat out a few times per week too. Not always someplace fancy, although she had fond memories of those evenings.

There was a Brazilian restaurant she liked near the house, and she'd always order a grilled meat dish called churrasco and a glass of Pinot noir. Or maybe it was a bottle of Pinot. Either way, she would give anything to have a bite of steak right now. Her sister-in-law, Olivia, had never told her where she'd gone out to eat, editing that part out from her letters so as not to make Kristen feel bad. But when Kristen repeatedly asked what restaurants she'd frequented, Olivia finally obliged.

The silly details of a "you pick two" combo at Panera or a dark chocolate raspberry shake from Godiva meant a lot to Kristen. They reminded her that life was still good somewhere and gave her hope that one day she might have a chance to live in the real world again. Unlike the fifty percent who screwed up, either by accident or on purpose, there was no chance she would follow in their shoes. She couldn't wait to leave prison and go home.

"How much stretchin' you gotta do to work this shit off?" a fellow inmate Kristen hardly knew asked, then sat down next to her.

"I don't know if it's possible to rid one's system of this toxic poison," Kristen replied. "You'd probably need an herbal cleanse."

Her new friend looked confused. "I don't know what you talking about, girl."

Kristen raised an eyebrow. "You know, from the health food store."

Her dinner mate laughed. "The health food store, yoga. That ain't my thing. Seen you doin' it out on the yard, though. Why you like it so much?"

Kristen paused. "Actually, I do Pilates. It strengthens the muscles and stretches them at the same time. When I'm done, it's almost like I've had a massage. Then I still like to run and lift some weights."

"All right. I feel ya. Maybe tomorrow I'll come by, and you can show me how to do it?"

Perking up, Kristen replied, "Sure. I'd love to."

On her way back to her cell, Kristen thought back to her Pilates class, her spinning class, and the kettlebells workouts. The studio she used to go to was tranquil and clean, in a nice part of town. Everyone who attended was polished and fit. She could recreate a fitness routine here, maybe, but polished wasn't ever going to happen.

The following day on the yard, the young woman showed up to work out with Kristen. Another girl joined in too, and she showed them some beginner Pilates moves. They started with a Spine Stretch Forward and moved on to the Saw and the Mermaid. A little bit of a challenge without a mat, but they were tough girls. They'd manage.

Kristen saw Jess playing basketball nearby. She seemed to be watching their small group laughing and having fun. She and Jess hadn't spoken since "the incident," and although it looked like Jess was interested in joining them, she continued shooting hoops.

Maybe if she hadn't been such an ass, they could have been friends.

*****

The next morning, Lakeisha was tired when she arrived at work. She and her husband had enjoyed a date night and then decided to watch a scary movie. Unfazed, he passed out in the middle of it, but poor Lakeisha was terrified. Like a small child, she wanted him to wake up and walk her to the bathroom. Instead, she did the brave thing and headed there by herself. But it had been a fitful sleep, and now at her desk, the exhaustion set in. She hoped to plow through all her incoming and outgoing and just make it through the day.

As she sorted outgoing, she was surprised to see a letter from Jess. She didn't usually write people.

Rachel,

Just wanted to say hi. And to tell you I'm sorry about what happened. I lost it, you know. I shouldn't have done that to her. It was wrong.

What you did to me was wrong too. I treated you well and gave you everything I had. If there was something missing that you wanted, all you had to do was ask, and I would've done everything in my power to give it to you. If I wasn't able to make you happy, you could've told me. You could've let me know. You didn't have to go behind my back like that.

I'm not blaming you for what happened. That was me, unable to control my rage. I'm just saying it didn't have to get that far if you had been honest with me. You could've done that.

Anyway, I'm not one for writing. Just wanted to say that. I heard you two are still together. Hope you're happy and things work out.

Goodbye,

Jess

Folding the letter back up and putting it in its envelope, Lakeisha felt noticeably more awake. She hadn't cared for Jess much, but the letter had given her a better appreciation for what took place on both sides of the fence. It was just another reason she indulged in her stories. Better than watching her favorite old soap opera, *As the World Turns*. Sadly, after a long run, that show was canceled. This one would continue for as long as she was employed here.

At quitting time, Megan stopped by.

"What plans does Ms. Megan have for tonight?" Lakeisha asked.

"Oh, you know. A little of this. A little of that."

"So no date then. What happened to what's his name?"

Megan shrugged. "He's around. He's just too needy. I have a lot of work to do, even when I get home. Research."

Lakeisha laughed and shook her head. Megan devoted so much of her time to helping others she forgot to have a life herself.

Chapter 5

A few weeks later, there was buzz over visitations. The hot-looking guy in the photo Lupe kept over her bed—her boyfriend—had come to visit. According to the others who'd had visitors that day, his picture didn't do him justice. Word spread, and by dinnertime, Lupe had gone from a powerful figure to something of a celebrity. If she wasn't a criminal, she'd make a great movie star, with paparazzi trailing her every move.

Kristen brought her tray of food over to Lupe's table and sat opposite her. They didn't eat together often, but Lupe didn't seem to have a problem with the attention. And since not much happened in their world, it would likely continue for weeks, with the story growing and expanding. It wouldn't be long before rumors of them enjoying conjugal visits passed through the halls. Of course, that would be untrue, but embellishments weren't frowned upon—they were welcomed. Everyone would have loved to have been in Lupe's shoes. Well, almost everyone.

"Someone is having a great day," Kristen said to Lupe.

"You heard, huh."

"Who hasn't." Kristen smiled.

Lupe visibly puffed up. "Yeah. It's been a while since

he's come to see me. Writes all the time, telling me how much he misses me, what he's gonna do to me when I get home."

Kristen had pushed those thoughts from her mind long ago. There was no point in entertaining them while she had forever to make it through, but the mention sparked an instinctive interest. "I'll bet you can't wait to get back to him. The girls are saying he's an Enrique Iglesias look-alike."

"He's better looking than that, but he's no singer. Can't hold a tune to save his life."

Kristen giggled. "How much longer do you have?" she asked, then took a bite of food.

"Six months."

Kristen was glad for Lupe, but inside, her heart was breaking. She had an eternity left in comparison. She hid her sorrow by holding a smile in place. "That's great. I'm so happy for you," she said.

"You're gonna make it too. Keep your chin up," Lupe replied. Her compassionate words took Kristen by surprise. Lupe wasn't known for saying such things.

Tears filled Kristen's eyes, but she willed them to stop.

Lupe must have noticed the glassy cast. "I know just what you need. Chocolate. You like Snickers?"

Kristen smiled again. "I love Snickers."

"Good. I'll get you one of mine and give it to you later."

With that said, Lupe got up and walked away, her legacy continuing. Everywhere she went, she was larger than life. Magnanimous. Combined with her beauty,

Kristen could see why she had such a gorgeous boyfriend. She'd almost have to.

Later that day, while munching on the delicious candy bar, mail arrived.

"Something for you," Lakeisha said to Kristen.

Kristen reached for the envelope and said thanks.

It was from Olivia.

Kristen,

Hey. How have you been? Crazy busy here. Cocoa had some tooth problems again, so she's off to the cat doctor. I'm afraid to find out how much that's going to cost… Yikes!

Heard my brother finally wrote you and that he expressed himself with flair. FYI—he read it to me first and asked my opinion. I told him whatever he had to say was appropriate to write. He kept looking for my input, but you know me. I don't want to put words in someone's mouth.

Are you doing okay? I worry about you.

Hey, remember that time we were all at the restaurant, and those guys were making vulgar gestures at you? How could you forget, right? Anyway, we were just talking about that again. Laughing about how low-key Bob always is and how he shocked us by standing up and confronting them. I'll never forget him yelling across the room, asking them to please keep their ridiculous expressions to themselves, and saying that we were a family out to eat and wanted to be left alone. When they looked stunned and tried to play innocent, he said, "Really? Do you think she's just going to get up and walk away from her family and take off with you? Why don't you mind your own business and eat your fucking dinner!"

I'm dying of laughter all over again as I write this. That was so out of character for him. I swear, that story never gets old. And how about the waitress? I don't think she found it amusing. If I'm not mistaken, she quickly handed us our check and gave us "the look."

Speaking of Bob, he's been busy at work lately. He's here now, though, and says hello. Cocoa says meow. I've read some good books recently and have seen a few good movies. I'll order you a book from Amazon and have it sent. I know how you like to read. And stay in shape. Can you do a few sit-ups for me? I've been so lazy lately. Maybe in the future, you could be a personal trainer. You never know.

Spoke to my brother recently. He said Ryan is dating someone. Sounds serious. Can you believe it? I guess you can. I have a vague recollection of being seventeen once. Toby is into skateboarding and playing the guitar. He still has one left of the seven. They sold the others on Craigslist to raise some cash for bills.

Anyway, Jeremy is still pissed. He's got a right to his feelings. What's weird is he says he's not going to read your letters anymore, but when we talk on the phone, he tells me what you wrote. I don't understand him. Then again, he is a man, right? We'll never know what they're really thinking.

Okay, chica, I better run. Dishes are calling me. I pretend I don't speak their language, but it hasn't worked yet.

Love ya,
Olivia

Kristen set the letter aside. The restaurant tale was a perennial family favorite. It made her smile. She could remember it like it was yesterday. It saddened her to hear Toby only had one guitar left, though, as she'd bought him so many. But she supposed when it came down to it, he only needed one. She was glad he was practicing. Toby was almost a child prodigy. She hoped something more would come of it since it was his dream.

It didn't surprise Kristen that Ryan had a serious girlfriend at such a young age. He'd never been one to hang out in large groups and tended to surround himself with only a handful of close friends. Kristen smiled as she remembered their movie watching times. He would sit through chick flicks with her and seemed to actually like them. Maybe he bought into the romance the way women who watched them did. Or maybe he just wanted to create the kind of relationship he never saw at home. Hey, if he could, Kristen thought, more power to him. She wanted nothing but the best for her oldest son.

Kristen sat and pondered what Olivia had said about Jeremy, that he was still reading her letters even though he said he wouldn't. She couldn't stop writing him if she wanted to, and even though he was pissed, he seemed incapable of completely ignoring her. Perhaps, she thought, it was like a phantom limb. Once an appendage was removed, you still felt the sensation of it being there.

Maybe they had the same kind of connection.

*****

Laura, the prison warden, passed by Lakeisha's desk. "How are things going here?" she asked.

Lakeisha cleared her throat. "Very well. No unauthorized items today."

Laura nodded and said, "Good." Then she walked off, moving to another area before returning to her office.

Laura was a disciplined woman who took her job seriously. She was respected by all and commanded authority, but she had a soft side as well, although she didn't show it often. She'd shown it once or twice to Lakeisha but not to Megan. Megan always looked like she was expecting to be scolded.

Some inmates had been recently released, and there were new arrivals to deal with, so Laura had a full day ahead of her. She liked to personally assign cellmates to create harmony if at all possible, something that could make her job easier and reflect how well she ran the place. She took pride in what she did and had an intuitive knack for matching people who would get along. She wasn't one hundred percent accurate, of course, and fights had broken out, but she was doing better than when she started fifteen years ago.

Kristen's cellie had been recently released, and Laura

thought it prudent to transfer Lupe to her location until her sentence was up. Jess hadn't been getting along well with her cellmate, so Laura had an idea to move that woman to another spot. It could be like musical chairs sometimes. It was all about getting the right balance.

When the newbies arrived, there was one among them who stood out like a sore thumb. A fair-skinned, redheaded woman. She was thin and fragile, with an unearthly appearance. She looked like a fairy from a children's story or a maiden from *The Lord of the Rings*.

Fully aware of Jess' aggressive history and personality quirks, Laura assigned the lifer to be Jess' new roommate. The inmate didn't know it, but Laura was sending her a message.

Chapter 6

The redhead was processed and changed into the drab prison uniform, a faded orange jumpsuit that clashed with her long red hair. She was cuffed and taken to meet her cellmate.

"Jess, this is Abigail," the officer said. She glared at Jess and added, "Warden Laura thinks she'll be a better fit than your last roommate."

Jess got the message. Warden Laura expected zero bullshit going forward, and if there was any more, she'd get another violation added to her already rather large C file.

The officer uncuffed Abigail, stepped out, and closed the door. The sound of it clinking shut startled the newcomer, and she jumped. Looking terrified, she held out her hand to shake Jess'. "Hello," she said in a small voice. "Nice to meet you."

Jess put her larger hand out to shake Abigail's delicate one. "Hi," she mumbled.

Abigail looked uncomfortable, like she didn't know what to do next. Jess continued to stand motionless, unsure of what to say. After a few soundless minutes passed, Abigail sat down and began picking her cuticles.

Jess was confused. She knew Warden Laura didn't care

for her. And even though it was against the rules to discriminate, it was obvious to Jess how the boss felt. She couldn't understand why Laura decided to send an angel straight from Heaven her way. If it was a test or a trick, it had failed miserably, for Jess heard music the moment she saw Abigail. Her heart stopped beating and time stood still as she beheld the most beautiful creature she'd ever laid eyes on.

If there was such a thing as love at first sight, this was definitely it.

Soon the dreamy mental haze parted, and Jess regained the use of some of her senses. With a dry mouth, she said, "You must be thirsty. Do you want a soda? I have Coke."

Abigail smiled appreciatively. "Oh, thanks. That would be wonderful."

Jess scrambled to her locker and rummaged through it, pulling out a can. "Here you go," she said while handing it to her.

"Thanks," Abigail replied.

Jess figured she must be stressed out and frightened. Maybe no one had been nice to her in a long time. Maybe she could use a friend.

Abigail sat on the lower bunk, so Jess found a spot on the ground opposite her. Jess watched as Abigail drank greedily from the can and noticed the slow rippling movement of her neck as the elixir made its way down. Jess was transfixed, in awe at how such a simple thing could mesmerize her.

"Ahh," Abigail said when finished. "I forgot how

good that tastes."

Jess smiled, then ran a hand through her short brown hair. She continued staring at Abigail, her expression one of pure bliss. She had never been in the presence of a goddess.

"So what are you in for?" Jess asked, figuring it wise to start talking instead of continuing to stare like a slack-jawed idiot.

The smile on Abigail's face vanished. And even though it didn't seem possible, she grew several shades whiter. "I'm afraid if I told you that, you wouldn't be very nice to me anymore."

Jess looked at her in disbelief. There was no way this sweet lady could have done anything horrible. It had to be a misunderstanding, or she'd been framed. "We don't have to talk about it if you don't want to," she said.

"I'd rather not." Then, in what seemed like an attempt at keeping conversation, Abigail asked, "And you? What are you here for? Or if you don't want to discuss it…"

Jess looked down at her shoes. It would come up eventually, and since she was anxious to find out her roommate's secret, she decided to fess up.

"I walked in on my girlfriend with another woman. They were in bed together, and I lost it. I beat the girl senseless."

Abigail visibly stiffened. Jess assumed it was because she connected the dots and realized she was a lesbian. It could make people uncomfortable, especially someone who already seemed nervous to begin with.

"Did the woman die?" Abigail asked.

"No. She survived but was hospitalized in critical condition for a week. She almost didn't make it."

Jess waited for a sign from Abigail. Anything that might reveal what she was thinking.

"Emotions," she finally replied. "They can get the best of us."

A sadness crept into Abigail's aura. The gloom enveloped her and managed to twist her beautiful face with sorrow.

Jess quickly changed the subject. "Which bunk do you prefer? Top or bottom?"

The question seemed to snap Abigail out of her sadness. "Whichever," she said. "I'm not choosy."

"Well, it looks like you're comfortable where you're at, so I'll take the top." Jess had been sleeping on the lower bunk but didn't mind the change.

Abigail smiled again. "Okay. Thanks. I really appreciate that."

That was what Jess wanted to see, her smile. It lit up their dismal surroundings like the North Star illuminated the night sky.

Jess woke up in the wee hours of the morning. When she remembered her new cellmate, she grinned again. She couldn't believe her good fortune.

*****

Lupe arrived with fanfare to Kristen's cell. "Hey, girl. We meet again," she said as she high-fived the middle-aged blonde.

"What's this? You've been transferred here?"

"Sure have. The next six months, we're gonna hang, we're gonna chill. Lupe's gonna take good care of you."

Kristen smiled. She couldn't help it. Lupe's enthusiasm was contagious. "Sounds good," she said.

Kristen wondered if she was even remotely as cool as Lupe when she was her age. So much time had passed, she couldn't remember. Boys liked her. She remembered that, and she'd scored a pretty good-looking husband, so she must've been. Lupe reminded her of the good old days, when she was young and not a criminal. She was more into parties and staying out late.

After getting comfortable, Lupe began poking around, checking out Kristen's book collection. "Chica. What are you reading? Looks like some serious shit." She picked up *Winter Garden* by Kristin Hannah and read the back cover to herself. "Sounds sad," she said, then set it aside. Lupe grabbed another. "*The Painted Veil* by W. Somerset Maugham?" she eyed Kristen.

"A classic. Also kind of sad."

Lupe put the book back and glanced at the remaining choices. She didn't seem enthused. "No romance novels? No mysteries?"

"Afraid not. My sister-in-law sends me what she likes to read. But I'll try to request something different, maybe an action-adventure."

Lupe sat on the bunk and made herself at home, leaning back with her arms crossed behind her neck. "Yeah, that sounds good. Meanwhile, I've got a few action-adventure stories of my own."

"I'm all ears."

Lupe shook her head and giggled. "All right. I've got so many. How about something recent?"

Kristen nodded.

"Okay. So I was coming out of the grocery store. It's hot as Hell, and I've got my shopping bags balanced in each hand, trying to get back to my car before my ice cream melts when out of nowhere, this fool in an old Buick slams on the brakes and just misses hitting me."

"Oh my gosh!"

"I know, right? So I walk right up to this guy's window, and he has the nerve to unroll it and start yelling at me, the fucking pedestrian! I was so pissed I set my bags down, took off my left flip-flop, and slapped him across the face with it."

Kristen burst into a fit of laughter. "No way!"

Lupe smiled and said, "You know I did. Left a red mark on his cheek too."

"Then what happened?"

"I put my shoe back on and grabbed my bags. He looked like he was going to get out of the car and try to fight me, but an older woman began screaming, 'Come on! Move already!' and he just hit the gas and took off."

Kristen lost it and began laughing even harder, with tears streaming down her cheeks. Lupe was a maniac. But in a good way. She couldn't remember the last time she'd laughed like this and was starting to look forward to the next six months together.

After Kristen regained composure, Lupe asked, "You wanna hear another one?"

Kristen wiped tears from her eyes. "Yeah. Keep 'em coming."

Now Lupe laughed. "This one goes back a bit, but it's a goodie," she said, rubbing her hands together as if she was concocting the tale on the spot. She could've been, Kristen thought. But either way, it was great entertainment.

"So this old white lady had computer problems at her office. And my cousin Juan, who had a small business repairing PCs, helped her out. Anyway, this bitch owed him $700.00 and wasn't paying. She kept having new complaints and tried to get him to come out and fix those issues for free. He fell for that shit a few more times, but she continued to balk at paying the original bill, so he finally got smart."

Kristen's smile was plastered on her face. She already anticipated where this story might go.

"He's complaining to me how broke he is and that he can't make his car payment, and I ask him what happened with Sarah. I guess he didn't want to tell me she was a no-pay because I'd introduced them. Once he did, I flipped. Especially when he said how much she owed. I knew she was playing him, and I didn't like it. She's got plenty of money. Works as a high-rolling sales lady at a fancy timeshare resort."

Lupe shook her head in disgust and continued. "So I show up at the hotel and find her office. She's not with anyone, but she's on the phone. By the way I was glaring at her, she decided to hang up and talk to me instead. 'Can I help you, Lupe?' she asks. 'Yeah, you can,' I say.

'My cousin has been more than fair fixing your computers, and you haven't paid him.' She went on to say there was more to be done, and she'd pay when they were all working up to par. At that point, I'd had enough of her BS, so I reached over the desk and grabbed her by the front of her blouse. I told her she'd better pay by tomorrow and that she needed to send Juan an overnight check, and if she didn't send it, I'd be back the next day to beat her senseless. I told her I didn't think she'd be able to close as many sales while wearing a neck brace."

Kristen's jaw hung open. "Then what happened?"

"UPS truck showed up next morning—10:00 am—with the check."

"Dang, girl," Kristen said. "You're not messing around. You're a real badass." Kristen paused, then asked, "You got another one?"

"You're kidding, right?" Lupe said. "I could go on all night."

She did just that, and for once, Kristen enjoyed her time in her small cell, snickering and slapping her knee every time a new, grander adventure unfolded.

Who needed a novel when there was Lupe?

Chapter 7

After breakfast and a walk out on the yard, Kristen wanted to know more about Lupe. The real her, not just her funny stories.

"Tell me about your family. Are you close?" Kristen asked when they got back to their cell.

Lupe looked serious for once. "Yeah, we're close. My mom is dead. Passed away giving birth to me. My dad raised me with the help of an aunt who lived nearby. I have lots of brothers and sisters too. From different moms."

Kristen wondered what it would be like to come from such a large family. She thought she would like it. "So, what did you want to be when you grew up?"

Lupe laughed. "That's funny, chica." She seemed to be mulling it over in her mind, though. "I don't know. Someone important. Like a scientist or a person that discovers the cure for cancer. Don't have the smarts for that, so I found another route." She tsked and added, "Look where that got me. Don't feel too important sitting in prison."

The way Lupe acted—like a hotshot—must have been for show. She used her power to her advantage while being locked up, which was smart, but deep down, she'd hoped for more. Luckily, she was still young. She could change things.

"Things will work out. You'll see," Kristen offered. "You're getting out soon enough, and you can do whatever you want."

Lupe shrugged. "I doubt I'll become a scientist, but I hope to do something good. I sure as hell don't want to come back here." She reached for her headphones, put them on, and pressed play. Soon she was tapping her fingers and bobbing her head to the music.

Kristen sat down on her bunk, bored. She wished she were getting out soon too. When she saw Lakeisha stop by with mail for her, she jumped up and grabbed the envelope, then turned it over to see it was from Jeremy.

Her heart thudded as she held the letter. She tore it open and began to read.

Kristen,

Please don't write and say how sorry you are anymore. I don't want to hear it. People make mistakes. I get that. People forget to send their aunt a birthday card because it slips their mind, or they forget to pay their electric bill. But it's not a mistake to repeatedly forge checks and siphon money out of your employer's account.

And you have the nerve to say we abandoned you because we don't come to visit? You ask over and over again why "we" left you.

We didn't leave you, Kristen. You left us. Each time you stole money to shop for things. How stupid you were to think you'd never get caught. Granted, you had me fooled. I didn't know how much things cost and you were in charge of all the bills. I was just the dumb blue-collar guy you married, right? Nothing I gave you was ever enough.

Your letters to me talk about all the "good times" we had. Maybe there were some. We were together for two decades. But the bad memories, combined with the way things are now, make it all a blur.

My life consists of buffing and painting cars in the sweltering heat while you sit on your ass reading books all day. I have to cook dinner, help with homework, shop for groceries. I work like a slave and never get a break. Meanwhile, my sister tells me you do yoga and have a counselor in there. Sounds rough, Kristen. I wish I had someone to tell my problems to, but I can't afford health insurance for me or the kids.

You complain they don't write you. I give them pens, paper, stamps, but I can't force them to do it. All I can do is suggest they write their mother. They say they're going to, and then they don't. They let letters from you pile up unread. Not because they don't love you. They do. But because they feel the pain all over again every time they read one, knowing their mom is in prison, enduring God knows what each day.

They don't read the letters or write because they want to forget. You know what? I want to forget too. But for some unknown reason, I do read them, and it just pisses me off all over again. I want to explode. What you don't understand is that we're in prison too.

It's harder on us than if you had died. At least then, we'd be able to mourn our loss. Instead, we have to go on knowing you're in there, and your letters are like a ghost that continues to haunt us.

So you see, you're not the only one suffering. You did this to all of us. Keep writing the kids, and I will continue to ask them to read your letters and write you back, but I'm not going to read anything you write me anymore, so don't waste your ink.

Save it for your boyfriend.

Jeremy

Kristen sat down, then let out a deep sigh. It always ended with the boyfriend. She'd never be able to live that down. What a colossal mistake. More disturbing was what he'd said about the letters. That the kids let them pile up and that her writing was like a ghost haunting them. That it would be easier on them if she had died.

Kristen's throat began to constrict, and she stood to get a bottle of water. When she made eye contact with Lupe, she fainted.

*****

Sitting in Megan's office, Kristen felt embarrassed. "We have to stop meeting like this," she joked.

"You keep me in a job," Megan teased back.

It was true, though, Kristen thought, and the gravity of her situation hit her again. To make matters worse, there was a swollen knot on her head from where she'd bumped it on the floor.

"I heard you gave your roommate quite a scare."

Kristen couldn't picture Lupe fazed by anything, but she took Megan's word for it. "I don't know how that happened. I've never fainted before."

"Do you want to talk about it?" Megan asked.

"Sure. Why not. I'm here, right?"

Megan stared back at her with a calm, comforting expression. She really looked like she cared.

"I got another letter from my husband. It was a doozy. I don't know why I thought it would be something nice. Wishful thinking?" Kristen smirked. "This one was way worse than the last."

"How so?"

Kristen sighed. "He brought up the affair again. Told me not to write him anymore because it pisses him off. He said to save the ink for my boyfriend."

"Hmm. And do you have any contact with him?"

"God, no. He was nothing. Just someone that made me feel nice while I was drowning. He didn't even know the real me. When he found out I got arrested, that I wasn't a successful business woman, he was history."

"And how does that make you feel?"

"I don't feel anything. I guess he wasn't very important to me."

"But your husband feels otherwise. He's obviously still hurt and angry."

"Yeah. He's not going to forget it. I know him."

Megan sat back and looked at her notes.

"He confuses me, though. One minute he's saying he's

working hard while I sit on my ass reading all day, the next, he's saying they're suffering and that they care. That it's like they're in prison too."

"You know Kristen, it's common for people to have love/hate relationships with their loved ones, especially when they've gone through something like this. It sounds like your husband is showing both his love and fury in the same letter. Maybe that's why it's confusing."

Kristen hugged her knees to her chest. "He said it would've been easier if I had died, that at least then they could've mourned their loss. He said my letters are like a ghost that haunts them, and the kids let them pile up unread because they want to forget."

This seemed to grab Megan's full attention. She sat up straighter and cleared her throat. "And how does that make you feel?"

"Like shit." A tear escaped the corner of Kristen's eye, and Megan quickly reached for a tissue and handed it to her. "Sometimes I wish I were dead. It would be easier on me too, but I'm not a quitter. I may have fucked up, but I still know right from wrong."

"Listen to what you just said there. You're not a quitter," Megan said. "Think about what that means. You made a major mistake, and you're paying for that mistake and hope to make things right. You've stopped drinking and are in counseling. You're doing all you can."

No matter how she tried, Kristen couldn't forget the memory of delicious wine. It teased the corners of her mind, clawed at her with its constant nagging desire. Even after all these years.

"I'm not sure I could not drink if I were on the outside. I mean, I've been able to kick it because I'm in here. I don't have a choice."

Nodding, Megan added, "But you've said you like how being sober makes you feel, that you have a clear mind and see things from a better perspective. If you kept that forefront in your thoughts, I bet you could do it. And with each year that passes, it will get easier."

"I guess you're right. Not drinking doesn't bother me as much as it did last year. It's just when I'm stressed, that's when I want it most."

Kristen shrugged and decided to lie back down. She closed her eyes. "I don't want to upset my kids by writing them, but I can't lose them either. I think I've already lost Jeremy. If I lose my sons, I'll have nothing to live for."

Kristen felt sorry for herself. She didn't receive visitors and only got regular mail from Jeremy's sister Olivia. Her own parents hadn't even come to the sentencing, preferring not to be embarrassed in public by the sight of their only child in an orange jumpsuit and shackles.

"You have you to live for," Megan offered, interrupting her thoughts.

Kristen sat up and looked into Megan's eyes, a confused look on her face. "I don't even know who that is anymore."

Megan got up, their visit soon coming to a close. She put her hand on Kristen's shoulder. "Well, that's what we're here to find out…together."

Chapter 8

Lakeisha headed to the employee cafeteria to meet Megan for lunch. She'd made a point of eating healthier now that she was pregnant but still hadn't told anyone of her condition. It had been difficult to conceive, and she wanted to wait until she was further along to share the news.

After selecting her food and paying, Lakeisha sat down next to Megan.

"Salad?" Megan asked. "I thought you hated salad."

"I like it just fine. Trying to eat better."

"That's cool."

"How's that boyfriend of yours? The one you haven't kicked to the curb yet?"

Megan grinned. "You make me sound awful. I'm not. It's just too many of the guys I've dated are pains. This one's good. Gives me space but is there when I want him."

"Uh huh," Lakeisha teased. She loved ribbing Megan about her men. One of them would get her to settle down eventually, but for now, she seemed committed to her patients. "You having any luck with Abigail? I remember you said she was a unique case."

Megan poked at her meal with her fork. "No. And it

bothers me. When we've met, she's talked about everything but why she's here. I think we need to discuss that. Everything I've tried has failed to elicit any form of meaningful communication."

"I'm sure she'll talk eventually. Just give it time."

Warden Laura walked by with her food and sat down at another table. She nodded at Lakeisha and Megan as she passed.

"She scares me," Megan admitted.

Lakeisha laughed. "Why? She's never done anything to you. That doesn't even make sense."

"I don't think she likes me."

"Girl. She likes you fine. You're just paranoid."

Megan shivered and fluttered her eyes, trying to brush the feeling off. "Must be me. I'm just nuts."

Lakeisha laughed harder, almost choking on a crouton. "Now, that was funny."

*****

On visitation day, Jess' mom showed up, and so did Abigail's parents. They'd both had family come in the past but never on the same day. Jess thought it was fortuitous.

Jess sat with her mom, listening to the news from back home but kept stealing glances at Abigail's parents, Gary and Lois.

Abigail had spoken highly of them. Her dad was a doctor, and her mom was a nurse. They'd met in college and, after getting married, had their only child, whom they'd raised to be their princess. She'd been given everything: love, attention, material goods. They'd gone on annual vacations all around the world.

From what Jess could see, it seemed like they had a perfect life. And a perfect daughter. She was a princess indeed, which often brought out chivalry in Jess, to the amusement and mockery of her fellow inmates.

But Jess didn't care what they thought. She was in love. Abigail still hadn't told her what she was in for, but they'd become friends. And she seemed to relax in Jess' presence, perhaps more comfortable with the fact that Jess was gay.

"Honey, are you listening?" Jess' mom asked.

"Huh? Yeah. Sure. You're sick of the neighbor's dog using your front yard as a toilet. You should have a talk with her again."

Jess returned her focus to her mom and listened as she prattled on about all sorts of minor happenings. She paid just enough attention to interact with her while simultaneously wondering what Abigail was talking about with her parents.

When she watched Abigail, it often felt like time moved in slow motion. Her laughter sounded like wind chimes. And the thing she did with her hair, tucking it behind her ear when it was in her eye, was endearing.

Abigail's father caught Jess staring.

Jess got spooked and looked away.

Her mom had paused. Luckily, Jess managed to hear the last phrase. "I miss you too, Mom. Think about you every day," she assured her.

"Aw, honey. That's sweet. Oh, you know what I forgot to tell you? I saw your old boss from the furniture store at church. He seems like a nice man. Maybe you could get your old job back when you get out."

When she got out, Jess thought. That used to be the thing she wanted most. Now it was what she feared. She didn't want to be apart from Abigail, even if it meant a lifetime in prison. Even if Abigail never returned her affection. The thought of leaving and going back to her old life made her nauseous. She felt her stomach lurch.

"You okay, honey?" Jess' mom asked. "You look a bit pale."

Jess had no control over the future. She hated that. "I'm fine, Mom. Probably just something I ate."

Time was up, and everyone hugged and said their goodbyes. On the way out, Abigail's father took another longer look at Jess.

She could tell he didn't like her.

*****

Lakeisha came by with mail for both Kristen and Lupe.

"A love letter for Lupe," Lakeisha said while grinning.

Lupe snatched it. "Only kind of mail I accept."

Lakeisha shook her head and smirked. "And a letter and book for you."

Kristen took both, but Lupe quickly grabbed the novel out of her hand. The cover was of a suited man in the center of a sniper's scope, ready to get taken down. "*King of Swords* by Russell Blake," Lupe said in delight. "I think

Olivia wants us to have some fun." She flipped the book over and read the description. "Yep. Now we're talking. It's about drug cartels in Mexico and a super-assassin named El Rey."

"Sounds like a badass. Your kind of man," Kristen said.

"And he's Mexican," Lupe pointed out. "All hot guys are Hispanic."

Kristen laughed. She disagreed but let her have the last word. She was more interested in her letter.

Lupe sat down to read hers and wore a big smile when she was done. Kristen opened hers up and began reading, too; tears filled her eyes.

"What's wrong? Bad news again?"

"No. It's good news. My oldest son, Ryan, is graduating from high school. Everyone is going to the ceremony, and there's a party afterward. I should be there," she said.

Lupe seemed at a loss for words for once. Kristen didn't expect her to know what to say, not having any children of her own.

"Man. That sucks," Lupe said. "I feel bad." She paused, then asked, "What about your sister-in-law? Is she going?"

Sniffling, Kristen replied, "Yeah. And she promised to take lots of pictures and send them to me, which I'm thankful for, but it just won't be the same, you know? I knew this would happen, that I'd miss it, but it's still hard."

Lupe gave her a compassionate look. Kristen felt tears

welling up again. She'd have to get a better grip on herself. But right then, what she needed most was to lie on her bunk and have a good cry.

*****

Warden Laura appeared outside Jess and Abigail's cell. Both women stopped what they were doing and stood up when they saw her.

"Just checking to see how you two are getting along. I hope this is a good pairing?" Laura asked while eyeing Jess distrustfully.

"Everything is great," Jess replied. "Couldn't be better."

Laura looked at her like she was trying to decipher what that meant. It could go either way, Jess thought. She could think she was being cocky, or she could think she was being honest. Since she had a history of being a smartass, Jess assumed Laura thought the former.

Laura looked like she wanted to club her. Jess just smiled back.

She was being honest this time. She really was.

"And how are you doing?" she asked, turning to Abigail. "Would you agree with that statement?"

Abigail nodded yes. "I would," she said in a soft voice. "Jess is very nice. I'm lucky to have a roommate like her."

Laura tsked, and it threw Jess off. She was swelling inside like a hot air balloon, ready to float away from the praise.

"Miracles never cease, I guess."

There was an unmistakable look of disgust on Warden Laura's face. And to Jess' surprise, it wasn't directed at her. She was glaring at Abigail.

Abigail hung her head and said nothing.

As Warden Laura walked away, Jess wondered how Abigail could deserve such an appraisal, a look far worse than she'd ever given Jess. Laura didn't just look at Abigail like she disliked her. Warden Laura looked at Abigail like the sheer sight of her made her sick.

Chapter 9

The time came for Lupe to be released, and Kristen found it bittersweet. Lupe was the only real friend she'd made. Who knew what kind of person she'd end up rooming with next?

"You keep it together, all right?" Lupe said to Kristen.

Kristen managed a smile but was getting emotional. "I will," she replied.

"I'll keep in touch. Won't be back to visit, but soon Olivia's letters won't be the only good ones you'll receive." Lupe reached out and gave Kristen a hug, something she never did.

Kristen squeezed her hard and didn't want to let go. "Good luck. Find the cure for cancer, all right?"

"I'll try," Lupe said, then winked.

A moment later, the officer came for Lupe, and Kristen was alone again.

She had to work to keep the tears at bay. There was no reason to cry, she thought. Losing people, losing things…it was all a part of life she'd learned, and there was no point in getting upset because it didn't change anything.

She'd lost her job, her house, all her possessions. Her parents didn't keep in touch. She lost contact with her children and her husband. Eventually, he'd move on, and she'd lose the last small hope she dared to have.

In the end, like in the beginning, all that was left was you.

It was strange to have lost everything and still exist. It was somewhat freeing in a way she couldn't quite put into words.

On Ryan's graduation day, Kristen was depressed. It seemed just yesterday he was a toddler. The years had flown by. At least they did on the outside. On the inside, they dragged.

When Olivia's letter finally arrived with the pictures, she smiled. He looked so grown up in his cap and gown. She thought of the good times they shared. There had been many. It wasn't all bad. With renewed enthusiasm, she decided to write him a letter.

Ryan,

I'm so proud you graduated high school. I wish more than anything I could have been there. I thought about you all day, hoping you were having a good time surrounded by people you love.

Aunt Olivia sent me a bunch of photos. You look so grown up! And I hear you have a girlfriend now. That's wonderful, honey. I'm not surprised since you've always been a serious sort, never one to want to play the field. I hope you two are happy.

How is Toby doing? I heard he's been practicing

the guitar and that he's in a band. Olivia says he's written songs with his friend and posted them online. I sure wish I could hear them.

I miss both of you so much and hope to see you again one day. I know your father doesn't want to visit, but now that you're eighteen, you're welcome to come on your own if you choose to. I'll send the papers for you to fill out in case you're interested.

Love always,
Mom

Kristen kept the letter short. Partly because she wasn't sure he'd read it and partly because she wasn't sure what to say. She'd apologized over and over again in previous letters, and Jeremy had told her they didn't want to hear that anymore.

There was a time when she could talk to her children all day, never running out of conversation. Now she felt the space between them growing, and she feared if they didn't communicate soon, they would end up strangers.

That was something she couldn't accept. She might have no control over anything now, but she planned to have a life with them in the future, to find a way to be their mother again.

She didn't know if Jeremy would ever want her back. She highly doubted it but secretly wished for it at the same time. She found it best not to force the issue. He hadn't written a third letter, but from her correspondence with Olivia, she knew he continued to read what she sent him.

Kristen didn't know what that meant, and she didn't try to understand anymore. She just lived each day as it came.

*****

Jess noticed Abigail gripping the back of her neck and looking miserable, something she tended to do whenever it was rainy outside.

"You okay?" Jess asked.

"Yeah. It's just my neck. It hurts when the weather changes. The family curse."

Abigail didn't talk much about her family. Jess used to think if she shared things about herself, Abigail would do the same, but she quickly learned that wasn't the case. Instead, she had to ask direct questions if she wanted to know more about Abigail's story. And even then, Abigail wouldn't always answer, often choosing to provide generic responses. Jess assumed that was code for "I don't want to get close."

"Your parents, did they have the neck pain too?" Jess asked.

Abigail sighed. "My parents had it. My aunt had it. My grandma had it. Bad genes, I guess."

Jess couldn't disagree more, but she wouldn't say it. Not yet. Maybe not ever. If she told Abigail that she loved her or even that she was the most beautiful woman in the world, it could damage their relationship. Megan had suggested being kind and patient, and she had taken that advice to heart. Maybe took it too far this time, as there was no chance her affections could ever be returned.

"My ex-husband used to fix my neck," Abigail said, pulling Jess from her thoughts.

This was the first mention of a spouse. Jess wanted to know more, but hearing of him now caused a tiny pain in her heart.

"He was a chiropractor," Abigail added.

Jess cleared her throat. "You've got lots of doctors in the family, huh?"

"Well, just my dad and my ex-husband. My mom is a nurse."

"Like I said. Lots of doctors," Jess repeated. She felt inadequate in comparison. "You know, I'm no chiropractor, but I'm pretty good at massage. If you need one, I'd be happy to help."

Without a moment's hesitation, Abigail said, "Would you? Good grief. That would be wonderful."

Flabbergasted but excited beyond words, Jess tried to remain casual. "No problem. Let's see. You could sit on the floor, and I can sit up here to reach your neck and shoulders. Not exactly a spa," she said, grasping for a joke.

Abigail followed her instruction and sat on the floor in front of the lower bunk. Jess climbed onto the thin mattress and sat behind her, with her legs stretched out, one on each side of Abigail. Jess was careful not to let her legs touch Abigail's body. She didn't want her to feel uncomfortable or like anything intimate was happening, even though, to Jess, it definitely was.

Jess reached out, hands trembling, and placed them on Abigail's shoulders. She could hear her own heartbeat pounding in her ears, and when her palms made contact, she felt a rush of energy surge through her. Somehow she managed to steady her breathing. "How's that pressure? Too hard?"

Abigail gave her a thumbs up. "Nope. It's just right."

"Okay, you let me know if there's an area that needs more attention."

Jess kneaded the muscles in Abigail's shoulders, lightly at first, but once they were warmed up, she went deeper, trying to relieve the pain.

Abigail let out a small moan of appreciation, and Jess just about lost it. She had to do everything in her power just to remain in control. The whole experience was surreal, like she was in a dream. She had to say something. Had to break the spell.

"Are you still doing okay? You're so fragile. I don't want to hurt you."

"Yep," Abigail replied. "I just have small bones. My muscles are full of knots, though."

"I can feel that."

Jess continued to press and rub the trouble spots. She could do this all night, she thought.

After a half hour, Abigail seemed relaxed. "You don't have to keep going," she said. "I've been known to be a massage hog. Please feel free to stop whenever you're tired."

"I'm good. I've got plenty of energy left," Jess replied.

"Trust me," Abigail joked. "You'll regret saying that."

But Jess didn't regret saying it and continued to work on her until she fell asleep. At first, she wasn't sure she had, but then Jess heard a faint snore and noticed she had gone completely limp.

Jess slid off the bed while holding Abigail up and gently lifted her onto the mattress, setting her head against the pillow. She crouched down and admired Abigail for a few minutes, then kicked off her shoes and climbed onto the top bunk, where she lay wide awake.

Right before midnight, Jess heard Abigail stir. She mumbled, "What? How did I?"

"You awake?" Jess said in a low voice.

"Yeah. I must've fallen asleep. Sorry about that."

"No need to apologize. How are you feeling?"

"Great. I haven't felt this good in a long time. Thanks."

Jess smiled. "Maybe I should've been a chiropractor instead of a furniture repair person."

"You could always become a massage therapist. The training is shorter, and you've got the knack. Steve had a woman working for him with five years' experience who wasn't as good as you."

Jess beamed. She'd also noticed she finally said his name—Steve.

After hesitating, Jess asked, "How long were you married?"

Abigail was quiet for a while. It was pitch black, but the room seemed to grow darker. "Ten years," she eventually answered.

Abigail's voice had soured, and Jess didn't want to ruin

the evening when she'd done such a good job pleasing her earlier.

"Maybe I'll research that massage school when I get out. That's a good idea. I could see myself doing something like that, helping people. So how about you? Do you have any idea what you'd like to do in the future?"

Abigail let out a deep sigh. "No."

"How come? Haven't you given it any thought?"

"I've given it plenty," Abigail said, sounding tired. "The truth is I don't have to make plans for the future because they'll never let me out of here...ever."

Chapter 10

Megan sat in her office studying her notes. She was pleased with Jess' progress, and Kristen was coming along just fine, slowly but surely.

But it was the violent prisoners that intrigued Megan most. It was like something inside them had died, and they were incapable of being reached. She found it both depressing and fascinating, always poring over the literature, trying to decipher what made them tick, to discern if there was any way she could help them. She didn't accept the idea of a "lost cause."

Megan heard her phone vibrate. She picked it up and saw a text message from her boyfriend. "Are we still on for the Italian place?" he asked.

She texted back, "No. I'm sorry. I forgot I have dinner with the boss tonight. I can't get out of it. Another time?"

Megan didn't really care if they rescheduled for another night. She liked him, but she wasn't crazy about him. Unfortunately, it just made him chase her more, which annoyed her to no end. She'd probably have to dump him soon, she thought.

On her lunch break, Megan decided to leave the grounds and take in the sunshine. As she relaxed on a park bench, a light wind blew through her hair, and the scent that came with it reminded her of a date she'd gone on with Rob when she was sixteen.

He'd taken her to a grassy spot near his house. Nothing special, just a place he went when he wanted to be alone, away from his nagging mom and younger sister who got on his nerves. He'd spread out a blanket, and they lay down on it. First, side by side on their backs while chatting about colleges they'd apply to, then they turned to face each other and began kissing.

They never went all the way, but it would happen soon. Megan had it all planned out. It would be special.

Her parents were going out of town, on a couple's trip to rekindle the romance. And since she was trustworthy, they decided it would be okay for her to stay home alone. Megan thought she'd be more nervous that evening since it was her first time. Instead, she felt calm, never more sure she was making the right decision.

Toes pedicured, legs waxed, and hair straightened to the point it flowed over her shoulders like strands of silk, Megan patiently waited for Rob. When he didn't show up or call at the planned time, she just assumed he was running late. She nibbled on a few pieces of shrimp that she'd prepared.

Another hour passed, and the doorbell finally rang. Elated and not in the least bit upset he was late, Megan skipped to the door to answer it. When she opened it she was surprised to see his younger sister. She looked terrible, like she'd been crying.

"I couldn't call," she told Megan. "I asked my mom to

drop me off here, and I told her you'd take me home afterward."

The hair on Megan's arms stood up. Something wasn't right. "Of course, I'll take you home. No problem, but come in, please."

The fourteen-year-old, usually bubbly and full of sarcasm, looked ill. She stepped into the foyer and said, "It's Rob. He was out with Phil today, and you know Phil. He's trouble."

Megan knew Phil well. She'd been trying to steer Rob away from him. He was into drinking and drugs and seemed to be headed nowhere fast.

"Please. Tell me what's the matter," Megan pressed, no longer able to stand the pressure.

The teen erupted into tears. "They were messing around with drugs, and something happened. Rob collapsed, and Phil called 911, but by the time the ambulance got there, Rob was already gone."

Megan slowly absorbed what she had just heard. *Rob was gone.* She went numb. She wanted to cry and scream and fall to the ground, but she saw Tina before her, sobbing and looking so small all of a sudden. Instead, she reacted by leaning down to embrace her. She hugged her tight while rocking her back and forth, telling her it would be okay. Megan realized Tina's parents were probably worried sick about her and that letting her deliver the news was an unbelievably generous gesture. She decided to get dressed and drive Tina home as soon as possible.

Megan's phone vibrated, bringing her back to the present. The text message read, "How about Saturday night? We could do Thai food if you prefer."

Megan pressed the phone's off button. She didn't want to think about that now. She preferred to spend her last ten minutes relaxing in the sun.

*****

An officer brought Abigail in for her session with Megan. Rested and with some new ideas on how to get her to open up, Megan greeted her.

"How are you feeling today?" she asked.

Abigail took a seat, formal as always, with perfect posture. "I'm doing well. Thank you."

That was what she always said, without fail.

"Anything new and exciting?" Megan asked, trying to be casual.

Abigail smiled. "Nope. Nothing new on my end."

Megan glanced at her notes. "And how are you getting along with Jess?"

"Just fine. Couldn't ask for a nicer roommate."

Megan studied Abigail's face and saw no indication of a struggle. She looked peaceful and happy, which seemed impossible considering her file. If anyone should be breaking down, it should be her, Megan thought.

"So, how have your parents been doing? Have you seen them recently?"

"Yes. They come every week. They're doing well."

Here we go again with the dance to nowhere, Megan thought. The time-wasting tango. She projected patience but was getting inwardly annoyed. She felt Abigail could sense it too, which frustrated her even more.

"Any contact with your ex-husband?" Megan asked.

"Nope. No contact," Abigail replied in the same even tone. It was as if no subject could elicit an emotion beyond the outward calm. Then she added, "My parents did mention he'd remarried, though."

Megan perked up. She jumped at the only opening she'd ever been given. "And are you okay with that?"

"I'm fine," Abigail replied. "It was to be expected."

Megan couldn't tell if Abigail wore a smirk or if it was just her imagination. When you spent as much time as she did with crazies, you started seeing stuff that often wasn't there.

"How come you feel that way?" Megan asked.

Abigail couldn't wiggle out of that question.

She shifted in her seat. "I guess because time has gone by, and it just makes sense...and because he had been dating her while we were married."

Megan watched Abigail's facial expression. She was as serene as before she'd uttered the comment. But at least she was sharing something.

"Did that go on long? I mean, was she always in the picture?"

"Not long," Abigail answered. "It started when things got stressful at home. I'm assuming it was a form of escape."

"From the situation," Megan added, hoping Abigail would finally talk about it.

"Yes."

Screw it, Megan decided. She'd just ask her a direct

question. "Would you like to discuss the situation? I mean, it is why you're here. I'd like to help."

Abigail gave Megan a disdainful look that spoke volumes. It was clear she thought Megan was a naïve fool. "I don't see how you could do anything to help. What's done is done."

With that said, the buzzer rang, and Abigail's session was over, just like Megan's chances of getting anywhere with her, it seemed.

*****

Lakeisha, Megan, and Laura met at the local Applebee's for dinner. At first, Megan was hesitant, not knowing if it was a good idea to spend time outside of work with the boss, but Lakeisha had insisted. She'd coordinated the whole thing.

Megan ordered a Coke instead of the margarita she really wanted. It was best to err on the side of caution, she thought.

"I'm so glad you guys invited me. I haven't had a night out in quite a while," Laura said.

"What she means is she hasn't had a night out with grown-ups," Lakeisha teased. "She's always running the kids to soccer practice, marching band, gymnastics."

Megan watched them interact with ease and relaxed into her chair a bit. "How many children do you have?" she asked Laura.

"Four. All two years apart. Two boys and two girls. They keep me busy."

Warden Laura seemed to brighten when she spoke of her kids. Megan couldn't imagine how she managed to attend all their activities, considering how much responsibility she had at the prison. Just thinking about it was exhausting.

"You're next," Laura said to Lakeisha. They knew about her pregnancy now. No one had been more thrilled to hear the news than Laura.

Lakeisha smiled. "Thank the Lord. We tried for so long. Feels good to finally be blessed."

Megan studied Lakeisha. She envied people with strong religious beliefs. She wished she could be one of them. It was like a club she was dying to join, had been invited to even, but wasn't quite able to ever make through the front door.

"How about you, Megan?" Laura asked while she was spacing out. "Are you planning to have kids?"

Before she could answer, Lakeisha jabbed her. "A man has to get her to commit first. And they better put their gym shoes on because this one's difficult to catch."

Everyone laughed at the joke.

"Don't worry. You've got time," Laura said. "When the right one comes along, you'll just know it."

The waitress arrived then, distracting the pair, so neither saw the ever-so-tiny frown that pulled at the corner of Megan's lips. Before they could pick up on it, Megan forced a smile. "I'm sure you're right," she agreed.

Megan could see what Lakeisha meant now about Laura having a softer side. She couldn't imagine why she'd been so scared of her before. It seemed downright silly. It would make sense she wouldn't show it much at work. She had to be tough at work—she was a leader. Maybe that was what Megan needed to do. Toughen up. Stop having patients lead her in circles.

After taking a sip of her Coke, she decided that was just what she'd do.

Chapter 11

Kristen's exercise group expanded. Abigail joined and suggested Jess join too.

"You go ahead. It's not really my thing," Jess told Abigail, then continued shooting hoops. Jess would've considered trying it for her, but with Kristen heading it up, she thought it best to pass.

While feigning interest in the game, Jess managed to watch Abigail, with Kristen at her side, helping her learn the routine. It was weird to see them together because she felt absolutely nothing for Kristen anymore. She couldn't picture herself with anyone but Abigail.

Joyful, she managed to make a jump shot, and her teammates hooted in unison. Jess was riding high when everything turned chaotic. Two women on the other side of the yard began screaming at each other. Punches were being thrown, and the tower guard gave them a warning over the loud speaker. When the pair didn't stop, he shot rubber bullets at them. Instead of controlling the violence, this just made things worse. A stream of guards rushed in to handle the situation.

The whole yard grew tense, and everyone was ordered back to their cells for lockdown. There was always someone who had to ruin it for everyone else, Jess thought. And it was probably over a stupid gang-related issue or a drug debt. The bullshit never ceased.

*****

Later, after everyone had been counted and things calmed down, Kristen sat in her cell and thought of Lupe. She hoped her life was getting back on track. Then she began to think about her new cellmate. No one wanted to get stuck with the psycho lady, Tanya, who'd cooked her newborn baby and served it to her family as a holiday meal.

Kristen prayed Warden Laura would send her someone acceptable. She'd been spoiled with Lupe, not just with her story-telling capabilities, but with her status. She made problems disappear and always had plenty of snacks to share.

With more time to herself, Kristen fell into her old pattern of thinking about the past. The past was all she had now, other than hope for an unknown future. Instead of dwelling on childhood memories that couldn't be changed and no longer mattered, she thought about her husband and sons.

Ryan, the older boy, was the quiet one. He didn't say much, but a lot was going on in his mind. As a child, he was her sunshine, always smiling and bright, but as he got older, he grew withdrawn and moody, which probably had something to do with her drinking. She sighed another silent apology, then let her mind continue to wander, blending memories from life before prison with news Olivia had relayed in her letters.

Kristen remembered when he wanted to grow up and become a veterinarian. He loved his dog and hoped to save his life one day. Unfortunately, the dog died before he'd graduated high school. Jeremy had gotten the boys a new one right after Kristen went to jail in order to soften the blow of losing both their mother and the family pet.

Thinking of Jeremy made Kristen depressed. There was nothing to soften the beating he took. Emotional pain, financial problems, constant stress. The blows just kept coming.

Kristen flipped through the graduation photos again, and it made her sad. Jeremy had changed a lot. He'd aged a decade in four years. Sure, he was still the most handsome man to her, but he'd lost that inner spark. The light that once emanated from his eyes and had attracted women, both young and old, everywhere they went had dimmed.

Kristen noticed he'd gained weight too. Probably from eating low-quality food, she thought. Olivia said they could barely afford groceries, so it was a given they'd stopped buying organic. She worried that he wasn't taking care of himself. He'd never been one for exercise, as his job working on cars had been exhausting enough. He smoked like a chimney, too, ever since he was a teenager.

All attempts to lecture him about eating right and exercising had fallen on deaf ears. Especially lately because that advice was coming from his incarcerated wife. No matter what she suggested, either for him or the kids, it was discounted as the opinion of someone who'd gotten it all wrong and shouldn't have a say.

They would be angry for a long time. If she were in their place, she would be too.

Kristen lay on her bunk and propped up her feet. She needed a vacation, so she chose to remember her last one. After getting fired, she told Jeremy it was a misunderstanding, that they had made a mistake. She knew the truth, though. She was fucked. They had plenty of proof and were going to come down on her hard.

In an attempt to pretend it wasn't real, she planned one last extravagant trip to Atlantis Resort in the Bahamas. Ryan didn't want to go. He'd become increasingly distant and spent time hanging out with his friends. Jeremy had to work and wasn't interested, so Kristen took Toby.

The place was beautiful—top of the line—the room decorated in a high-end tropical theme with a view of the ocean. Kristen and Toby dined on lobster tail and jumbo shrimp in coconut sauce. They frolicked on the beach, running in and out of the crystal clear blue water, and played tag on the warm ribbon of sand.

Kristen could still hear Toby giggling with the sound of the surf in the background like it was yesterday. He was just a boy then. Already a teen now.

They went jet skiing, swam with dolphins, and even had their photo taken giving one of the gentle creatures a kiss on the beak. Kristen and Toby spent an afternoon at Aquaventure Water Park, floating peacefully down the lazy river. On the Leap of Faith slide, their hearts pounded hard in their chests as they plunged almost straight down from the top of a Mayan replica pyramid, racing through the clear acrylic tunnel into a pool surrounded by sharks.

Exhausted after a day of non-stop activities, they spent the evening ordering burgers and chocolate milkshakes from room service. Each cozy in their own queen bed, they eventually fell asleep with the TV on.

Kristen opened her eyes and gazed at the bottom of the unoccupied bunk above her. Her trip down memory lane should have been a purely happy one. But it wasn't quite so simple. She had paid for the vacation with stolen money.

She could've saved up to go on a vacation like that. She made good money, out-earning many in the family who had a college degree. She worked banker's hours and enjoyed a business casual dress code. The owners treated her like family until it was revealed she'd betrayed them. She knew that's one of the reasons they had been motivated to push for the maximum sentence.

If she could have given the money back, she would have. She wished they'd let her work so she could begin to pay them back, little by little. Yes, they had been demanding at times, and yes, they relied on her too much, but it didn't make it right to steal from them. She knew that now. She was mortified when, finally sober, she'd read through her own file. She didn't even know who that person was.

Earlier in her sentence, Kristen had befriended an inmate who used to be a lawyer. She'd helped her fill out the necessary paperwork for an appeal in hopes of having her sentence reduced, but after months and months of waiting, it came back denied. It was worth a try, Kristen thought, but eventually, she came to terms with what she had to do: live the rest of the best years of her life behind bars.

She missed her job, though. She'd been a hard worker, never arriving late or taking a sick day, was a whiz with computers, and was a super-fast typist. When a list of prison jobs opened up, the one at the library seemed a perfect fit, but Kristen applied for the one out in the garden instead. Many women were interested in staying busy, so the jobs always went quickly and were given to whomever Warden Laura felt deserved them.

Luckily, Kristen landed the position. Maybe Warden Laura had noticed her initiative with the exercise group and liked what she saw. She wasn't sure. Thankful, and with a desire to show appreciation for being selected, Kristen planned to make the outdoor area shine. Just as soon as she learned her way around plants.

Kristen delved into the task with determination, despite having little experience with gardening. She followed instructions from others, and before she knew it, she was digging into the earth, planting a variety of vegetables and flowers while working up a mighty sweat. She trimmed and pruned and studied, so she knew exactly what was needed to make each plant thrive.

The job didn't pay anything, of course, but for once, Kristen didn't mind. She was enjoying herself and savored the time alone, as privacy inside was in short supply. Someone was always yakking or bragging or arguing. It was incessant. And prison was no place for modesty, either. Shyness and embarrassment didn't have a home in a place where you brushed your teeth next to another woman taking a dump.

Compared to that, the garden was Heaven. It became Kristen's own little world, a place where she made plans for the future while toiling away under the hot sun. Life could be grim, but at least she'd get out someday, unlike the lifers, whose gain time sheet release date read 999. She still had a chance. She wished it would be with Jeremy, but every time she allowed herself that wish, she quickly pushed it aside. True, he hadn't pursued divorce yet. But was that just a matter of time? If he did choose to move on and get remarried someday, she would be sad, but she'd find the strength to wish him well.

Thinking of Ryan's graduation, Kristen realized she'd end up missing Toby's too, and probably their weddings. She could even become a grandma while locked away. At first, the idea depressed her. But the more she considered it, the more exciting it sounded. Maybe they'd need help raising them. Maybe they could use a hand.

Kristen smiled as she thought of the chance to be a better grandma than she had been a mom. She wanted to make it up to Ryan and Toby somehow, even if she couldn't go back in time and make it up to them.

She thought of her parents. She'd lost almost all contact with them. They never visited or wrote, only deposited some money in her commissary account each Christmas, probably out of guilt. She wondered if she'd ever see them again. While trimming a shrub, she came to the conclusion she highly doubted it. If they ever came around looking for another chance at a better relationship, would she give them the same opportunity she hoped to be given by her own children?

"Time to go back in," a corrections officer said. Kristen stood, wiped her hands, and returned her tools. She was starved and ready for dinner.

After collecting her meal, Abigail waved at her. Jess was behind her in line and cringed as Kristen eyed both of them.

"Hey," Abigail said, tray in hand. "I heard you're working in the garden. How nice."

"Yeah. I'm enjoying it. It's peaceful," Kristen said before walking toward an open table.

Abigail followed and took a seat next to her.

Kristen continued. "I've always wanted a garden. I'm learning about vegetables, annuals, perennials." She watched Jess stall for a moment, then walk away, taking a seat at another table with one of her basketball friends. Kristen turned back to Abigail and noticed she was wearing a bewildered expression. Kristen smirked. Let the idiot move on, she thought, and kept talking.

*****

Later, back in their cell, Abigail asked, "So what's with you and Kristen? You two never talk."

Jess was doing sit-ups and stopped. Short of breath, she said, "You noticed that? Yeah. We don't. We had a fight a while back."

"A fight? What about?"

Jess stood and ran a hand though her hair. "I don't know. It was so long ago, I don't remember anymore, but we don't speak to each other."

Abigail grinned. "You got into a fight with Kristen. I can't believe it. I mean, I guess I can, seeing as you told me the story of why you're here, but I find it hard to picture."

"How come?" Jess asked.

Abigail let out a giggle. "I don't know. I guess because you're so nice."

Chapter 12

Lakeisha was bored. Her job had always been a bit tedious, but with little happening in her "stories," it began to feel less like an entertaining soap opera and more like...opening prison mail. She started thinking of her college years and how she hoped to get into the publishing industry. Things hadn't gone as planned, but there was a bright side. She met her husband after graduation and got married.

Shrugging, she let go of her career ideals and focused on the work at hand. She repeated the process of opening each envelope and checking it for contraband, taking care to check the seams and running her thumb over the stamps. If there was a bump underneath, it was usually narcotics. It amazed her how crafty people could get when they wanted to take drugs.

As she made it to the end of incoming mail and was about to start outgoing, Warden Laura passed by. Lakeisha sat up once she saw her. She had been getting groggy and wanted to look alert.

As Laura paused in front of Lakeisha's office, her phone rang. "God damn it!" she cursed. "I'll be right there," she said, then took off running.

Lakeisha grew alarmed. Laura didn't run unless there

was an emergency.

*****

Rushing through the infirmary doors, Laura raced to where Megan lay. She was thankful to see there was no blood, but she was shaken. This shouldn't have happened.

Megan's eyes grew wide when she saw Laura.

"Are you okay?" Laura asked her. "Can you talk?"

Megan's eyes were red, and her neck was covered in bruises.

Megan began to speak, but it looked painful. "I was in session with Tanya," she said in a raspy tone. "She seemed fine. Then I glanced down at my notepad for a second, and she sprung at me."

Laura turned to the nurse who had just tapped her on the shoulder.

"The guard outside her office took quick action, otherwise, her larynx would've been crushed. I think she'll be okay. I just gave her a painkiller. She needs to rest."

Laura turned back to Megan. "Okay. I don't want you to talk anymore. You need to rest your throat. I'm going to ask you some questions, and instead of answering, you can lift one finger for yes or two for no."

Megan looked weary, like even that might be asking too much.

"Do you have anyone at home who can take care of you?"

Megan lifted two fingers.

"Do you have family nearby that you'd like me to call?"

Megan lifted two fingers again.

"You have any family near you?"

Megan lifted one finger.

"Good. You have family. Do you want me to call them?"

Megan lifted two fingers again.

"I see what you're up to," Laura said. "It's brave, but I can't send you home alone."

Laura mulled over an idea. "How about this? I can take you to my house after work. We have a spare bedroom. You can be my fifth kid until you've recovered. What do you think?"

Megan closed her eyes and lifted one finger. She had a smile on her face, no doubt from the happy drugs finally kicking in.

"Good. It's settled then," Laura said, then turned on her heel and left.

*****

Lakeisha stopped working when she saw Laura. She'd already heard the news but figured she'd listen to her tell the story again.

"I'm sure you know by now," Laura said.

Lakeisha nodded. "It's terrible. But to be honest, I knew it was only a matter of time until something like that happened."

Tapping her fingers on the top of the desk, Laura said, "Agreed. I haven't been comfortable with all her methods, especially allowing all prisoners to be un-cuffed during their visits, but I didn't want to interfere. She's been such an amazing help to a lot of the women. She's good at what she does." Crossing her arms and pacing, Laura added, "But I'm going to have to put my foot down. There has to be common sense. If the inmates have shown respect and can act like regular patients, then fine. They can be treated like one. But Tanya? She's a psycho. Why Megan would allow her to be un-cuffed is beyond me."

Lakeisha knew why. Because the crazy ones intrigued Megan the most. They were her passion.

"I think she just wants to help," Lakeisha replied.

Laura stopped pacing and looked furious. "That whack job doesn't need help. She needs a beating."

Lakeisha raised an eyebrow but thought it unwise to reply.

"I'm going to keep her in solitary until I figure out what to do with her. Right now, I don't want to subject anyone else to her special brand of madness." Laura crossed her arms in front of her chest. "Things are going to change around here going forward. I'm not taking any more chances. I've only got one Megan and lots of women who need help. Inmates that have an actual release date. I think we need to keep our focus there."

Lakeisha didn't have a response. She sensed Laura was just making a statement more than anything, which was confirmed when she abruptly walked away.

*****

As the workday drew to an end, Laura checked in on Megan.

"I've got your purse and sweater from your office. We'll swing by your place and gather what you need, and then we'll have dinner at my house. You like pot roast?"

Megan went to nod her head yes but felt pain, so she gave her boss a thumbs up instead.

Once they arrived at Megan's apartment, Laura sat on the sofa while Megan put clothes and toiletries in her bag. Megan grabbed her Kindle, too, figuring there would be plenty of downtime over the weekend. Looking around the place, she was thankful she'd cleaned recently. It would've been embarrassing to have her boss over if it looked like it usually did. She couldn't help it, though. When she was immersed in research, neatness took a back seat to knowledge.

As they pulled into Laura's driveway, Megan noted the middle-class neighborhood and nicely kept yards. A great place to raise a family, she thought. Once inside, the scent of prepared food hit her nostrils. It smelled great, and she hoped she'd be able to eat without too much pain. After brief introductions, she was shown to her room to drop off her things.

Laura had called ahead and asked the kids to turn off the Crock-Pot and set the table. Even in her personal life, things seemed to run in an efficient manner. Already exhausted from the day's events, Megan was relieved to be sitting down to a home-cooked meal.

Laura must have told her family what happened because they didn't make small talk with her. Under other circumstances, she would've loved to get to know them all, but her throat pain trumped that desire. Instead, she focused on cutting the tender meat and savory vegetables into minuscule chunks that could be swallowed with the least amount of discomfort.

Megan watched her boss interact with her husband. It was funny, she thought, how stern and forceful she could be at work yet gentle as a kitten at home. It was clear her hubby was the man of the house, and she seemed content and possibly relieved not to have that title at home.

They reminded her of her own parents, albeit a bit younger. She was grateful Laura had offered to help. Megan wasn't looking forward to telling her mom and dad what had happened. They both were already paranoid enough that she worked at a prison in the first place. There was no point in getting them upset. Not now, at least.

Soon after her meal, Megan grew drowsy. She could barely find the energy to change into pajamas, wash her face and brush her teeth. Once she climbed into bed, she was instantly out.

The day's trauma unfolded in her sleep, with Tanya's lifeless blue eyes staring into hers, offering her a serving of her cooked baby.

"Would you prefer an arm or leg?" she casually asked Megan.

Horrified but unable to scream, Megan ran, trying to escape while Tanya chased at close range with a large butcher knife, ready to strike.

Megan woke in a cold sweat and hoped she hadn't screamed out loud. When no one came to check on her, she assumed she hadn't. Thankful but unable to fall back sleep, she pulled out her Kindle and started reading a romance novel.

The next time she woke, it was mid-afternoon. Laura popped in to check on her soon after.

"Hey there. Glad you got a good night's sleep. Do you want breakfast? I can whip something up and bring it to you. Does an egg white omelet sound good?"

Megan lifted one finger for yes, thankful for Laura's continued generosity. Laura nodded and gently shut the door on her way out.

Laura returned within fifteen minutes with an omelet, a slice of buttered toast, and a glass of orange juice, all neatly set up on a wooden tray. Megan sat up in bed, and Laura set it in front of her.

"Enjoy," she said. "I put fresh towels in the bathroom if you want to take a shower or soak in the tub. I've got all kinds of bath salts and bubble baths to choose from. You'll see them in the basket."

Megan smiled as Laura walked away. It was hard to believe she had ever thought Laura didn't like her. She'd forever be grateful for her help and kindness during this ordeal.

By the end of the weekend, Megan felt better, ready to return to work. Laura suggested she spend Monday going over paperwork and not see any patients. She wanted to have a meeting with her first, she said, at 3:00 pm.

Megan heard the knock on her office door at the designated hour and smiled as Laura came in. Megan listened as she described the changes she'd decided to implement. There'd be no cuffs for the inmates Megan deemed safe, but restraints would be used on the questionable ones.

"I don't want to take any more chances," she said. "Understood?"

"Understood," Megan said. "You're right. I should have been more careful. I'm not going to make that mistake again."

Chapter 13

After an exhausting day in the garden, Kristen received a letter from Olivia. She sat back on her bunk and ripped it open.

Kristen,

Hey. How've you been? Things are fine here, but I've got some good news and some bad news. I might as well tell you the bad stuff first.

Toby is in the hospital. Some kind of stomach thing. He can't keep anything down and is constantly throwing up. He went to the doctor, and they suggested he not eat certain foods. They gave him medication, but it didn't help. He kept vomiting and lost a lot of weight in a short amount of time. Now they're running tests, and he's being kept overnight. They think it's an ulcer, which they said would be unusual for someone his age. Anyway, I thought you should know. As soon as I find out more, I will write back.

Now for the good news. Well, possible good news. Bob read an article online about the state of Florida running out of money and having one of the highest incarceration rates in the nation. The article said they're looking into releasing some of the less dangerous criminals in order to stay on budget. That sounds like you, right? Fingers crossed.

Same old same old here. Cocoa is feeling better since her dental cleaning. Bob is working non-stop, as am I. Looking forward to taking a vacation soon.

Love ya,

Olivia.

Kristen's hands were shaking. This was just the kind of thing she feared.

"Damn it!" she cursed, then broke into tears. She let them flow freely but didn't make any sound. She didn't want to attract attention or get hauled off to see Megan again. The woman had enough trouble of her own lately.

Toby's ulcer was all her fault. She was sure of it. No doubt because he was under constant stress, both emotional and financial. Olivia had said he was struggling to focus in school and that he was depressed because his mom was gone. Kristen wanted to rush to his side to comfort him, but her hands were tied. All she could do was pray he got better and hope what Bob had read was true, and she'd be selected to leave prison early.

Thinking of it all made her feel like she was losing her mind. She could really use a drink. Then she became furious and whipped the letter across the room. Alcohol had been one of the main reasons she was in this predicament.

She'd never been more upset in her life.

On break, Kristen threw herself into the workout

class, paying closer attention to the other students and seeing where they needed help. Afterward, there were murmurings of gossip about Tanya, that once she got put back into the mix, she was getting shanked. Kristen couldn't care less. The world might be a better place if she were gone anyway. At least then she wouldn't have to worry she'd get stuck rooming with her.

Not long after, that very situation was addressed. Kristen had been assigned a new cellmate. An older woman named Debbie.

After an uneventful introduction, the guard left them to get acquainted. Kristen offered her the top bunk as she'd been accustomed to the lower one and prepared herself for the inevitable night of conversation. She wasn't in the mood for talking or listening.

Debbie had just arrived from the local jail and didn't seem as ruffled as Kristen had been when she came. Kristen wondered what her crime was. She looked like someone's harmless aunt who was known for baking great cookies.

Out of the blue, the newbie said, "I'm in for murder, in case you're wondering."

A chill went down Kristen's spine, but she kept a straight face, revealing nothing. She hoped Debbie wasn't another psycho like Tanya. She almost wished she could take back her earlier thought. Had she jinxed herself?

Debbie smiled and added, "My husband used to beat me. I got tired of it one day and killed him in self-defense."

Kristen relaxed. She hadn't even noticed she'd tensed

all her muscles.

"I'm sorry to hear that," she said.

Kristen didn't know what to make of this new one.

"Me too," Debbie said. "I used to love him once upon a time, but the recurring blows to the head knocked some sense into me. I realized it couldn't be love and that he was sick."

Kristen immediately felt sorry for her. She'd heard about people like this but hadn't known anyone in her close circle of friends. "Couldn't you get help? Like from the police?" she asked.

Debbie sat down, crossing her legs and getting comfortable. "You don't know many battered women, do you?"

"No. I don't. You're the first one I've met. There are others here, but I don't know them well."

Debbie sighed. "Well, I'm glad to hear you don't know anyone. That's wonderful. I wish I could say the same. And yes, there is help available. You can file a report and get a restraining order, but it doesn't work. Sometimes it makes the situation worse."

Forgetting her own problems for the moment, Kristen asked, "How long were you married?"

Debbie sighed. "Ten years."

"Wow." Kristen paused, then asked, "And the abuse? Was it the whole time?"

"No," Debbie said, looking like it was exhausting to discuss. "It began slowly. First, he was normal, albeit jealous, which I thought was romantic. Then he began wanting to know where I was all the time, going so far as to put a tracking app on my smartphone. He could tell when I was at work and when I went on lunch break. He'd know if it was close by or if I had left and gone somewhere else, like the bank or the store. Then he'd always call to check up on me."

"Creepy," Kristen said.

"Yeah. Then he started telling me what to do and what to wear. We'd go to the clothing store to shop, and instead of hanging out to give his opinion like a normal guy, he'd make selections for me and force me to try on outfits that weren't my style. If I liked a dress he didn't care for, he'd say, 'I think that one's a pass.'"

"That would piss me off," Kristen said. "I don't like people telling me what to buy when I shop."

"I know. I didn't like it either. He acted like he owned me."

Debbie rolled her eyes, which made Kristen smile. She was starting to like her. She had a bit of an attitude.

Sighing, Debbie continued. "Look, I didn't plan on telling my life story to a stranger. Sorry. It's just that I like to get it out of the way, you know? I can stop."

"No, please. Keep going. I mean, if you want to. I've got nothing else to do at the moment."

"You sure?"

"Yes."

"Okay. In time, it got worse. He grew moodier. He never told me he was upset about anything or said there were problems we should work on; he was just always tense and uptight. Then one day, we had a minor disagreement, and he pushed me, and it escalated from there. Next time, it was a backhanded slap for something minor, like me accidentally cutting someone off in traffic. He'd tell me I was stupid and have me pull over and let him drive."

"God. That's awful. I'm so sorry," Kristen said.

"Thanks."

Debbie stretched her arms over her head and continued. "Eventually, he wouldn't let me go anywhere without him. No girl's night out. No manicures without him tagging along. If I wanted to do anything with someone else, he'd get enraged if he wasn't invited. And then he started to accuse me of cheating on him. I wasn't. In fact, that was the last thing on my mind. After a few years with him, I could've used a break from men just to be alone for a while."

"For real," Kristen agreed. "What a nightmare."

"Yeah. Anyway, it got to the point where I didn't love him anymore but was afraid to leave him. I tried to get help, like you mentioned, but the beatings grew more severe as I attempted to pull away. I was afraid he would kill me. So in the end, out of self-preservation, I killed him."

It was like a bad movie, Kristen thought, and so sad. She wondered what she'd do if she were in the same situation. Although she abhorred violence, she was known to have a temper. She didn't put up with anyone's shit. Still, she couldn't picture it.

"How much time did you get?"

"Five years. The judge could see it was self-defense but wouldn't let me get away with murder. I understand,

and I accept it. If I knew beforehand I'd have to spend half a decade here to be a free woman, I'd do it again. I didn't tell the judge that, of course, but I'm telling you. If I hadn't killed him, and if I had managed to survive somehow, the rest of my life would have been more of the same. At least now I have a life."

It was hard to believe she could think this was a life. To Kristen, there was nothing worse.

"Do you have children?" Kristen asked.

"No. And I'm thankful for that."

"You have savings?" Kristen quickly calculated the woman would be retirement age when she got out, same as her.

"A little. And I'll have Social Security. Plus I can work part time. Or who knows? Maybe I'll take my meager stash and leave the country. Live a totally different life somewhere."

Kristen eyed Debbie. Not only did she have attitude, she was adventurous. "You're a strong woman."

Debbie shrugged. "Haven't always been, but I learned to be."

The rest of the night, they discussed Kristen's situation. What she was in for, how she regretted what she'd done. They also chatted about Kristen's family and personal life. Debbie was in disbelief at the length of her sentence in relation to the crime.

"You should appeal it. Try to get your sentence reduced," Debbie suggested.

"I've tried. It was rejected. Now I'm hoping for a miracle. My sister-in-law said she saw an article about

Florida's prisons being overpopulated and that they're short on cash. She said they're thinking of letting some of the less violent inmates out earlier."

"That sounds promising," Debbie said.

After they'd gotten to know each other, Kristen gave her the run down on most of the other women. What to expect and whom to avoid. She explained the exercise routine and what meals would be like, about the garden, the library, and Megan. Once they'd breezed over every topic, it was time for lights out.

As Kristen lay in bed, she thought about how in men's prison, the inmates were separated by threat level, but in women's prison, everyone was lumped together, regardless of the crime. At first, this scared the daylights out of her. Then, in time, she realized most of her fellow inmates were women who had made bad choices, like her. Or like Debbie, who had killed in self-defense.

Of course, there were a few true nutjobs. Kristen shuddered to think of them. Even hardened criminals stayed away from them. You couldn't turn your back on them for a minute.

Before Kristen drifted off, she thanked God she got someone decent as her new cellmate. She was relieved it wasn't Tanya. And with that final thought, she drifted into a deep, peaceful sleep.

Chapter 14

Jess sat on the floor of her cell, bored while Abigail read a historical romance novel, one with a worn cover featuring a muscle-bound man holding a helpless-looking young woman in a flowing dress. Jess had been playing Solitaire but was losing interest. She gathered up her playing cards and set them aside, then began tapping her foot with her hands clasped behind her neck.

"Is that book any good?" Jess asked.

Abigail poked her head up. "Oh yeah. The duke is about to embark on a cross-country journey to find his lost love. There's a rumor she didn't die."

Jess scrunched her face. She might vomit, it sounded so awful. Abigail frowned. "I see it doesn't appeal to you."

"No," Jess lied. "It sounds all right. It's just not my thing. I like thrillers."

Abigail set her book down, folding the page so she wouldn't lose her place. "Which ones?"

"Lee Child. James Patterson."

"I guess those are good," Abigail agreed. "I just prefer romance."

"I'll still take my thrillers, thank you. I used to read

them out loud to my mom," she said. "She loved it."

"Aw… What a nice daughter. No wonder she visits all the time."

"Yeah. She's great. Hey, if you want to give your eyes a break, I can read the next chapter to you."

"Really? Are you sure?"

"Yeah. It's no problem. I was getting bored anyway. Can only play cards for so long."

Abigail looked thrilled. She bunched her pillow and got comfortable on one side of the lower bunk. Jess took the book and sat upright on the opposite side, leaning against the wall.

She cleared her throat and began reading. For the male voices, she made her own sound deeper, and for the female ones, she raised her pitch. If the scene was wrought with conflict, the struggle was reflected in her tone. And when it was a softer, more romantic moment, she was able to express that sentiment too.

When the chapter came to an end, Jess paused, set the book in her lap, and looked at Abigail.

"Don't stop!" Abigail said with a smile. "It's wonderful. You're a natural at this."

Jess saw how much it pleased her, and she wanted nothing more than to continue. So she picked it back up and turned the page.

If it made her beloved happy, she would read all night.

Jess finished another chapter within an hour and then took a sip of water to soothe her dry throat. "So tell me why they told the duke she was dead."

"It's because she was a peasant girl, and he wouldn't

be able to marry her," she explained, obviously entranced by the story. "He had to choose someone of noble origin. She was paid to disappear. Well, actually, she was told to leave with the money or suffer the consequences."

Jess enjoyed the book more than she let on. Maybe she just hadn't given the genre a chance. The plot wasn't half bad. Or maybe she just liked it because Abigail did.

"You must be tired. I can read for a while if you want," Abigail offered.

Jess would have been happy to continue but didn't want to deny Abigail the chance to read. "Okay," she said. "You're next."

Abigail sat up, and Jess took her spot, lounging with the pillow.

"She walked along the moor, fog hanging low, in the cool, misty evening. Would they ever meet again, she wondered. Would she ever kiss his lips? The memory of their last embrace burned in her mind."

Jess sat mesmerized, listening to Abigail's soft voice as she narrated the tale, her expression wistful to match the scene. She began daydreaming, visualizing Abigail walking near the moor, wearing what the character was wearing. As she listened, her mind trailed off, wondering if she would ever get to kiss Abigail's lips, like the duke and the peasant girl.

Abigail paused. "I'm no good at this. I should stop."

Jess looked up. "What? No. You're doing great. Please continue."

Jess hadn't realized it was so obvious she'd zoned out. She sat up and listened more intently.

A little bit later, when a scene came for Abigail to sound like a man, she botched it. "I refuse to do as you say, sir. And if you force me, I will draw my sword."

Jess burst into a fit of laughter. Abigail couldn't get her voice to go low enough, and it sounded hysterically unconvincing.

Spurred on by the bad performance, Abigail repeated the line, this time going overboard with an even deeper voice. It sounded awful, like she had gravel lodged in her throat.

Jess jumped up. "Gimme that."

"No," Abigail said, pulling her hand back.

Jess tackled her. "Gimme the book. You're ruining it."

Abigail wouldn't let go of the book, so Jess began tickling her.

"Ahhhh!" she screamed in a fit of laughter, writhing to make it stop, the book dropping to the ground.

Jess lunged for it and jumped back, trying to locate the correct page. Abigail was still recovering from the onslaught, then made one last attempt to snatch it back and failed.

Jess smirked. "Would you just let me read to you, woman? Why don't you sit down, get comfortable and let me do what I do best."

"Yes, sir," Abigail joked, saluting Jess. Then she reclined to her original position and calmed down.

"I refuse to do as you say, sir. And if you force me, I will draw my sword," Jess continued where they'd left off, sounding just like a man.

Jess kept reading, doing all the roles perfectly as she

had before. When she finished the chapter, she saw Abigail staring at her.

"What?" Jess asked, dying to know what was on her mind.

"Nothing."

"What do you mean nothing?"

Abigail sighed. "I don't know. I guess I was just thinking I didn't expect to ever have fun again."

Jess's heart almost burst from her chest. She couldn't hide how happy she felt. Trying to play it down, she said, "C'mon, Ab. Gotta have some fun. Can't be all doom and gloom."

The look on Abigail's face grew somber again. "It is for me."

"I thought you just said you were having fun." Jess couldn't understand how quickly her mood could change. She was so mercurial.

Abigail smiled again, although it looked forced. "I am. It's not you. It's me." She pointed to her head. "All doom and gloom in here."

Jess set the book aside. "You know I'm here if you want to talk."

"Huh," Abigail laughed blackly. "I wouldn't subject you to the horror."

Jess stared into her eyes, desperately wanting to know what caused her so much suffering. "You know you can talk to me. I'm your friend."

"Thanks," Abigail replied. "I'll keep that in mind."

Jess had grown frustrated with Abigail's unwillingness to share. She had shared many stories with her, from childhood to her teen years. Abigail always listened with interest and responded without ever revealing much about herself. When something did slip, Jess felt like she'd discovered gold. She hung onto the find like it was a treasure, trying to get Abigail to talk more, which unfortunately had the opposite effect.

Jess decided this time would be different.

"Why don't you tell me something that makes you happy? A good memory."

Abigail looked like she was considering it. "Hmm," she answered. "I'll have to dig deep on that one." She tilted her head and said, "I liked sailing with my parents as a child. My dad didn't see patients on the weekends, and we'd hit the open sea. He'd let me steer for a while, supervising, of course, but it was fun. They liked fishing too, and we'd always manage to catch something and bring it home for dinner. My mom is quite a good cook."

Jess smiled at her. "See. Was that so hard?"

"I guess not." Abigail pouted like she'd been scolded and had survived.

"How about another? That can't be the only happy memory you can think of."

Abigail sat up. "Okay. You asked for it. I was a ballerina."

"You were?" Jess asked, but could easily believe it. She still had a dancer's figure.

Abigail grinned. "I was." Then she stood up, got into a position with her heels touching, feet turned slightly out, and raised her arms in a graceful arc.

Jess admired her, nodding approval. Then Abigail bent

107

down into a squat, rose and spun around, landing back on her feet, with her long red hair in a swirl still catching up.

"Whoa," Abigail gasped. "I haven't done that in a while. I'm already out of breath."

Jess sat transfixed. She was out of breath too.

"I'm as uncoordinated as a drunkard with two left feet. I'm so out of practice."

"You looked like a pro to me," Jess managed to say. "Too bad we don't have more room. You make it look so easy."

Obviously enjoying the praise, Abigail said, "Why, thank you." Then she got into position again and bowed, the way dancers do at the end of a performance.

When she sat down, Jess said, "What? No more. You're all done?"

"For tonight I am. I'm pooped. And I don't have my tap shoes."

"You tap dance too?"

"Yep. Ballet. Tap. Hip Hop. If there was a dance class, I took it."

Jess immediately took an interest in the words "hip hop," with memories of ass-shaking rap videos tucked in the corner of her mind.

"How long did you take classes?" she asked, trying to appear friendly and casual, not wanting her inner lustful feelings to show.

"All my life, I mean, up until I got pregnant. After my son was born, I didn't have any time."

Jess's jaw dropped. Abigail had a kid! How had she managed to keep that a secret for so long? When Jess had pressed, she managed to get a whole lot more than she bargained for.

And when it came to Abigail, Jess wanted to know everything.

Chapter 15

Sitting in her office studying her notes, Megan looked up when she saw Lakeisha standing in the doorway holding Tupperware. "Oh, my God. More home-cooked food? You're just spoiling me now. I'm better, honest."

"No one's spoiling you. Just taking care of you is all."

Megan smirked. "Who knew wardens and corrections officers could be so nurturing?"

"Hmm... You got a diagnosis for that?" Lakeisha teased.

"How about Awesome Syndrome?"

They both laughed while they dug into their food. It felt nice to take a break. Both their jobs, although very different, could be overwhelming at times.

Megan stared distractedly at a faded floor tile, then found her voice. "Is Tanya still in solitary?"

"Yeah. Warden Laura thinks it's for the best."

Megan worried about Tanya. She wanted to talk to her again but wouldn't challenge Laura's new rules. "You were right about Laura," she said. "She's got a soft side. I was in shock when she offered to help me, and I was treated like gold last weekend. I never would've made it on my own, and it saved me from having to tell my parents."

Lakeisha smiled. "I'm glad she was able to help. Things will be fine. You'll see. You just have to take precautions, is all. Some of these bitches are just too dang crazy."

Megan burst into laughter. Lakeisha slapped her knee and giggled along with her.

"In all seriousness, though, a few of them are," Megan said. "Learned that the hard way."

"Don't we all."

*****

Back to the grind, Lakeisha shuffled through the mail and came upon a letter to Kristen from Lupe.

Good ole Lupe, she thought. She was one in a million.

Lakeisha opened the envelope and found a short note and photo inside. She pulled the picture out and nodded in approval. "Don't she know how to do it," she said to herself.

The photo was of Lupe and her incredibly hot boyfriend, Julio. The two of them stood hand in hand. He wore a suit, and she wore a body-hugging white wedding gown. The sign behind them said Las Vegas.

Kristen,

Hey, girl. I'm a married woman now. Can you believe it? Only the best for Lupe. You see how fine my man looks. His uncle has a restaurant out here and wants us to stick around and help him with it. I thought, why not? No real jobs at home. None that I could get, at least with a record. Julio's uncle is legit, mostly. And it's different here. You know what they say. What happens in Vegas.

I hope you're hanging in there. Keep your chin up, okay? You're a survivor.

Lupe.

Lakeisha checked the seams and, as expected, found no contraband. It was just formality. She wished Lupe good luck, a long life, and happy marriage, and most of all, that she stay out of trouble. Then she put the letter and picture back in the envelope and set it aside for Kristen.

Of all the women's stories she followed, Kristen's interested Lakeisha most. She didn't know why. Kristen wasn't magnanimous like Lupe. She hadn't committed any extraordinarily violent crime like Tanya. There wasn't any one thing that Lakeisha could find to explain why she was drawn to her situation more than the others. She just was. It would be a miracle if she could survive the sentence, she thought. She wasn't sure she would have the strength to do so herself.

*****

Kristen read Lupe's letter and smiled. She was so happy for her. Lupe would make a great wife, she thought, and she could picture her in Vegas. The town was larger than life, just like her.

"Good news? I see you grinning," Debbie said.

"Yeah. It's from Lupe. She got married and moved to Vegas. Here's the picture," Kristen said, handing it to her.

"What a good-looking pair. This is the funny one, right? With the stories?"

"Yeah. The woman is one hysterical adventure after the next."

Debbie sighed. "I want to be young, attractive, and funny. My life has been an adventure but not quite the same."

Kristen could relate. She would love to be young again, knowing what she knew now. "Don't worry, Deb. When you get out, you're going to have a second chance. Any man would be lucky to have you. Just got to find the right one."

"I'll take one like him, please," she teased. "Meow!"

Kristen and Debbie broke into a fit of giggles. It felt good to laugh over something for a change. It took the edge off things like seeing a corrections officer fling a woman through the air like a rag doll and slam her body to the ground. It happened from time to time, until an inmate learned to respect prison rules, but it was still difficult to watch.

One morning at breakfast, something even more disturbing took place.

"Did you hear?" Debbie asked Kristen as they ate.

"No. What's up?" Kristen replied. Debbie seemed tense, which in turn, made Kristen uneasy.

Debbie leaned in and whispered. "Someone murdered Tanya after she got out of solitary. Shanked her in the shower with a sharpened toothbrush and left her to die."

113

Horrified but not surprised, Kristen asked, "Who did it?"

"No one knows. Gossip is the guard on duty stepped away and didn't see anything."

Kristen and Debbie exchanged a knowing look. That was bullshit. And nothing would come of it. An investigation would take place, no one would talk, and the world would be less one sick psychopath.

All was well that ended well.

*****

Christmas came and brought a tiny ounce of cheer. Kristen's mom, who still hadn't come to visit, deposited some money in her commissary account so she could buy a few things. Olivia had sent her a couple of books, and her older son, Ryan, who usually never wrote, sent her a card with a note inside.

Tears of joy welled up in Kristen's eyes as she looked at the envelope. The red square was like a beacon of hope. She opened it and read the card. It was simple, not mushy, and then read the note.

Mom,

I've been thinking of you a lot lately. I filled out the paperwork to come and visit. I guess I have to wait and see if I'm approved. I asked Dad to come along, but he said he didn't want to. I'm not mad at him. It just would've been nice to have someone there with me. It's hard for him. He moves forward, and then he gets set back. I think seeing you again would ruin the progress he's made. He says he doesn't want to have a life with you, so what's the point of visiting? He did promise to help you when you get out because you were his wife once, and you're our mom, but until then, I don't think he wants to see you.

Anyway, my girlfriend and I are getting pretty serious. I think she's the one. Dad says to give it time. Don't rush things like he did. I think you'd like her. She was the one who suggested I write you finally. She said I was angry and depressed, and she couldn't stay with a person like that. She said I needed to fix things with you. Can you imagine such a young girl knowing all that? As I said, she's a keeper.

Merry Christmas, Mom. I love you.

Ryan

Tears streamed down Kristen's face. She'd hoped and prayed for this moment, and here it was. Her son was talking to her again and might even visit soon. And there was a girl. From the sounds of it, a wise one. Kristen could only wonder what it was like to see her oldest son in love.

She'd seen his first steps and heard the first words that came out of his mouth. She'd taught him how to swim and how to tie his shoes. And now this.

"You okay, honey?" Debbie asked, reaching out to rub her shoulder.

Unable to speak because she was crying so hard, all Kristen could get out was a "yep" between tears.

She cried because her child was in love, and she was missing it. She cried because he was happy, and she was happy for him. She cried because she might finally see him soon—her baby—and she cried because her husband had said she was his wife once. Past tense.

It was final, she realized. Their marriage was over. All that was missing was the divorce papers. She knew a manila envelope would arrive one day, and just like that, her future would be over.

She had no one to blame but herself.

Debbie sat opposite her, looking unsure of what to say. She wore a compassionate expression that soothed Kristen a little, and for a fleeting moment, Kristen felt like she could be her mom.

As she gazed at Debbie, she thought of all she'd been through. The controlling, manipulative spouse, the beatings. Thinking of it made her cry harder because she'd never endured any of that. She had a nice life, with a good husband and well-behaved kids.

"Honey, you have to pull it together. They'll be coming by for the count soon, and you don't want to miss the movie tonight."

The movie was *The Holiday,* a chick flick featuring Kate Winslet and Cameron Diaz. It was one Kristen really liked. This was the prison version of Christmas, and although it wasn't much, when you had nothing, it felt like an incredible gift.

No, Kristen thought. She didn't want to miss it.

She stood up and wiped her eyes, then reached for the nearby toilet paper roll to blow her nose. Afterward, she began breathing deeply, trying to get it together.

Things will work out, she told herself.

Later, as Kristen's group huddled together in the rec room and watched the film, she felt outside herself. While she gazed at the screen, her mind hovered over the gathering, observing it like a soul whose owner had just died, taking one last look before departing this earth.

Chapter 16

Jess munched on a candy bar she'd gotten with her commissary money. She wasn't a big sweets person, but every now and then, she'd indulge. Abigail had gotten her into the habit, being a chocoholic herself. And it was Christmas.

"I really liked the movie," Abigail said to Jess. "What did you think?"

"It was decent. Can't complain."

Jess had already told her what kind of movies she liked. Her favorite was the Jason Bourne series. She tolerated chick flicks.

"How about those houses, huh? I can't decide if I prefer the English cottage or the modern Los Angeles home," Abigail said.

"They both were great. But that's the thing about movies. Everyone looks perfect, and they live in amazing places. Not like real life."

"I guess you're right," Abigail agreed.

Jess had always been self-conscious about her looks, mainly her teeth, wishing she had more money and could have gotten braces. Jess bet Abigail didn't suffer from those kinds of problems. She was stunning and most likely had a beautiful home. Maybe that's why she could relate to the movie.

Jess noticed Abigail had that faraway look again.

"What are you thinking about?" Jess asked.

"Sad stuff. Again. Not something you'd want to hear."

"I don't mind. Spill it," Jess said.

Abigail gave Jess the "you asked for it" face, then replied, "I was thinking about a Christmas when Steve and I went to Taos, New Mexico. We stayed at this hotel, I can't remember the name of it for the life of me, but it had rocking chairs on the porch. There was a group of women clustered together knitting, with hot ciders resting nearby on a table." Abigail's face lit up at the memory. "It was so peaceful there. I could have stayed on that porch forever."

Jess looked confused. "That doesn't sound sad," she said.

Abigail's smile faded. It was replaced with a look of melancholy. "You're right. I guess it isn't. Except I was thinking he's probably there with his new wife instead."

Jess realized her blunder, that she'd been insensitive. "You still miss him, don't you?"

Sitting down now, looking weary, Abigail said, "Yes. I miss the way things were before."

Jess felt sad that Abigail was hurting. "I'm sorry."

Abigail reached over and threw her arms around Jess, taking her completely by surprise. An innocent gesture, just a hug for comfort, but it was like Santa Claus and all his reindeer had shown up, granting holiday wishes.

Jess wrapped her arms around Abigail and squeezed

her tiny body tight. "It's going to be okay," she said in a low, soothing tone, now hyper-aware of everything: the way Abigail felt against her, the way she smelled, the sound of her breath, all combining into one completely perfect moment.

Abigail pulled away. "Thanks," she said, looking somewhat better. "Sometimes a hug from a friend helps."

"No problem," Jess replied, feeling dizzy. She made a mental note to remember to act like a friend more often. She had spent the majority of her time going out of her way to make sure she didn't make Abigail uncomfortable, so much so that she missed out on opportunities like this one.

"How about your son? Maybe talking about him will cheer you up."

It hadn't before, and the truth was Abigail hardly spoke of him. Any mention seemed to end in a change of conversation. She was probably too sad to discuss the boy, Jess thought. And now, after bringing it up again, she realized maybe it wasn't a good time, even if she was curious to the point she couldn't stand it.

Something in Abigail changed, but Jess couldn't place it. "Devin loved Christmas," she said. "When he was young, it was so nice."

Abigail got up from the bunk and stretched from side to side, Jess' eyes following her, still reeling from the hug but wanting to hear more about her son.

"I'll bet he got a ton of toys," Jess said.

Turning back to face her, Abigail replied, "Yeah. He did. And he'd find one he liked and play with that one exclusively, until it was worn out, ignoring the others."

"My parents should be so lucky," Jess joked. "When I was a child, I'd play with all my toys and destroy them in a matter of weeks. Nothing was sacred. I was a real brat."

Abigail seemed to brighten at the comment. "You must have done something right. Your mom still comes to visit all the time."

"Well, you know. She's my mom," Jess shrugged.

"She's a good one," Abigail said, her lip quivering, looking like she was on the verge of tears all of a sudden.

"I'll bet you were a good mom, too," Jess said, her earnest smile full of kindness.

Abigail's expression was odd, almost like she'd been told she had blue hair. "I tried," she mumbled.

Feeling confused, Jess added, "You'll see him again one day. Maybe your ex-husband won't bring him, but eventually, he'll come. You'll see."

All the color drained from Abigail's face, and she looked faint. She seemed to waver in place where she stood.

"No. I won't."

*****

Debbie was gossiping about another inmate, someone she didn't like. Kristen listened, but her mind was elsewhere. All she could think of was what Ryan had said in his note.

"You mind if I offer you some advice?" Debbie asked.

"Sure," Kristen said, surprised by the sudden attention. She sat up to listen.

"Here's what I think. You've got a long time here. What do you have, nine years left?"

Kristen frowned. "Yeah."

"There's no sense agonizing over the past. You had a marriage, and now it's over, even if there aren't divorce papers yet. There's been no contact. Your son told you what your husband said. And as sad as it is, maybe it's a good idea to forget him. You may leave here and meet someone amazing, someone even better for you. You never know. The future is unpredictable."

Kristen listened, all the while visualizing herself standing inside a clear bubble. The words sounded muffled as they came out of Debbie's mouth. Kristen stood inside the enclosure, protected from intentions that were not her own. She didn't want to consider her ideas.

When Debbie finished, and it was Kristen's turn to reply, the bubble soundlessly popped. "You might be right," was all she said back.

That evening, Debbie lay in her bunk snoring, a habit that Kristen had grown accustomed to but hated. She thought of Ryan. She couldn't wait to see him again. Maybe when Toby turned eighteen, he would come and visit her too. Then, as she drifted off, she mentally repeated her nightly mantra. "My family and I will be reunited, and we will be happy again. My family and I will be reunited, and we will be happy again."

She had been reciting the line for so many years now it turned on by itself when her head hit the pillow. The rhythm of the phrase was like a lullaby, calming and peaceful, like a trickling fountain. Kristen planned to keep thinking positively and visualizing what she hoped would happen, however impossible it seemed.

*****

Lakeisha's due date was fast approaching. And she was thankful because it was becoming increasingly difficult to sit at her desk. She'd made it through the holiday mail rush and was thoroughly exhausted.

Megan swung past her. "You getting excited yet? I'll bet you can't wait."

"I can't wait. I think a few of my co-workers can't wait too."

Raising an eyebrow, Megan said, "And that means?"

"Means I may have snapped once or twice in the last month on a few of them. Luckily, they've been gracious enough to walk away. They could've told me off."

Lakeisha felt terrible that she'd lost her cool, but the power of hormones was too much for her to handle. She was usually very nice, so she hoped they'd let her rare snippiness slide.

"They'll get over it," Megan said. "So, do you know if it's a boy or a girl yet?"

"Nope. We decided we didn't want to know. We chose two different names in case, and hubby painted the bedroom a pale yellow."

"Are you going to go natural or do the epidural?"

Lakeisha thought about it. "The plan is natural, but I'm not going to turn away pain meds if it becomes unbearable."

"That's my girl," Megan said. "No need to be a hero. Take the drugs." She smiled and added, "Laura and I will stop by afterward. We have a little something for the baby."

"Sounds good."

When Lakeisha finally went into labor, her husband rushed her to the hospital. She was in a lot of pain and asked for an epidural, but they said they couldn't give it to her because something was wrong. There was frenzied activity all around her. The doctor was shouting commands.

The next time Lakeisha woke, it was morning. She'd passed out during the commotion, she guessed. When the nurse came in to see her, Lakeisha smiled. She couldn't wait to see her baby.

"I'm sorry to tell you this. But your baby didn't make it. She was stillborn."

Lakeisha processed what she said and felt ill.

Her name would have been Ashley.

Chapter 17

When Lakeisha returned to work, her mind wasn't on the mail. She was heartbroken and unhappy but refused to take anti-depressant medication. The daughter she lost consumed her thoughts. She wondered why she had been blessed and then had the gift taken away. Still, Lakeisha plodded along, trusting there was some greater reason for her suffering. Her husband had been extra attentive lately, and even though they were both despondent, they were closer than ever. He'd promised they would try again when she was ready.

The sound of a siren growing louder in the background caught Lakeisha's attention. She stood up, walked over to the window, and noticed an ambulance racing toward the gates. Then, a moment later, the phone rang.

She hurried back to her desk to grab it. "Lakeisha speaking."

It was the staff nurse. "Warden Laura is being taken to the hospital. She's having a heart attack."

"Oh no!" Lakeisha gasped.

"Tell the others," the nurse said, then hung up.

Lakeisha was immediately worried sick. Laura had

been complaining she wasn't feeling well lately and thought it might be indigestion. Good Lord, Lakeisha thought, when problems hit, they all seemed to come at once. She finished contacting her co-workers, telling them each the news, and most took it badly. Megan became especially distraught, her voice quivering as she spoke. She sounded on the verge of tears.

The paramedics whisked Laura away to the hospital, and the guards were instructed to keep the event between staff and not let prisoners know. Easier said than done, though, as a handful of inmates had been out on the yard when the ambulance pulled up.

*****

As word of Warden Laura's incident spread, the officers remained vigilant while prisoners began reacting to the news.

"I hope that bitch dies!" one of the women cried out. She wrapped her hands around the bars that held her in captivity and gripped them as tight as she could. "You're gonna meet your maker, you rotten white piece of shit," she screamed.

Her comments were like a call that beckoned, inviting others to join in, and soon there were more, like echoes, each trying to outdo the last in severity.

"Die, Warden Laura! I hope you rot in Hell. You motherfucking cunt!"

"The devil has a special nightstick waiting for you, bitch!"

The slander grew increasingly malignant, and the atmosphere was volatile, making it difficult to confront each prisoner. Before the guards could figure out how to best handle the situation, a group chant broke out.

"Die, Laura, die. Die, Laura, die. Die, Laura, die…"

Hoots and whistles erupted in the background, and the malicious incantation intensified, accompanied by clanking and foot stomping. Total pandemonium.

One of the officers—who felt she wasn't paid enough to deal with this shit—asked her superior what to do.

"If we start cracking people upside the head with batons, it will only get worse. Better to let them wear themselves out. Let's keep our eyes peeled and make sure no one gets hurt, though. The last thing we need is for one of them to start fighting with their cellie. Save your energy in case we have to handle something like that."

The officer nodded and returned to her assigned area, skin prickling with discomfort. She would definitely step up her job search when she got home.

*****

"Goodness. Can you believe how everyone is shouting?" Abigail said to Jess. "It's terrible."

Jess could believe it. She'd even been tempted to join them and let some of her inner rage dissipate but thought better of it. For one, she didn't want any of the guards to remember her as being included in the mayhem. Who knows what kind of trouble that could bring at a later date? And two, she could see Abigail was appalled by the scene. Keeping quiet was a win-win, as far as she could see.

Abigail looked back at Jess when she didn't respond, and Jess just shrugged. "Look around. It's not exactly an etiquette convention. The place is a dump."

Cracking her neck, Abigail said, "You're right. I guess I'm just getting spooked. I hate being here."

Jess had never heard Abigail complain about being in prison. It seemed she was increasingly agitated lately. A shoulder massage would help for a while, but then whatever plagued her mind continued to torment her, and she'd be troubled again. The only time she seemed to be completely at peace was when Jess read to her, which she did often. But when they were just hanging out, killing time, something they had an abundance of, she seemed more and more uptight.

Jess wondered if Abigail would ever tell her what her crime was. She wished she'd share it with her already. Maybe then she could help. Maybe having someone to talk to would make her feel better.

All Jess wanted was for Abigail to be happy. But when it came to this inner demon Abigail struggled with, Jess felt powerless.

A stern voice came over the intercom. "Unless everyone wants to skip dinner and wait until breakfast tomorrow to eat, stop chanting and sit down in your cell. No one will be allowed to leave until there is order."

"Finally," Abigail said. "A sane voice. God, I'm starving. I hope these idiots shut up soon. I really want to eat."

"We've got chips, just in case," Jess reminded her.

Abigail paced back and forth, looking highly agitated, ignoring Jess' attempt to soothe her.

Soon the cries from beyond began dissipating, the mob giving thought to their basic needs, like food and water. Around a half hour later, the excitement faded, and things returned to normal. They were all still locked up in prison, and Laura, regardless of what they thought of her, was a free woman being taken care of by doctors. Something to ponder as they ate their miserable-tasting dinners.

*****

The following day, Megan woke up and got ready to go to the hospital to visit Laura. That meant missing a date with her boyfriend, but he told her not to worry about it, that he'd see her at home afterward. This one wasn't clingy, and for his efforts, he was rewarded with a key to her apartment, often staying over a few nights per week.

"Hey," Megan said to Laura while holding a vase of flowers. "You gave us quite a scare."

Laura lay in bed looking weak and exhausted. "I always knew this job would kill me," she joked.

Megan smiled faintly, then set the vase on her bedside stand. "Well, it didn't. You're too tough for that. You just need to take it easy."

"Yeah. And it's not just a suggestion anymore. It's an order. Have to change my diet and find time to exercise too." Laura rolled her eyes like that was going to happen.

"Is there anything I can do to help?"

"No. I've got these guys to wait on me," Laura said. "But thanks for offering."

"Okay. Well, if you change your mind and need me let me know."

"I will," Laura said with a smile.

Laura's husband was just returning from the snack machine with two of the kids, and Megan thought it appropriate to leave. She didn't want to take up all their visiting time. "Oh, almost forgot," she said, handing her a get-well card. "It's from everyone. Lakeisha wanted to visit, but she didn't seem up to coming to the hospital. She told me to tell you she is praying for you."

"Thanks," Laura said, holding onto the card, choosing not to open it right away.

"Get better," Megan said. Then she waved and left.

As she got into her car, she thought about all the recent challenges: her near strangling, Lakeisha's tragedy, and Laura's heart attack. They'd had their fair share of bad luck. Maybe the tide would turn soon.

*****

"I wish my husband would have died of a heart attack," Debbie said to Kristen. "No such luck. He was a fit bastard too. One of the things that attracted me to him in the first place."

"My husband isn't buff," Kristen said. Technically, they were still married. "He's just normal. Burns a lot of calories working on cars, so he doesn't have to work out."

"Unlike his wife, the exercise queen," Debbie smirked.

"Just something to occupy my time, like working in the garden."

"Yeah. While you were out working, you missed the insanity in here. I thought they were going to tear gas us all."

"I was planting some flowers and had just been battling an ant attack on my ankles when I heard the ambulance. I was curious about what was happening, but no one was talking. When it was time to come back in, they told me to hang tight, so I kept working. I could stay out there all day. No offense."

"None taken," Debbie said.

"I wonder if Warden Laura made it? She's always been fair with me," Kristen said.

"I'm sure we'll find out soon enough. And yeah, she seems fine. Just doing her job. What an awful one, right? Who would want to run a prison?"

Kristen didn't reply. She was entertaining another small hope about Florida's sentence reduction plan. She really hoped Laura recovered. Not just because she had always been fair with her but because she'd have a better chance of leaving sooner with her in charge than with someone new.

Chapter 18

Kristen's oldest son Ryan had been approved for visitation, but she suffered a familiar disappointment each weekend. No visitors. Ryan had gotten more serious with his girlfriend, Valerie, and they had been spending all their free days on dates or hanging out with friends. He kept in touch, though, writing monthly, and just when all hope seemed to be lost, he said he would come and visit with Toby, who had just turned eighteen. All he had to wait for was Toby's visitation papers to be approved.

The news of Toby's authorization came to Kristen first. Seeing the paperwork made her ecstatic. She hadn't been this happy about anything the entire time she'd been locked away. She didn't know when they'd visit, but they would eventually, and that was all that mattered. It had been so long since she'd seen her boys. In the years that passed, she'd watched them grow in a succession of photographs Olivia had sent her. They both looked like little adults now, she thought. All their innocence lost. Time she'd never get back with them.

Kristen had always wanted Olivia to visit her too. They'd discussed it once via letter, Olivia reluctantly admitting it might be too much for her to handle, that she'd see her on the outside one day. That made sense to

Kristen. Just as she sugar-coated the outgoing mail to Olivia, leaving out some of the more upsetting prison events, she knew Olivia did the same with the information that filtered in to her. The two women had established a comfortable balance, something that could be upset if their dynamic changed. Plus, Olivia remembered Kristen as fun and fabulous. Seeing her there would probably be too painful.

Lakeisha stopped by Kristen's cell and had a smile on her face. "You've got mail," she said.

With the positive expression she wore, Kristen knew it could mean only one thing: the boys were coming to visit. She'd gotten good at deciphering what kind of news was headed her way depending on Lakeisha's expression. No eye contact meant something bad. Her friendly but often vacant expression meant a basic life update from Olivia. Today's grin spread from ear to ear. And Kristen quickly snatched the envelope from Lakeisha's hand.

Mom,

We just got word that Toby's approved. Woo hoo! We are finally coming to see you this weekend.

Sorry it has taken so long. I just didn't want to come by myself.

Love,

Ryan

Tears of joy sprung from Kristen's eyes. She didn't try to stop them. She set the letter down, and Debbie gave her a big hug.

"See, honey. It's all gonna be okay, like I told you."

Her words sounded like the soothing comfort of a knowing mother, something Kristen had never experienced.

Kristen wiped away her tears. "I know. I believe you now."

"So, are they both coming?"

Kristen nodded. Her heart felt like it would burst at the seams.

"That's wonderful! When?"

Kristen looked up, radiating happiness. "This weekend."

Debbie smiled too. Then they sat together, enjoying the moment, saying nothing more.

*****

Time dragged like a high school detention on a beautiful summer day until Sunday's visitation. The week felt like a year to Kristen. Even the activities she usually enjoyed, like gardening and exercise class, seemed to bring no pleasure. All she could think of was seeing her boys.

Saturday night, Kristen wasn't able to sleep. As much as she wanted to be refreshed and look her best the next day, she just couldn't relax. The anticipation was too great, and she was worried. What would they think of her appearance, she wondered, wearing her faded prison uniform and looking like a hardened version of her former self? Would it frighten them? Would they still think of her as their mom? What if it got back to Jeremy how awful she looked? Her figure was the best it had ever been, but her skin, tanned and rough, was different. She wasn't the glamorous woman she once was. Surely they'd notice. Surely they'd tell their dad.

After stressing for hours, she finally decided it didn't matter. Jeremy wasn't coming and still hadn't written. This wasn't about him. It was about the boys. She couldn't change what they saw and hoped they wouldn't care. Maybe when they looked into her eyes they would see what she wanted them to see, a mother who truly loved them.

Despite her lack of sleep, the following morning Kristen felt energized. She showered, brushed her teeth twice, and carefully combed the knots out of her hair. Usually, the lack of privacy got on her nerves. She hated being undressed in front of a bunch of other women. But today, it didn't upset her. Today was her day.

At the appointed time, a corrections officer approached her cell. "You have visitors," she said flatly.

Kristen jumped up, the officer's unexceptional line sounding like music to her ears. She was taken to a waiting area she had never been to, where she sat with other inmates. The mood was upbeat in the tiny space, everyone excited to have contact with someone from the outside world. Within five minutes, a guard popped her head in and motioned for Kristen to follow.

The visitation area was a large cafeteria. Silver tables with attached benches were spread throughout, and there was a spot to purchase microwaveable food and vending machines for soda and candy. It was decorated to have a cheerful, homey feel, much more pleasing to the eye than the rest of the prison.

Kristen saw Ryan wave as he and Toby came walking toward her. The sight of them stole the air from her lungs, and she wanted to cry all over again but promised herself she wouldn't, not until they were gone. She had to be strong today.

"Hey, Mom," Ryan said as he opened his arms.

Kristen wrapped hers around her oldest boy and hugged him so tight she thought she might crush his ribs. He smelled of men's cologne and bubble gum mixed with the scent of fresh air. "Hey, honey," she whispered to him. "I missed you."

"Missed you too," he said.

Forcing herself to let go and pull away, she smiled at Toby. He'd grown twice the size it seemed, no longer the boy he'd been on their last trip to Atlantis Resort.

"Look how tall you've gotten," she said, then put her arms around him and gave him just as big a hug as she'd given Ryan.

"Ow!" Toby joked.

Kristen loosened her grip and smiled. "Sorry, honey. I just missed you so much."

Toby smiled. "Missed you too, Mom."

With two guards nearby watching their every move, Kristen, Ryan, and Toby walked over to a bench and took a seat. The other prisoners and their conversations faded into the background. Kristen's focus was entirely on her sons.

"They said we could bring money and buy lunch. Are

you hungry?" Ryan asked Kristen.

"You didn't have to do that," she said.

Toby chimed in. "We know, but we wanted to. What are you in the mood to eat?"

Kristen's stomach was nervous, but she didn't want to pass up fast food. It was the first time she had access to something other than the usual slop.

"I don't know," she said, looking around. "Let's see what they have here."

The three of them made their way to the food station and picked out two burgers and a hot dog. They purchased two Cokes and a Sprite, and a package of Starburst and returned to their seats.

Ryan looked uneasy. Kristen had heard about the security procedures. They'd get patted down and have their bodies scanned with hand-held wands, just like at airport security. Their shoes would be removed and searched, and a corrections officer with clear plastic gloves would look inside their mouths and under their tongues, making sure they weren't concealing anything. They couldn't bring anything in with them except their driver's license and some cash to purchase food.

It didn't seem like much when watching an episode on TV, Kristen thought, but in the real world, she was sure it was disquieting.

Ryan and Toby seemed at a loss for something to say.

"So, how've you been?" Ryan finally asked her.

The words he spoke sounded off, like a wrong note had been struck while playing the piano.

Kristen pretended not to notice. "I'm doing okay.

Much better now that you two are here."

Her response seemed to comfort them. The tense expressions on their faces relaxed. Olivia had told her they worried endlessly about her, wondering what her life was really like. They'd watched a bunch of episodes of *Lockdown* together, ignoring their father's request not to, and were well aware of the harsh reality of prison life.

"So tell me all about your girlfriend," Kristen said to Ryan. She took a bite of her hamburger, the first beef she'd eaten in half a decade, choosing to avoid the mystery meat they served in the cafeteria.

Ryan lit up at the mention of his significant other. Toby seemed happy not to have the spotlight directed at him.

"She's awesome," Ryan cooed. "Treats me nice, doesn't nag. And she's beautiful. Like I said before, I think she might be the one."

Kristen took a swig of her Coke and smiled. "She sounds wonderful, honey. And since you sent pictures, I know she is beautiful too."

Turning her attention to Toby, she asked, "How about you? Any girlfriend yet?"

"Nah. No time. Gotta practice the guitar and write songs."

"Once he's famous, he'll have all the chicks," Ryan teased.

Toby opened a lemon Starburst, popped it into his mouth, and then shrugged. He looked like he couldn't care less. Kristen smiled, remembering what Olivia had said about all the young ladies constantly blowing up his phone with texts to "hang out."

"How is the band going?" she asked Toby.

"Good. We might have a big show soon. Still waiting to hear. Dad's friend knows people since he was in that band before."

Must be a new buddy, she thought, as they'd never had a guy in their circle of friends who'd been in a band.

"How lucky that Dad has a musical connection now. That's almost meant to be, like fate helping you," Kristen said.

"It's Cindy's friend, actually, not Dad's."

"Cindy?"

"Dad's girlfr—"

Ryan elbowed Toby a second after it slipped out, then glared at him, but it was too late. His face sank in response to the blunder.

The words were like a punch in the gut to Kristen.

"This hamburger is pretty good," she said, ignoring her youngest son's slip-up and taking another bite.

Toby took a bite of his hot dog. He looked upset with himself. Kristen led the conversation, though, and they continued chatting about mundane things. She tried to ignore that their time was coming to an end soon.

When they'd eaten the last of the candy, Ryan stood. "Mom. Check that out," he said while pointing to a wall that had a mural of a colorful rainbow painted on it. "It looks like we can get our pictures taken there. You wanna do it?"

Kristen beamed and stood up. "Yes," she said. "I do."

The three of them headed to the mural, and the

photographer stepped up.

"Two dollars per Polaroid," she said, and with that, Ryan reached into his pocket and gave her six dollars, enough so they could each have a photo of their own.

Both boys looked at the Polaroid camera. It was from before their time, Kristen mused. But in prison, it was considered the latest technology.

The photographer got situated in front of them as they prepared for their shot, with Kristen in the center, Ryan on her left, and Toby on her right. She said cheese, and they all smiled brightly. After she took their picture and set the film on the table to develop, they repeated it two more times. Afterward, she handed them their mementos.

"Thank you," Kristen said, tears welling up in her eyes. They didn't spill because she fought them back, but her sons noticed, and it seemed to make them uncomfortable.

The guards announced it was time to wrap things up, and Kristen was allowed one more hug before they left. This time they each hugged her just as tight back.

"I love you, Mom," Toby said.

"Love you too."

Kristen hugged Ryan next. They said their I love you's and then their goodbyes, and in an instant, her kids were waving to her and walking away, out the door and into the free world.

140

Chapter 19

Ryan and Toby walked side by side without speaking back to the car. The fervid sun beat down on them as if in anger, and the humidity, something they'd grown used to living in Florida all their lives, felt especially oppressive. As they approached their vehicle, Ryan fell to his knees. Toby froze, unsure of what just happened, and then he heard sobbing.

His older brother had always been the strong, silent type, and through the years, whenever Toby had a problem, like being bullied at school, Ryan had been the one to take care of it. Now he watched him cry, something he'd never witnessed before, head in his hands, gasping for air between sobs.

Toby reacted by doing the first thing that came to his mind. He crouched down and reached for his arm, grabbing hold of him.

"C'mon, man," he said, helping him back up. "I got you."

Ryan took hold of it and stood, the effort seeming too much for him. His tears slowed, and he inhaled some deep breaths, the expression on his face was like a shell-shocked soldier who'd seen one too many battles.

Ryan wiped the tears away and let out a deep sigh. He

looked up at Toby. "That was so fucked up."

"I know," Toby agreed.

"Those guards opening up our mouths and patting us down beforehand."

"Dude. I know. It was freaky."

Ryan rubbed his head, which was shaved with just a bit of stubble. "Man. Seeing Mom there."

"It sucks," Toby said.

"Yeah."

"She looked different too."

"I noticed that."

Ryan pulled the photo out of the back pocket of his pants and studied it. Toby checked it out as well. "Can you believe this shit is real?" Ryan asked. "That this is our life?"

The two boys—young men now—locked eyes. The moment felt suspended in time, and Toby knew he would never forget it. He felt Ryan was thinking the same.

Toby looked away, breaking the spell. "No. I can't believe it. I wish things were different." He paused, let out a deep sigh, and said, "Why don't you let me drive?"

Ryan fished the keys out of his pocket. He seemed thrilled to hand them over. On the way home, he sat in the passenger seat with his eyes closed and the air cranked.

*****

After the visitors left, the inmates were taken to an area to be checked. Kristen was patted down, the inside of her mouth searched, and her shoes were removed. There was always a chance something could be passed to a prisoner even though they were being carefully monitored. Kristen didn't mind the routine. She was ecstatic to have finally seen her boys after so many years.

The guard took her back to her cell, where Debbie was sitting in her bunk reading a novel.

"How did it go?" she asked.

Kristen held the picture in the air, and Debbie set her book aside, swung her legs over the edge of the top bunk, and reached for the photo.

"Aw... Aren't they sweet," she said, then looked up at Kristen, who had now begun crying.

"Sorry," Kristen said. "I'm a bit overwhelmed. And I didn't want to lose it in front of them."

Debbie handed the picture back to Kristen. "You don't have to apologize, honey. We're friends."

Kristen was surprised when she thought about the friends she had made while being locked away. She never expected to, but the longer she was there, the more she managed to find a few people she really liked.

"Thanks, Deb. I really appreciate that. If you don't mind, I think I'm going to lie down and rest now. I'm spent."

"I don't mind at all. I'll just get back to my story. You relax."

Debbie swung her legs back up. Kristen kicked off her shoes and lay down, facing toward the wall in an attempt at privacy, and gazed at her photo. Their visit was bittersweet and had gone by much too fast, in her

opinion. She sighed and set the picture next to her pillow.
With eyes closed, Kristen's mind went somewhere she
didn't want it to go: Cindy.

Of course, there would eventually be a Cindy. How
could there not? Somehow knowing her name made it
worse.

She was getting a little dose of karma, and it didn't feel
very nice.

Kristen's abdomen twisted. Her greasy-hamburger
lunch, combined with the thought of another woman
sleeping with her husband, was a stomach-churning mix.
Her head began to feel hot, and soon perspiration dotted
her forehead. She was sure she was going to be ill. Kristen
tried to will her intestines to relax because she hated
being sick, especially in front of another person.

If it happened, it happened, she thought. There was
nothing she could do.

Unwanted images popped into her mind of her
husband and Cindy making love. She didn't know what
Cindy looked like, of course, but her brain was a sadistic
inventor, conjuring up visions of a luscious Victoria's
Secret supermodel with long tousled hair and mind-
blowing curves.

One X-rated scene after another assaulted her. She
could see them doing it in every position. The images
made her dizzy even though she was lying down, and
anxiety rose in her chest, causing it to constrict. The
abdominal spasms quickened, and then there was nausea,
followed by the sensation of water rushing to her mouth.

Kristen jumped up and ran to the toilet. She leaned

down and vomited the contents of her stomach into it, sweating and shaking afterward.

"I knew that food wouldn't agree with you," Debbie said from above. "You haven't eaten like that in a long time."

Kristen dropped to her knees, worried another round was on its way. "I know," was all she could reply.

She had no intention of discussing what had really made her sick. She didn't want pity or a lecture on how she'd get over him and find a new partner someday. That was the last thing she wanted to hear. What she wanted most was silence.

Wiping her mouth with the back of her hand, she got up carefully, regaining balance, then washed her hands and splashed her face. Once it seemed certain she wouldn't throw up again, she returned to her bunk, curled into a fetal position, and closed her eyes.

Kristen thought back to her wedding day. It had been a celebration—a fun affair where guests enjoyed themselves. Nothing stuffy, like some she had been to. Through the years, lots of people had told her it had been one of their favorite weddings. They loved the music, the food, the drinking, and the dancing.

Her mind skipped further back to another memory. She and Jeremy were walking hand in hand at Disney World after having just gone on a series of heart-stopping rides. He paused, looked at her, and said, "Will you marry me, Kristen? I want to grow old with you."

His proposal was completely unexpected, and the words were like a wave of warmth washing over her. The light in Jeremy's eyes shined from deep within, and the sun setting in the background gave the moment a spiritual quality. She'd never forgotten it.

Then, just like a scene in a movie, Kristen said yes, and she threw her arms around his neck, and he pulled her close for a tender kiss.

Her reverie was interrupted by the sound of two cellmates arguing next door. "Why don't you kiss my black ass," one of them cursed. "Why don't you shut the fuck up," the other shouted, their confrontation deflating the last shred of romance the memory had offered.

Kristen pulled her blanket over her head like it could shield her from the insanity surrounding her. She didn't know how much more she could take of the place, but what choice did she have?

She'd have to endure it.

She thought of what brought her here—all the stealing, the phony checks she'd written. She pictured the shopping trips and all the items she'd bought that seemed so important then, so necessary to her happiness. How wrong she had been. She wanted to beat herself up again, but self-flagellation was pointless. What was done was done.

Cindy popped into her mind again, the thought of her as frightening as a painted clown. She smiled, and her perfectly straight teeth taunted Kristen. Her full lips mocked her, and without uttering a syllable, her smile said it all: *You blew it.*

A solitary tear rolled down Kristen's face, the last tear in a day defined by tears, both happy and sad. But this one was the saddest of all. Part of her thought it might be a good idea to see Megan about the development, but the more she thought about it, the more she realized it would be a waste of time. All they would do was discuss the obvious and beat it like a dead horse. No, she decided, she wouldn't waste Megan's time. There were women waiting to see her with bigger problems. She would just deal with it on her own.

Then, even though there was no chance for a future with her husband, she closed her eyes and repeated her mantra: "My family and I will be reunited and be happy again. My family and I will be reunited and be happy again."

The repetition was like a good friend, the kind that knew when you needed to believe a lie and happily went along with it. Soon, she'd fallen asleep.

Chapter 20

Warden Laura had finally recovered and made it back to work. After getting caught up, she went out to dinner with Lakeisha and Megan.

"So tell me how you've been?" Lakeisha asked Laura once they were seated and had their drinks.

Laura shrugged. "I've been okay. When it happened, I was scared to death, but they put the stents in, and I'm doing much better. I kind of enjoyed being home with my family, though. Since I've been back, I tire easily."

"You showed those rioters who's boss," Megan teased.

"Yes. Hearing the story of the mass chant warmed my spirit. I'll tell you what, I won't punish any of the participants, but if any one of them is looking for leniency for a future incident or time taken off for good behavior, it ain't happening."

Their meals arrived, and as Megan reached for a dinner roll, Laura blurted out, "What the heck?" as she stared at Megan's hand. She'd just noticed the flash of light that played off her diamond engagement ring. "Oh, my God! When did this happen?"

Megan smirked. "Last weekend."

"Congratulations!" Laura said. "I'm so happy for you."

"Thanks."

"Wanna know how he got her to say yes?" Lakeisha teased. "You're gonna love it. It's pure Megan."

Laura waited in anticipation.

"He used reverse psychology on her. Never pushed her to make plans, never made a fuss over her even though he was whipped. Eventually, it was like he was living there, and they'd recently walked past a jewelry store, and he casually said, 'What do you think of marriage? You wanna try it?' He mentioned it like it was a passing thought, like he hadn't planned to ask her that way."

"That's how it happened," Megan quickly added, "The walk past the store was random. He didn't plan that. He didn't use reverse psychology."

"Girl, that's what you think," Lakeisha said, razzing her.

Megan shook her head and rolled her eyes.

Laura laughed. "I told you you'd know when the right one came along."

Taking a sip of her soda, Megan agreed. "That you did."

They caught up on work gossip and discussed wedding plans for the rest of the night. Laura and Lakeisha were eager to be involved and offered to help Megan with anything she needed. It seemed like the tide had indeed turned.

*****

During the week, Lakeisha saw an incoming letter for Kristen from Lupe. Like most folks, she was interested to see what Ms. Lupe had to say. She half expected to read that Lupe had been picked to be in a reality TV show.

Kristen,

I hope all is well. Things are good out here in the desert. Married life is great, but then look who I picked as a husband. I did good.

Have some news that might surprise you. I'm pregnant! Yep, there's going to be a little Lupe in the near future. We just found out it's a girl. I'll keep you posted and send pictures.

Chin up, chica,

Lupe

Lakeisha checked the seams, folded the letter, and put it back in its envelope. Afterward, she found herself feeling down. Of course, she was thrilled for Lupe. Nothing made her happier than finding out a prisoner had moved on and was starting a new life. But she couldn't help thinking about the daughter she'd lost.

When she was depressed, she needed candy, so she reached into her bottom drawer and grabbed a snack-size packet of Skittles. While munching on the colorful treats, it brought back the memory of being a kid, her brothers and sisters all playing hopscotch or hide and seek together. She wanted more than anything to recreate that life by starting her own family and prayed God would bless her with a healthy child when the time was right. Finally, her sadness eased into a strange peace, and she returned to work.

She noticed a second letter for Kristen. They came in waves. It was from Olivia.

Kristen,

How are things? I'll bet you were glad to see Ryan and Toby. They're so grown up. Jeremy told me about the lunch you ate and the photos you took. That's awesome.

Crazy drama going on around here. Bob found a better job closer to home, and his old job, the one that didn't want to pay him what he was worth, is now begging him to stay, trying to match what he's been given and offering a work-from-home option one day per week. He's not taking it, though. He's moving on. I would too.

Cocoa's breath started smelling awful again, so we brought her back to the vet. They say we need to brush her teeth. They gave us this plastic thumb cover and chicken-flavored toothpaste. The vet claimed it would be easy to do, but Bob and I both struggled to take care of it. Now he's wrapping her in a blanket, so she looks like a kitten burrito. The only thing that sticks out is her head. That way, she can't scratch us to death. She still squirms and hisses at us every time. The best part is I watched the vet do it by herself, and Cocoa sat completely still and was an angel when she did it. Ugh!

How's the gardening gig? Are you still liking it?

Love ya,
Olivia

*****

Lakeisha stopped by Kristen's cell with two envelopes. She had zero expression on her face, which Kristen thought was odd. Kristen ripped open the letter from Lupe. She hadn't heard from her in ages.

In typical Lupe fashion, the note was short and to the point. Kristen beamed with happiness. She couldn't believe Lupe was pregnant. And that she was having a girl. It was so exciting. If Kristen were out of prison, she would have loved to buy her a bunch of cute outfits and toys. She was ecstatic for Lupe. She liked Debbie, but no cellmate compared to Lupe and all her stories. She wished nothing but the best for her and couldn't wait to write her back so that she could share her own good news about the boy's recent visit.

After Kristen read the second letter from Olivia, she found herself feeling disappointed. Olivia still hadn't mentioned Cindy, and she wondered how long she had been in the picture.

Kristen let out an angry hrmph and tossed an envelope aside, then climbed onto her bunk, tucking her legs into her chest and resting her head on her knees. She was upset Olivia hadn't said anything to her. They were sisters, after all. Didn't sisters share everything?

No, they weren't sisters. Not really.

Olivia was Jeremy's sister, and blood was thicker than water.

Brooding and in a terrible mood, she thought again about the fact that her own family hadn't been there for her. Yet she could always count on a letter from Olivia twice a month, with family updates and assorted photos. Maybe she was being too harsh. Olivia was doing the best she could, trying to walk a fine line between being a good sister and a good sister-in-law.

Deep down, she knew she had no right to be upset after what she'd done. But she figured Olivia would've at least given her a heads-up about another woman. That way, she wouldn't continue to hope. Or maybe that was why she didn't say anything—so she wouldn't lose hope.

She hadn't received divorce papers yet. And as awful as life was right now, with another woman having an intimate relationship with her husband, she still had a minuscule chance of reconciliation. She never expected him to be celibate while she was gone, although knowing about it wasn't very reassuring. Maybe Olivia was doing her a kindness by omitting those details.

Besides, if Jeremy were serious about this other woman, he'd want to move forward with her. And so far, he hadn't. She was still technically his wife.

She determined to focus on that small bright spot.

Kristen decided to throw all her energy into gardening and the daily workouts on the yard. Abigail had recently suggested adding some ballet into their routine, and after she demonstrated a few beginner moves, the group found out how much harder the practice was than it looked. She thought it could be just the extra kick they needed to take their sessions up a notch.

Chapter 21

After a visitation from Abigail's parents, Jess noticed Abigail seemed more distraught than normal. Seeing them usually cheered her up, but with her mood swings lately, it was so hard to know. Jess had begun walking on eggshells, afraid to say the wrong thing for fear Abigail would have a meltdown or withdraw. She was completely at a loss on how to help.

Jess watched Abigail pace the small room. "How are your mom and dad doing?"

"They're fine," Abigail replied without making eye contact. She only had a few feet to traverse each way, but as she did, her long hair swished as if she were walking briskly.

"Did something happen?" Jess asked.

Abigail stopped and looked up. "No. Why do you think that?"

"I don't know. You just seem annoyed."

Abigail continued pacing and began chewing on her nail, something she did when things were troubling her. Jess was growing tired of her secretive nature, and even though she loved her, she had given up on trying to get any closer, even as a friend. It seemed nothing she did was ever enough to make her happy.

"Is it your ex, Steve? Did he do something?"

Abigail burst into laughter, the tone so high-pitched and earsplitting it bounced off the walls and echoed, making the room seem to shrink. She was behaving like a lunatic, and it frightened Jess.

Jess hopped up onto her bunk and reached for a deck of cards. She was too frazzled to play an actual game; she just wanted to have something to occupy her hands. If she could, she would run away from Abigail to free herself from the bedlam.

Jess forced herself to play solitaire, but soon the energy in the room grew to suffocating proportions, so she chucked the cards and grabbed a book to hide behind. Once Abigail calmed down, she'd try to talk some sense into her, maybe suggest (for the hundredth time) seeing Megan.

After lights out, Jess pretended to fall asleep so she wouldn't have to interact. She couldn't take the pressure. Instead, she lay in the dark wishing Abigail could be how she was when they first met, a lot more fun and way less neurotic. She hated seeing her suffer. When Abigail was hurting, it made Jess feel pain. And when Jess couldn't help her anymore, and the little things she used to do no longer comforted her, it frustrated Jess to no end.

The sound of sniffling caught Jess' attention. She thought maybe Abigail had a runny nose, but then she heard soft crying.

"You okay?" she whispered.

"Not really," Abigail said through a sob.

It was dark, but Jess managed to climb down without

wiping out, and she sat on the edge of Abigail's bunk, where she continued weeping.

Jess reached out and took hold of Abigail's hand. "You know you can tell me anything, right? I'm here for you."

Abigail sat up, her face drenched with tears, and said, "There are some things so terrible they can't be spoken aloud, especially to someone like you."

The comment hung in the shadows, confusing Jess.

"Like me?" she finally asked, feeling a pang of worry.

There was a long pause. Abigail whimpered between sobs and said, "I mean someone I care about."

Jess reached for Abigail and pulled her close. She rubbed her back gently and rocked her back and forth. "You can tell me anything. I promise I'll be here for you no matter what."

"I can't," Abigail cried out in a tiny voice. "I just can't."

Jess continued to hold her. She didn't want to let go. Whatever this misery was that tormented her beloved's soul, she wanted to banish it once and for all.

"Tell me," Jess whispered.

Abigail pulled back, and Jess released her. Jess wished she could see her face but could only make out its outline in the gloom.

Then Abigail began crying again, and in a shaky voice, she said, "I killed my son, Jess. I murdered my beautiful boy."

She barely got the phrase out before letting out an agonizing howl. Jess quickly pulled her close again, burying her face against her chest so as not to draw attention from the guards. Abigail sobbed freely. Jess couldn't imagine what hell she'd been suffering, keeping that knowledge to herself.

Without thinking, Jess began stroking Abigail's hair and pressed her lips against the top of her head, kissing her gently. When Abigail didn't recoil, Jess continued, planting tender kisses on her forehead, damp eyelids, and cheeks.

Warning bells sounded loudly in Jess' brain, saying: this woman just told you she killed her son!

Jess ignored the warnings and moved on to her neck. She couldn't believe this was actually happening, that it wasn't a dream.

Heat rushed through Jess, and she began getting a bit more forceful, sucking on Abigail's neck and letting her hands roam free, exploring every exquisite curve of her delicate princess. Jess was filled with ardent desire as she caressed and nuzzled, taking in her intoxicating scent. After a few minutes, she couldn't wait anymore, so she pulled Abigail's pajama top off and started groping her breasts. Jess's heart pounded hard, and she felt more alive than she ever had. When she eventually made her way between Abigail's legs, she was like a person who'd gone without a basic need, eager to make up for all that was lost.

The sound of Abigail's ecstatic cries, muffled under a pillow she'd grabbed, was more triumphant than anything Jess had ever heard. It was the happiest night of her life. She couldn't believe it was real. She wanted to pinch herself. Luckily, she'd been intensely present throughout. Every moment was burned into her mind so she could replay it later in all its glorious detail whenever she chose to.

*****

Morning seemed to come right after falling asleep, and Jess and Abigail were up making their beds. They adhered to military style, tucking the sheets and blankets in tight, with a six-inch collar at the top. Neither of them spoke as they went about their business, finishing just before the guard came by for morning count. Once their names were ticked off the list, it was time to get cleaned up for breakfast.

While lathering with soap and water, Jess found herself thinking. Not about the amazing sexual experience, but about the secret Abigail had revealed. She was so caught up in the moment she hadn't had a chance to let it really sink in.

The woman she loved killed her son.

She didn't know why the idea hadn't occurred to her before. Jess knew it had to be murder since she was in for life, but she'd always assumed it was in self-defense or something more complicated. Then, as she mentally revisited past conversations, it all became clear. Abigail never wanted to talk about Devin. And she never mentioned hoping he'd come to visit someday.

While Jess dried off, an uncomfortable thought crept into her mind: Abigail wasn't her dream girl anymore.

She couldn't be.

That bubble had burst.

What started out as a sinking sensation morphed into full-blown paranoia as Jess brushed her teeth. What if Abigail was crazy? Like Tanya crazy? It was unthinkable she'd killed her own son, but now Jess wondered how she had done it. A flood of horrific scenes filled Jess' mind, and she felt the room tilt. She had to grab hold of the sink to stay balanced.

When she glanced at her reflection in the mirror, it looked distorted. It always did because they had circus mirrors in prison, the warped metal kind, but today it seemed especially strange. As Jess studied herself, she realized most of the time she saw what she wanted to see and not what was right in front of her.

The trip to get breakfast was the longest walk Jess had ever taken. The corridor stretched endlessly, taking on the appearance of a tunnel. Her feet were as heavy as cement blocks. She would sit with Abigail, of course, and they would have to talk at some point.

Once she got to the cafeteria, she saw her ahead in line but chose to remain where she was in the back. Abigail was right, Jess thought. If she had told her what her crime was the very first day, she wouldn't have been as nice to her. As Jess inched forward, waiting her turn for a tray, she realized Abigail hadn't been anything but honest with her. She'd held back the ugly part, but it was always there, waiting to be seen. All she had to do was take off the rose-colored glasses.

"You didn't get much food today," Abigail mentioned

as Jess sat down at her table.

Jess took a bite while staring at her meal. She could feel Abigail studying her, probably searching for a hint of what might be happening inside her head. When Jess looked up, she felt her heart soften. Abigail still looked sweet, like the same person she knew her to be.

Jess shrugged. "I guess I'm not that hungry today."

"Well, I'm starved," Abigail said, then proceeded to devour everything on her plate.

As she munched on her food, Jess watched, wondering what could have happened to make her want to kill her own child. Abigail's parents still visited almost every weekend and were supportive of her. Why would they do that? Then, Jess remembered what she'd told Abigail last night, that she could tell her anything and that she'd be there for her no matter what.

A wave of guilt washed over Jess, followed by a flash of the intimacy they'd shared the prior evening. "You wanna finish my leftovers too?" Jess asked.

Abigail smiled. "Only if you're not going to eat them."

Jess pushed her tray toward her. "Have at it. Knock yourself out."

*****

Later, out on the yard, Abigail showed off a bit, demonstrating some more advanced ballet moves. She used to notice Jess stealing glances while she worked out, but today, even with her added fanfare, she ignored her. She seemed lost in her basketball game.

She knew that would happen if she told her the truth. What she didn't expect was that she'd care as much as she did about Jess' reaction. She knew Jess adored her, and in its own way, it made Abigail feel good to be on someone's pedestal. She had been on her ex-husband Steve's once, but that was long ago.

When Jess made love to her the night before, Abigail drifted during the session. She visualized being on the beach with Steve. That it was his hands touching her, that he was the one who found her irresistible. Her ex-husband had never made love to her with that level of intensity, and as Abigail responded to Jess' expert touch, she was a combination of ecstatic, confused, and surprised.

Now Jess probably thought she was a monster. The thought brought on more anxiety, something she always struggled with, but Jess had been able to take the edge off with her kindness and friendship.

If she lost Jess, she'd probably snap.

When they were back in their cell, Jess hopped up onto the top bunk and grabbed a book. Abigail lay down in hers and closed her eyes. Her neck muscles began twitching, and a sense of dread filled her consciousness when Jess didn't offer to read to her.

Abigail was slowly drowning in apprehension. It was suffocating. She was on the verge of screaming out loud, and it took everything she had just to hold it inside. Because she couldn't sit still, she got up and grabbed a Sprite out of the locker. On her way back, she chanced a glimpse at Jess.

Jess caught her and made eye contact. She looked uncomfortable, like she wanted to avoid discussing things. "You wanna talk?" she asked.

"Sure," Abigail replied, feeling even more nervous all of a sudden. She opened her drink and sat down.

Jess stayed on the top bunk. She set the book aside and stared at the ceiling. After a pause, she said, "I want to hear about your son Devin."

"What do you want to know?"

"Everything."

"It will take a long time to tell you everything," Abigail answered in a shaky voice, "but since we have nothing but time, I guess I could if that's what you really want."

Abigail took a deep breath, exhaled, and began. "My son was the blessing we had always hoped for. Steve and I both wanted children, so when we got news I was pregnant, nothing could have made us happier."

Jess climbed down and sat on the lower bunk opposite Abigail, leaning on one arm to support her head.

"Devin was an angel as a baby. Very quiet. He cried once in a while but not as much as other babies. He was our everything."

Jess wore a puzzled expression.

"As he grew, we noticed some unusual behavior. He didn't seem to connect with us. It was like he was emotionally detached. Then, as the years passed, it went downhill. One tumultuous event after another. There was no peace. Somehow over the course of his short life, something went wrong, and my son began acting like a demon, hell-bent on destroying our lives."

"What do you mean by demon?" Jess asked. "You mean like scary movie possessed?"

Abigail sighed. "Not exactly, but truth be told, it wasn't that far from living in a scary movie."

Abigail could almost see the jumble of emotions on Jess' face: love, disgust, curiosity. They appeared to be in competition. "Couldn't he get some kind of help?" she finally asked.

That question made sense. Of course, no one would really understand unless they'd lived in her shoes.

"We loved Devin and did everything in our power to help him. Unfortunately, nothing we tried worked. He was diagnosed with so many things it was overwhelming. They said he had conduct disorder, oppositional defiant disorder, ADHD, anxiety, depression, reactive attachment disorder, and autism spectrum disorder."

Abigail could see Jess glazing over but continued. "In a nutshell, he was crazy. But to break it down, conduct disorder means he was a diagnosed sociopath. He was violent, and if he couldn't be cured, he would've most likely turned into a psychopath. He had massive aggression problems. We dealt with IEP—an individualized education program—meetings for his school twice per year and a social worker once a month. We had him in occupational therapy, behavioral therapy, speech pathologist therapy, life skills classes. He'd gone to a neurologist, did talk therapy, sand play therapy, even regression therapy, which was supposed to take him back to being a baby, so we could try to connect with him. He'd gone to six different specialists, and they had him on drug therapy which only ended up making him angrier. Eventually, he spent time in a residential treatment center and had every test under the sun run on him, but nothing worked."

Abigail studied Jess' expression. The woman who used to worship her, go out of her way to do whatever it took to make her happy, was gone. In her place was a person who looked crushed with disappointment.

It was right for Jess to judge her. She knew she deserved it.

Abigail averted her eyes downward. Then, in a soft voice said, "It still doesn't mean what I did was right. I was his mother. He was just a child who didn't ask for those problems. It wasn't his fault. It was my job to raise and protect him…no matter what."

When Abigail looked up, Jess' eyes were filled with tears. She could see the pain on her face and wanted to reach out and comfort her, give her a hug like she had done when Abigail was sad.

She was no longer worthy of a person like Jess. Truth be told, she felt she never was.

Wiping her eyes, Jess said, "I'm sorry, Abigail. I know I said I wanted to hear it all, but I'd prefer if we continue tomorrow."

"I understand," Abigail replied.

It was more than one sane person deserved to be subjected to in a day.

Chapter 22

With all the buzz over Megan's upcoming wedding, Warden Laura thought it might be a good idea to add a few more inmates to work in the garden. They'd been selling flowers and plants and using vegetables in the cafeteria kitchen. With everyone just sitting around doing nothing, she figured they could be put to work planting more flowers. That way, they could be used in the ceremony.

Jess had signed up for a position hoping to spend a few hours a day in the sunshine using her hands. She was chosen for lawn mowing and sod installation since she was stronger than the other girls and could handle the old-school push mower. Abigail wasn't sure if she should sign up, but she didn't want to be left behind, so she put her name on the list. She hoped to work with Kristen on flowers. But, instead, Warden Laura decided she would be a great fit for wheelbarrow duty, transporting heavier items throughout the garden for other inmates to plant.

Laura had a special affinity for sticking it to someone like Abigail. She might have had a moment of hesitation at first, knowing that she didn't have all the details about the young woman's heinous crime, but it didn't last.

Abigail was the worst kind of killer, and she didn't deserve kindness.

Debbie wasn't an outdoorsy type. She preferred to cook and signed up to work in the kitchen. She got in right away because sweating and chopping vegetables weren't high on most people's list of favorite things to do. Debbie, on the other hand, found it relaxing.

With everyone busier than usual, the time passed more quickly. Unfortunately, it wasn't long before there was drama. Abigail was struggling to push a wheelbarrow full of plants to the other side of the garden when a snake slithered up the handle and onto her arm. She let out a blood-curdling scream, shaking the serpent off her and sending the flowers tumbling to the ground.

Jess heard the commotion and rushed over. "Are you okay?" she asked, sounding worried.

Abigail was shaken up and started crying a little. "Yeah. I'm fine," she sniffed. "I just don't like snakes."

A corrections officer walked over, making sure there was no funny business going on, but Jess explained and offered to help clean up. The guard, a rather robust woman, just shook her head and tsked, anxious to return to her post standing in the shade.

"Thanks," Abigail said.

As Jess helped her put the plants back in the barrow, she couldn't help but think of how fragile Abigail seemed. She couldn't imagine her harming a soul.

Then another thing came to mind.

She still loved her.

"There. You're going to be fine. You'll build up your muscles doing this," Jess said, trying to make light of an obviously bad situation.

Abigail was about as suited to her task as Jess was suited to paint toenails. It was ridiculous, she thought, but it was prison, and they had no choice in the matter.

Kristen worked nearby and had witnessed the whole scene. She and the woman next to her looked at each other and rolled their eyes.

"She's so different around that one. She almost seems nice," the newcomer said.

Jess glanced in Kristen's direction and was rewarded with a dirty look.

*****

Debbie's first day in the kitchen, she blew her fellow inmate's minds. She could chop carrots at a furious pace, just like on a television cooking show.

"Dang! Check this one out," one of the women said. "Don't mess with her. She'll carve you up good."

Debbie smiled to let them know they had nothing to fear, but the comment triggered a memory, one that often haunted her.

She was in the kitchen preparing dinner—in a great mood—when her husband came out of nowhere and grabbed hold of her arm.

"Ouch!" Debbie cried out. "That hurts."

Her husband spun her around and slapped her across the face. "You fucked my friend! You think you can get away with that?"

"What are you talking about?" Debbie asked, visibly shaken, her face numb with stinging pain.

"You know exactly what I'm talking about. He told me he was here today."

Here we go, Debbie thought. Here comes the insanity.

"He forgot his sunglasses when he dropped you off last night. So he came by unannounced and rang the doorbell to pick them up. That's all," Debbie pleaded.

But he wasn't listening. His face was beet red, and his eyes had the look of a wild animal. He lunged for the butcher knife. Terrified, Debbie took off running. She headed up the stairs, but he caught hold of her ankle, and she came down hard, knocking the side of her head on the railing. The next moment he had one of his hands around her neck, and in the other, the butcher knife, its menacing glint causing her to cringe in fear.

"If you ever cheat on me, I'll kill you."

Crying, Debbie closed her eyes and wished she could disappear.

"Ahem," a corrections officer said to Debbie. "No time for daydreams. Get back to work."

Staring at the guard with a faraway look in her eyes, she replied, "Oh… Sorry about that." Then she continued preparing the myriad of veggies for the pot of soup, letting go of the past.

As Debbie went about her work, she thought about how she'd killed her husband and how it seemed to be the only solution to her hellish nightmare.

She wished there could have been another way.

*****

After dinner, Abigail threw herself onto her bunk. "I don't think I've ever been this exhausted in my entire life. It's like boot camp. Why did I sign up for this?"

Jess laughed as she watched her lying there. "You didn't want to be bored, remember."

"Oh, yeah. Now I want to be. I mean, look at me. Do I look like someone who can lift heavy objects and cart them around?"

"No, you don't."

"And I'd give anything to soak in a bathtub filled with Epsom salts."

Jess wasn't much into taking baths, preferring showers instead, but she relished the visual of Abigail soaking in a tub full of fluffy bubbles. Pretty beat herself, Jess kicked off her shoes and climbed into her own bed. She thought they would talk more tonight as she wanted to hear more about Devin, but within an instant, they both were out.

Jess woke up parched in the middle of the night. She wanted bottled water and tried to climb down quietly but tripped.

"You all right?" Abigail asked in a groggy voice.

"Yeah," Jess replied while rubbing her knee. "I was trying not to wake you."

Jess stood up and reached into the locker for a bottled water. After she opened it and drank some, Abigail came up beside her. "Can I have a sip? I don't want a whole one."

"Sure," Jess said as she handed it to her. They usually didn't share drinks.

When she finished, Abigail gave the water bottle back to Jess and plopped into bed. "I'm in pain," she groaned. "There isn't a muscle in my body that doesn't hurt."

Jess chugged the rest of it and wiped her mouth with the back of her hand. Then, on impulse, she went over and sat on the edge of Abigail's bunk.

"Do you want me to kiss you and make you feel better?"

Abigail didn't answer right away, and Jess didn't know if it was because she wasn't interested or if she was worried a guard might stop by after count.

"Okay," she answered, interrupting Jess' thoughts.

That was all Jess needed to hear. She realized she still felt the same for Abigail despite her confession. And it wasn't just sexual attraction. She was deeply in love. There was a part of her mind that fought those feelings. Her rational mind that spoke to her of logic and morals and what was right and wrong, but it was too late. She was already too far gone.

*****

The next morning, Jess and Abigail were up early and had their beds made before the guard came around for the morning count. They weren't scheduled for garden work, so after showering and eating breakfast had the day to relax, which was ideal for Abigail. Her muscles needed a break.

171

"How are you feeling today?" Jess asked her as they got back to their cell.

"Like I got run over by a bus," Abigail joked. "But I slept well."

Jess smiled at her, and she blushed.

"I can't figure out why they have you doing hard manual labor. I mean, working in the garden is tough, but to put you in charge of hauling things," Jess said as she shook her head in disapproval. "That's just cruel."

"I know why I got the job."

"Because Warden Laura doesn't like you?"

"Exactly. And why should she?"

Jess seemed to mull over her comment. "She just doesn't know you," she said. "And, of course, she's judging you for your crime."

The phrase hung in the air, and Abigail wondered if Jess still judged her. But, based on how she treated her last night, she guessed she'd been forgiven, even though, in Abigail's mind, she didn't deserve to be.

She had always thought Jess was a much better human being than she was and could never figure out what Jess saw in her. She'd been confused by the whole situation since she'd never imagined she'd ever be with a woman. She wasn't sure how to feel about what was happening in her life.

"I don't know what I did to deserve someone as kind as you," Abigail said to Jess with a look of sincere appreciation in her eyes.

Jess looked down, obviously embarrassed. She stuffed her hands in her pockets and shrugged. "That's funny you should say that," she replied, looking back up, "because I've been wondering how I managed to get a goddess as a girlfriend. An enigmatic, incredibly damaged goddess, but a goddess nonetheless."

Abigail shook her head and laughed. Jess was definitely nuts.

She sat on her bunk. "If you want to hear more about my son, I can tell you the rest if you like."

"Sure," Jess said, taking a seat opposite her. "I want to know everything."

"I might jump around a bit. I can't always remember everything in order."

"I don't mind," Jess replied.

Abigail took a deep breath and exhaled slowly. "Remember I told you how sweet Devin was as a baby?"

Jess nodded.

"Well, it changed as he got older. He seemed withdrawn, and when we'd cuddle up to him, give him kisses and make cooing noises, he was distant. He didn't respond the way a normal kid does. It was like he was having a different experience than we were."

"Huh. That's weird."

"That's what we thought. I mean, we didn't discuss it at the time, but when the problems grew exponentially through the years, we went back and analyzed things and finally agreed it was strange. While it was happening, it just felt like something was off. I remember always feeling anxious about it too, wondering why my child didn't seem connected to me."

"Man. That sucks."

Abigail grimaced and continued. "When Devin got older, he pulled away from me and cringed when I tried to hug him. It broke my heart. He'd run to his dad, though, so Steve would take him out front to play ball or take him fishing on his day off. I assumed it was a phase or something."

Jess looked sad. "I'm so sorry, Ab. I can't imagine how painful it must have been not to be able to feel close to the child you love."

"Thanks," she mumbled sheepishly before continuing. "When we put him in kindergarten, the underlying issues flourished. He had lots of problems with the other kids. He'd stand too close to them, and they'd get upset and push him away. That's when he started acting aggressively. At first, it was just toward the other kids, but when he got older, he attacked one of his female teachers. He was only in second grade, but he threw a chair at her, and she was hurt pretty badly."

"Oh my God!" Jess gasped.

Abigail gave her a look that said, "you just heard the beginning of it."

"Eventually, we had to take him out of that school and put him into a special one for troubled kids. I know I shouldn't have felt embarrassed by it, but I did. I mean, I came from the perfect family. Growing up with my parents was like a made-for-TV show. It couldn't have been any better."

Jess grinned.

"And with my dad being a doctor and my mom a nurse, well…we had high hopes our son would follow in the family footsteps and be a success. Someone to be admired in the community. Having him in that school and dragging him from specialist to specialist to discover why he was so violent was a huge disappointment. We were saddened, but we loved him and would've done anything to heal him. That's why we tried so hard."

Abigail studied Jess, looking for any sign of judgment. Instead, she just sat opposite her, wearing a concerned expression.

Running her hand through her hair, Abigail went on. "There were so many things. I could go on for days. There was the time they had arts and crafts at school, and Devin made a butcher knife out of aluminum foil. His teacher asked him why he made it, and he said it was for Mommy. I received a worried phone call and had to come in for a meeting to discuss the incident. There was the time he told his babysitter we starved him, that we wouldn't give him any food, which of course, wasn't true. He'd make up all kinds of elaborate stories. You have no idea," she said, shaking her head.

"Steve and I tried to have a weekly date night. You know, to keep the romance alive, but after a while, no sitter would put up with Devin for any price. It was useless. Word spread what a handful he was, and we were screwed."

Abigail got up and began walking back and forth. "Anyway, then he became demanding. He wanted things, and if he didn't get them, he would threaten us. He'd say he was going to jump out the window and tell the neighbors we pushed him. He threatened suicide off and on, and as he got bigger, he began randomly attacking us, out of nowhere, with no advance warning or situation preceding it."

"Holy shit," Jess said.

"Holy shit is right," Abigail said and stopped walking. "And at first, he'd do all this craziness when Steve wasn't around. It was almost like I made it up. I'd call Steve at work frantic when he was with patients, and he'd listen and try and help but couldn't. Then, when he'd come home, he'd plan to have a talk with Devin, but when he walked in the door, Devin would go running to him saying, 'Daddy! I missed you so much today!' and as he hugged him, he'd be facing me, wearing a devilish grin.'"

Jess looked like she was getting freaked out. "So then what did you do?" she asked.

"I tried to discuss it with Steve, but it caused a rift between us. He thought I was exaggerating. The notes and calls from the teachers concerned him, and once doctors were involved and he had a series of diagnoses, he paid closer attention. As Devin got older, he realized he couldn't manipulate Steve, and he turned on us both. He'd tell his teachers we abused him. He'd hit his head repeatedly against the wall to create bruises so he could say we did it. I would try to stop him, but he'd bite me and push me down."

"Fuck!"

"Yeah. One of his therapists suggested he get a diary, you know, to record his thoughts. In it, he wrote extensively about how he wanted to kill us in our sleep and how he planned to kill some of the other kids at his school. So anyway, one time, I woke up in the middle of the night with an uncomfortable feeling. When I opened my eyes, I found him standing next to my bed, staring down at me, his face illuminated by the moonlight, with a sinister look in his eye."

Abigail sat back on the bunk, and tears began to spill. "I was scared, Jess. I was so scared."

Jess reached out and hugged her. "It's okay. You don't have to continue if you don't want to."

Abigail hugged her back, then let go and wiped her wet face with her hand. "I want to finish," she said, looking determined.

Taking a few more deep breaths, she went on. "We eventually had him in a mental hospital for a month. And I hate to say it, Jess, but it was the first time I felt free. I usually felt like a prisoner in my own home. Always terrified."

She began crying hard again but eventually managed to find composure. "When he came home, nothing changed. It seemed to have actually gotten worse. He kicked Steve in the back one day for no reason. He was just walking down the hallway, and boom! He knocked him down, and poor Steve hit his head on the side of the granite counter in the kitchen. He had to be rushed to the hospital."

Abigail pulled her legs in and wrapped her arms around them. "I wasn't home at the time. I was at the store. When I got back, Devin was gone, and Steve was lying on the ground with blood on his head. Afterward, I suggested we put him in a home, but we couldn't afford it, even with my husband making a great salary. The mental health situation in this country is a joke. There's so much red tape and limits on the insurance policy it's hard to get help. I won't bore you with the details. Let's just say you wouldn't want to be in our shoes."

Jess nodded.

"And then there was the incident."

Abigail stared at Jess, unsure if she should tell her. "A neighbor claimed he'd violated their little girl. That he'd held her down and shoved a tree branch in her vagina."

Jess looked horrified.

"There was no proof, of course. Not that they found."

"What do you mean?" Jess asked.

Abigail began to cry again. "I was cleaning his room and found a dirty pair of little girl's underwear hidden under his mattress. And they were stained with blood."

A look of shock was frozen on Jess' face. That was how Abigail had felt too.

Chapter 23

"Word is you're the Gordon Ramsey of the prison kitchen," Kristen teased Debbie.

Debbie balked. "I don't yell at people like he does."

"Not the yelling. The cooking. I had no idea."

Smiling, Debbie said, "There's a lot you don't know about me. The secret is culinary school."

"No way. You're a trained chef?"

"Yep. Studied back home on the west coast. I worked at a few nice restaurants in my time, and when I got the offer for the one here in Florida, I couldn't pass it up. It was hard to leave my family, though."

"So your parents didn't know what was happening to you?"

Debbie shook her head. "I didn't want to worry them. They're elderly and have been through a lot. The first time it happened, I thought it was a one-time thing anyway, like maybe I'd said something wrong or had taken the argument too far, but later, it was obvious it wasn't me."

"Wow... I'm sorry you went through that. You're such a nice lady."

"Thanks, sweetie. As you know, bad things happen to

everyone. Life doesn't care if you're kindhearted. It just goes on with its twists and turns."

Debbie described her past like it was a chapter in a book she'd read, one that she planned to leave behind. She was so good at looking ahead and focusing on the future, a trait Kristen really admired in her.

"I don't know if this is too forward, and if you don't want to talk about it, I totally understand, but may I ask you how you did it?"

Debbie sat down on the lower bunk and smirked. "You wanna know all the grisly details, is that it? Like if I chopped him into bits?"

Kristen let out an uncomfortable laugh. "I guess I do."

Sighing, Debbie said, "Well, I'm going to disappoint you then. Because it wasn't quite as dramatic as that."

Listening intently, Kristen said, "I still wanna hear."

"Okay. Well, I was at my wit's end, as you can imagine, and had a pretty good idea if I didn't do something, I'd end up dead. So I went to a gun range and signed up for lessons. I got a permit and purchased a handgun. One night I waited until the bastard was asleep, and then I shot him in the head."

"Oh, my God! You must've been terrified. And the mess!"

Debbie shuddered. "Honey... You have no idea. I stood at the foot of the bed with my heart hammering in my chest. My hands trembled. I couldn't hold them still. I almost talked myself out of it, but then I remembered the last hospital visit and the concussion. I had to reason with myself that it was either him or me. You'd be surprised what a person is capable of doing to preserve one's own life."

Kristen believed her. The desire to live was built into human nature. She heard of other women in prison that had been in similar circumstances. And many of them had children, too, most of which ended up being sent to foster homes.

"Did you at least try to plan it out so you wouldn't get caught?" Kristen asked.

"No. After watching all those police shows, I assumed the cops would just outsmart me anyway. I'm a chef, not a criminal," she joked. "The only thing that helped me in court was my hospital records. I had admitted my husband had hit me, and it was noted in writing that it wasn't the first time. A nurse there wanted to help me, but she couldn't. Her suggestion was to get a restraining order. That's what everyone suggests. It probably would've been better if I had police reports to build a case, but I'd never pressed charges because I was too afraid."

Kristen gave Debbie an understanding nod. "You know, I have a hard time picturing you as a battered wife. I can't see you afraid of anything. You don't seem like the type."

Debbie smiled. "I hate to break it to you, doll, but there isn't a specific type. It could happen to anyone. The luck of the draw."

Kristen agreed. "I guess you're right."

*****

Jess' mom and Abigail's parents frequently visited at the same time. Jess didn't know if this was pure chance or some kind of cosmic joke. Or was it a kindness? Jess had told her mom all about Abigail, and her mom seemed happy for her that she had finally found true love.

"Isn't she beautiful, Mom?" Jess commented.

Jess' mom glanced in Abigail's direction. "She sure is, dear. You've got great taste."

Jess grinned, which made her mom smile too. She had always been supportive of her.

"So, how are the neighbors?" Jess asked. "Are you guys getting along?"

Jess' mom waved her hand in a dismissive fashion. "I ignore them now. Best way to handle it. Otherwise, they drive me insane. Now, honey, I know you don't care to hear about him, but your father isn't doing well. He said to say hello."

She was right about that. Jess didn't want to hear about him. He could literally drop dead, and she wouldn't feel a thing.

"You know I don't speak to him, Mom. I'm sorry if that upsets you."

"It doesn't upset me, honey. I just think it's best to let bygones be bygones."

Jess crossed her arms in front of her chest. How does a person forget when their dad tells them that having a lesbian for a daughter is an embarrassment to the family name? She was thankful her mom didn't follow his advice, which was to drag her from psychiatrist to psychiatrist, trying to talk whatever "mental disorder" she had out of her. Jess considered it a gift when he left them to start a new family.

"Okay. I forgive him," Jess said. "I hope his health improves and he's out dancing the tango soon."

Jess' mom shook her head in defeat. "How about we forget I brought it up."

"That works, too," Jess replied.

*****

Abigail's dad studied his daughter. "You look good, sweetheart. You seem happier, too, more relaxed."

"And your skin looks wonderful," her mom chimed in.

Abigail blushed. She could never tell her parents the truth. That she had a girlfriend. It would break their heart. Not that they were prejudiced. They weren't. They just wouldn't understand.

"I've been working a few days a week in the garden here. I think the combination of fresh air and exercise has been good for me."

Abigail's dad said, "That's good, honey. That's good. We sure do miss you. I want you to know that." He tried to cover his sadness with a smile, but Abigail could see he was suffering. She hated that they had to endure this, that they were hurting because of her.

"I know, Dad. I miss you guys too. Every day."

Abigail's mother got teary-eyed but took a deep breath and managed to regain composure. "So do you have any friends here?" she asked.

"Yeah. I've got a friend named Kristen. She works in the garden with me, and we do a daily workout with some other girls out on the yard. She's in charge of it, but she's been kind enough to let me add some ballet moves into the routine."

"That's wonderful," she said.

"And that lady over there," Abigail said while pointing to Jess. "She's my cellmate."

Abigail's dad looked over at Jess. His face changed. She sensed his disapproval, but he didn't remark. Instead, he nodded and asked, "And do you two get along well?"

Her father's gaze penetrated her skull, waiting for an answer. He had a way of staring with his calculating blue eyes that was unnerving. He read people with unusual clarity, which often resulted in her getting busted in little white lies as a kid.

"We get along great," Abigail replied. "She's big into reading. I'm into reading. We do a lot of that. Makes the time pass when you're bored."

"At least you're keeping busy," her mom said. "That's what's important."

Abigail's dad took a sip of his bottled water and glanced at Jess again. He didn't have to say a word. Abigail could tell he didn't like her.

*****

Kristen sat in her cell during visitation. It had been a long time since Ryan and Toby had come. She'd hoped to see them again, but they hadn't returned. When she brought it up in outgoing letters, they'd write back about everything else but ignored responding to that part.

Maybe it had just been too much for them to handle. And if that was the case, she didn't want to pressure them into coming back. It would be difficult to go without seeing her sons, but if it was what she had to do, she would do it.

Their sanity came first.

The very next day, Lakeisha came by with a letter from Ryan. Kristen couldn't wait to read it and snatched it from her hand as soon as she saw it.

Mom,

I've got great news. I'm getting married next month. I told you she was the one. I know I'm young, and I could wait, but why should I? Why put off what I want today, tomorrow and what I know I'll want for the rest of my life?

I wish you could be there, Mom. That'll be the only thing missing from my perfect day.

Ryan

Kristen read the letter twice, then wiped a stray tear from her cheek. She was both elated and heartbroken. She knew this would happen. But nothing prepared her for the anguish of missing her eldest son's wedding. It was a moment every mother dreamed about and wanted to remember.

Another moment she would never get.

Chapter 24

Things come in threes, or so the saying goes. First, there was Lupe, who had just given birth to a healthy baby girl. She'd sent an announcement out to Kristen with a photo. Then there was Megan's wedding and Ryan's wedding.

There were times when days and weeks stood still, and inmates could almost hear the minutes pass. Then there were months with flurries of activity. And this was one of those months, especially in the garden. Everyone had gotten fairly good at their tasks. Even Abigail managed to grow some arm muscles and was able to maneuver her wheelbarrow around like a pro.

Bougainvillea, roses, daisies, azaleas, gardenias, morning glories, zinnias. These were just a sampling of the flowers the prisoners grew. Their sunflowers were nothing short of spectacular. No other prison could replicate them. The group toiled under the hot sun, cutting grass, turning sod, raking, and pruning. They had a football field-sized area to tend, with sections for veggies, banana and avocado trees, mangoes, and even aloe plants.

Warden Laura was proud of the prison garden and frequently scheduled tours for visiting officials. She even gave them seedlings to plant in their own prison gardens, happy to share her success. Since the garden was her showplace, Warden Laura allowed inmates to dress up the area. Abigail painted the benches pastel colors, strung snail shells together, and hung them as decorations from a few trees. Kristen shaped some of the shrubs throughout into peace signs and smiley faces, adding a bit of whimsy.

The work was grueling, and the women were often left with blisters on their hands at the end of the day, but still, they loved it. The garden had become a work of art, a magical place.

They called it their Neverland.

*****

Megan's wedding was a beautiful event, taking place at a small church on a Saturday afternoon. The weather was warm but comfortable, with low humidity. There wasn't a rain cloud in the sky. Her dress was stunning but simple, her hair shiny and curled instead of her signature straight, and her skin and makeup were flawless. Laura wore a stylish beige pantsuit instead of a dress, while Lakeisha donned her best lacey frock.

The interior of the church burst with elegant floral displays, all color-coordinated in varying shades of pink and ivory. The girls from the garden had outdone themselves. Warden Laura was very pleased indeed.

Laura swelled with emotion as the music played, and Megan walked down the aisle. There was nothing more exciting to her than a couple beginning a life together, and in her opinion, Megan was just about the best catch a man could get.

Dinner was delicious, followed by dancing to a live band, a refreshing change from the DJs most young people hired. By the end of the night, Laura and Lakeisha were pooped and said their goodbyes. They congratulated Megan and her new husband and wished them a relaxing honeymoon in the Caribbean.

"Not too relaxing," Lakeisha said with a wink.

Megan shook her head and smiled. "See you guys. Thanks so much for coming."

*****

Kristen moped in her bunk on the day of Ryan's wedding. Olivia promised she'd send photos and had tried to cheer her up in the last letter, focusing on the bright side, that her son was getting married to a great girl, but it was no use. She was beyond depressed.

Debbie had brought her a candy bar from Canteen, but even chocolate couldn't pull her out of the funk.

"This should be a happy day," Debbie chirped. "How proud you must feel."

Kristen wasn't in the mood for the positive attitude seminar today. She just wanted to feel sorry for herself.

"I am proud," Kristen responded. "Just wish I could be there." Then, realizing she seemed rude added, "Thanks for the candy bar, Deb. That was nice of you."

Hoping for privacy, Kristen turned and curled into a fetal position facing the wall. Jeremy's girlfriend, Cindy, was probably there, hanging on his arm and smiling, congratulating him for having raised such a great son.

The thought of it made her ill.

Another woman filling her shoes. Taking her place at the wedding. She felt infuriated even though she knew she had no right to be.

Kristen unwrapped the candy bar and took a bite. She'd never had much of a sweet tooth, unless you counted alcohol as a dessert. She rarely thought of drinking anymore. It had been years now. Megan was right. It did get easier with time.

The rest of the day, Kristen pretended to read a magazine in an attempt to avoid Debbie's bubbly demeanor. She was only marginally successful. Debbie had gotten into the habit of humming along to the music while wearing headphones.

*****

"I think my dad hates you," Abigail said to Jess.

Jess sat back, clasping her hands behind her head, and grinned. "So I've noticed."

Abigail came closer, then posed in an appealing way that showed off her curves. "I think he thinks you've corrupted me."

The bewitching look in Abigail's eyes filled Jess with desire. She was like a siren.

Jess pulled her onto her lap. "Well, we can't have any of that, can we?" she whispered into Abigail's ear. "Corrupting Daddy's little girl."

Abigail giggled, and as Jess kept an eye out for guards, she groped her and was happy that she responded like a real girlfriend now instead of just being on the receiving end of the pleasure. It had taken her a while to wrap her mind around the idea, but in the end, Abigail's feelings for her had won out.

No one could've been more thrilled than Jess. This was proof positive that patience really was a virtue. Megan had been right.

Instead of reading books to each other in their free time, they spent it having copious amounts of sex. And to Jess' surprise, once Abigail became comfortable with their pairing, she behaved like a complete nymphomaniac.

An unforeseen godsend.

Later that night, after they'd exhausted themselves and were lying in their own bunks, Jess asked her a serious question, one that she'd been putting off for a long time.

"Abigail?"

"Yeah."

"Are you ever going to tell me how you did it?"

There was a long silence. "You sure you want to know?" Abigail said in an unsteady tone.

Jess was quiet, mulling it over. "Yeah," she replied. "I want to know."

Jess climbed down and sat on the corner of Abigail's bunk. Abigail looked terrified.

"I've never spoken to anyone about this," she said. "But the scene's a recurring nightmare that lurks in the corners of my mind and disturbs me every day. When I think of it, it's like the weight of the world is crushing me with enormous guilt."

Jess lifted her chin, so their eyes met. "You can tell me. Whatever it is, I will still love you."

Abigail let out a deep sigh. "How to begin," she said. "I've already told you a lot of the stories about Devin. Going forward, Steve and I grew apart from the stress. He'd begun going over to a buddy's house more often, something he had never done before, and staying late at the office to finish paperwork. After a while, he bumped into an old girlfriend at a coffee shop, and they began talking, rekindling what had been lost. My guess is hearing compliments from a pretty woman was much more enjoyable than getting a report on the latest meltdown from me."

"Anyway, once I discovered the affair, I retreated inward. I should have reached out to family but instead isolated myself. It was just Devin and me. Then I stopped telling Steve anything because I could see he'd emotionally checked out."

Jess took hold of Abigail's hand.

"I felt so alone, with problems larger than I could face alone. We'd tried everything, like I told you. We loved our son and prayed somehow things would work out and thought if we just kept trying, you know? But then Steve was hardly around, and the pressure of it all built to where I was suffocating. After the incident with the neighbor's daughter, I gave up. But I couldn't escape. Each day brought a new level of insanity, and then I made a decision."

Abigail paused. Jess squeezed her hand. "It's okay, Ab.

You can tell me."

"I know," she replied, choking back tears.

Jess waited while Abigail tried to pull herself together, then found she was getting nervous in the process. She'd told herself she was ready to hear it, but now she wasn't so sure.

"I went to the library," Abigail continued, "and researched how to poison someone without it being painful. I didn't want to look online at home in case they could track me."

Abigail paused again and took some deep breaths. "I'd planned it all out in my head, how it would happen, but the night before, I couldn't sleep. I was alone since Steve and I had started sleeping in separate bedrooms. And as I lay there, I kept wondering how I could consider doing such a thing. I wondered what kind of person I had become. I wrestled with anxiety, morality, fear. Basically, I fell apart. I'd gotten in so deep I'd accepted the madness of the plan as the only solution. I thought I was doing something good, like he had a disease I was curing."

Clearing her throat, she continued. "The next morning, Steve went off to work, Devin ate breakfast, and I took him to school. When I picked him up, he was highly agitated, but I didn't receive a phone call from his teachers, so I assumed it was a good day. Actually, it was an unusual day because most of them were so totally out of control. I asked him what was wrong, and he just glared at me like he hated me more than anyone in the world. And even though I'd disconnected, that last look of pure hatred hurt more than all the others he'd ever given me combined."

Abigail was sobbing now. Jess leaned in and gave her a hug. This story was turning out to be more emotionally upsetting than she thought it would be. She was shaken on so many levels.

Jess rubbed her back, trying to comfort her beloved. And in a few minutes, Abigail pulled back, wiped her eyes, and went on.

"So I made his favorite meal for dinner, knowing Steve wouldn't be coming home until much later, and I put the medication into it. Medication...see what I mean? I'm even doing it now. Calling it 'medicine' instead of what it really was: poison." She sighed a sad sigh before continuing. "I said I wasn't hungry but sat at the table with him. God, Jess! I sat there with my boy and watched him eat the food that would kill him. And as he chewed each bite, I felt a little piece of my soul disintegrate. I remembered the day he was born, his first Christmas, all the dreams we had for the child we loved. They were shattering with each minute that passed. And when he'd finished his meal, he said he felt sleepy, and he went to his room. I wanted to run after him and scream, 'No, Devin! Don't lie down. I don't want you to go!' but it was too late, and he did lie down, and I stood next to his bed and watched him. He looked so peaceful, Jess. So gentle and kind. The way I always wanted him to be. Then I climbed into bed next to him, wrapped my arms around him, and told him how much I loved him while sobbing uncontrollably. And then my ten-year-old boy—my baby—was gone."

Tears flowed freely from Jess's eyes as she re-lived the experience with Abigail. She'd never felt as much pain as she had today. Overwhelmed with grief, she pulled Abigail close and hugged her tight.

"I'm so sorry, Ab," Jess sobbed while trembling and shaking. "I'm so sorry."

Chapter 25

As promised, Olivia sent wedding pictures to Kristen. It had been a small affair. A church ceremony followed by a dinner gathering at Ryan's favorite restaurant. There wasn't money for a full reception, with drinks, dancing, and music, and for that, Kristen felt terrible.

Ryan looked happy in the photos. That was all that mattered. And his new bride, Valerie, looked lovely in what appeared to be a vintage wedding gown. Kristen wondered if it was her grandmother's. As she continued staring at Valerie, she got excited. It was real now. Her son was married! And she had a daughter-in-law. Pretty soon, she could even become a grandmother. It was difficult to imagine as she still felt young herself, but it could happen.

There was something to look forward to.

Kristen continued checking out the photos. Olivia and Bob looked the same, which was no surprise. She swore the two of them never aged and wondered if they'd secretly made a pact with the devil. Her younger son, Toby, had matured since she'd seen him last, looking handsome with a date on his arm. Kristen wondered who she was and hoped Olivia would spill the details in the letter.

Kristen's heart stopped when she saw the next photo. It was of Jeremy and Ryan. She hadn't seen a picture of Jeremy in ages. He looked different. Older, of course. And he'd gained a bit of weight. Olivia had told her he still smoked and that he still didn't exercise or eat right. She wished he'd take better care of himself.

Kristen still loved him. He'd always be her husband. She wondered if Cindy was just as smitten with him as she was. If she were smart, she'd treat him better, but for her own selfish desires, she hoped Cindy wasn't smart.

Of course, there weren't any pictures of her and not knowing what she looked like continued to bother Kristen. She set the photos aside and turned her attention to the letter.

Kristen,

Hey, sis. How about these snaps? We're getting old, huh? Wish you could've been there. I hope you don't mind, but I took the liberty of writing a little speech for you. I stood up and gave it at the dinner reception. I hope that was cool.

Here's what you said: Ryan, Today is a moment in time to be cherished. I pray it was one of the happiest of your life, with many more still to come. I wish I could be there with the two of you, to witness this occasion but know that I am with you today in my mind, thinking of you and wishing you good luck in your new life together. Love always, Mom.

What do you think? Too cheesy? Does it sound stolen from a Hallmark card? Bob said it was decent, and Ryan and Valerie seemed to like it. I noticed Jeremy wipe a tear from his eye, so it must've been good. I've rarely seen my brother cry.

The ceremony was nice. Not too long. Just right. And the food was delicious. Oh, and the dress was cool. Valerie found it at an antique store and said it reminded her of a movie called *Somewhere in Time*.

She's a sweet girl. When you meet her, you're going to love her.

Other than that, not much else is going on. Gotta play catch-up around here from being out of town. I hope you're doing okay. I worry about you.

Love ya,
Olivia

Kristen thought the speech was nice. She was thankful Olivia had done it. Then she thought of Jeremy. If he cried, did that mean he still cared about her? Maybe it was because he felt bad for Ryan. She could analyze it for hours, she thought. It was a great way to come undone quickly. Thankfully, it was time to head out to the garden.

When Kristen arrived, she saw Abigail in her area digging.

"Hey there. Did they take you off hard labor or what?" she asked.

Abigail smiled. "Not sure. Just know I'm working with you today. That's what I was told."

Kristen kneeled down. "Cool. I finally have someone to talk to."

As the two of them sweated side by side under the hot

sun, Kristen wondered if Warden Laura was giving Abigail a break since Megan's wedding had been a success. She didn't know for sure, but she was happy her friend was off wheelbarrow duty for the day. She'd grown some arm muscles, but she was still a pipsqueak.

Jess strode past and grinned at Abigail, and Kristen noticed the way Abigail smiled back.

When Jess was out of earshot, she asked, "So, how do you two get along?"

Kristen already had a sneaking suspicion that they got along more than fine, but she wanted to see her reaction.

"We get along great. Jess is so nice," Abigail answered.

She seemed to glow with adoration as she spoke. Kristen wondered if they were talking about the same person.

Truly curious, she asked, "What do you like about her?"

Abigail seemed offended by the question, and Kristen hoped she hadn't inadvertently put her foot in her mouth.

"What's not to like?" Abigail replied. "She's thoughtful, a good friend, a great listener."

Kristen kept working, surprised to hear such praise. Abigail continued, apparently unable to stop herself once on a roll. "We've got some books too, and she reads them aloud. It's amazing how she can change her voice to sound like any character."

"Huh," Kristen said. "That's cool."

Abigail nodded. "And she's a pretty good masseuse. I've had some neck issues she's been able to help me with. My ex-husband was a chiropractor, but obviously, he's gone, so I've been lucky to have Jess."

Kristen bet Jess was adjusting more than Abigail's neck at this point, but it wasn't any of her business.

"Nice," she said instead. "Sounds like you've got a great cellmate."

Abigail continued sporting a dopey smile, a dead giveaway that proved her hunch. She never would've pegged Abigail as a lesbian. But, then again, she didn't even know what Abigail was in for or much else about her. When she thought about it, she realized none of it really mattered. They were all just people she passed the time with until she could get back to her life in the real world.

And what a colorful group they were.

*****

Sunburned from being outside and full from dinner, Kristen plopped down on her bunk.

"The food has gotten so much tastier now that you're in the kitchen, Deb."

"Why, thank you. It's been nice to get back to what I'm passionate about. In fact, I'm pretty excited about the future. When I get out, I'm going to return to the restaurant I used to run."

"Really? I mean, have you been invited back?" Kristen asked.

"Yep. I just found out. I'd written my old boss, who was a real sweetheart, by the way, and happened to be open-minded about my crime. Anyway, I let him know my release date and that I'd been cooking here, staying up to date as much as possible considering where I'm at. He wrote me back saying he's opening a new place next year and that he'd love to have me on his team."

Ecstatic, Kristen found the energy to jump up and high-five Debbie. "That rocks! I'm so happy for you. You must be on cloud nine."

"I am. I have to say I never expected such a positive outcome from reaching out to him."

Kristen wasn't surprised one bit. With Debbie's upbeat attitude and sunny disposition, she could see how good fortune would smile upon her. And she didn't have too much more time to serve.

Kristen sure would miss her when she was gone.

*****

A newly pregnant Lakeisha sat at her desk. She looked up as a suntanned Megan walked in. "You wanna go for drinks tomorrow night? It's been a while. Love the hubby, but need my girl time too."

"Sure," she replied. "Is Warden Laura coming?"

"I'm gonna ask her next," Megan said.

After she left, Lakeisha set the mail aside for delivery, took a bathroom break, and made her rounds. Lakeisha shook her head in disapproval when she delivered Kristen her mail.

*****

Flipping the envelope over, Kristen saw it was from her mom. She quickly opened it up and read it.

Kristen,

Hey, honey. Your dad and I are going on vacation to Disney World at Christmastime and thought, since we'll be in Florida, we'd try to come by and visit you. Just thought I'd write and let you know.

Mom

Kristen laughed even though it wasn't funny. They thought they could "drop by" like it was a social call. They were clueless that there was actual paperwork to be filled out. Maybe if they'd kept in touch or had shown up to her sentencing, they'd know these things.

Kristen felt anger rise within. Not just from today's insult. From decades' worth of mistreatment.

It was remarkable how her parents still had the power to make her feel rejected after all these years. She'd talked about all this with Megan, and she understood that they were doing the best they could with what they had, but it still hurt. It was hard to be the child of a parent who had nothing to give.

Kristen thought about writing them back and telling them about the required paperwork. Then, as she contemplated it more, she changed her mind. They had never really seemed to love her. Why would that be any different now? If they actually did come to see her, which she doubted, they'd find out then.

Kristen set the letter down, climbed into her bunk, and

closed her eyes. Somehow receiving their short note had changed her world. In less than a half hour, her perspective shifted.

And she was able to let them go.

Chapter 26

A new prisoner came into the mix and, after a short time on the yard, joined Jess' basketball game. She was aggressive and a little more physical than necessary, adding tension to an atmosphere that already hummed with indignation.

But she had game.

Jess thought she played like she'd been on a team before. She knew her shit. She was the one to watch and learn from.

"You're good," she told the new girl. "Name's Jess, and you are?"

"Shanice," she answered without saying thanks.

Jess was curious. "You play ball somewhere before?"

"Ain't you full of questions," Shanice replied. "I been shooting hoops all my life."

Apparently done with small talk, Shanice bounced the ball and started dribbling, and the group returned to their game. Shanice seemed extra forceful, downright bullish even, almost knocking her to the ground when she tried to block one of her shots.

This impressed Jess even more, and when they finished, she approached her again. "Dang, girl. You almost killed me on that last one."

Shanice crossed her arms in front of her chest and smirked. "Wouldn't be the first time I killed a cracker."

Jess' friendly smile faded along with the spirit of camaraderie. "Oh," was all she could think of to say.

Shanice tossed the basketball to Jess. After Jess caught it, Shanice sauntered over and put a hand on her shoulder. "I'm gonna let you in on a little secret," she whispered. "God ain't too fond of your type."

With that supposed nugget revealed, Shanice walked away, leaving Jess crestfallen.

*****

"You seem upset," Abigail said to Jess once they returned to their cell.

Jess shook her head. "I'm sick of hypocrites. That's all."

Abigail listened while Jess told her what had happened. Jess knew she felt bad but couldn't really relate. Being an affluent white woman, she hadn't been the subject of much prejudice in her life.

"You know what pisses me off the most?" Jess blurted out. "When people claim to know what God thinks. That gets me," she said while chucking one of her shoes across the room. "They don't know."

Abigail looked like she was about to say something when Jess added, "I happen to believe God loves me. No. I know He does."

Jess stalked back and forth, becoming more aggravated. "I used to be very involved in my church. I helped with all kinds of events: bake sales, car wash fundraisers. I don't need some asshole telling me God doesn't like my type."

"See, you just made your case," Abigail said. "She's a jerk. You should forget about her."

Jess knew she was right but was still aggravated. Usually, when people said that kind of thing, it rolled off her back. But after admiring Shanice, getting slammed by her made it sting more. And bringing religion into it was a great way to push Jess off the deep end.

"Maybe you should exercise with us instead. You're always playing ball."

"Cause that's what I like!" Jess quipped.

Jess could tell she'd upset Abigail. She didn't mean to take out her frustration on her.

"You want me to kick her ass?" Abigail asked. "I'm kind of small, but I could probably get one good slap in."

Jess laughed. "No, Ab. I don't want you to do that." She sat down next to her and smiled. "But it's kind of cute to picture."

Abigail smiled back. She seemed happy to have said something to break the tension. "If you have faith in God and know how He feels, don't let someone else try to shake it," she added, a bit more serious now.

Jess looked at Abigail and thought how lucky she was to have her. "I won't," she said.

Later on, after they ate dinner, Jess was interested in hearing more about Abigail's past.

"Remember when you told me the story about your son?" Jess said.

205

Abigail nodded.

"Well, you never said what happened afterward. I mean, how did you get caught?"

Abigail stood and began fidgeting with her hands, then stretched her neck from side to side, the way she did when she was tense. Afterward, she sat down on the cell floor, where she seemed to stare into the past.

"It was pretty straightforward, I guess. I stayed there next to Devin, crying. First, in a fit of hysteria over what I'd done, then consumed by pain that was beyond comprehension. Eventually, I fell asleep. Steve had just walked in when I woke and flipped on the bedroom light. He looked at me—the state I was in—then he looked at Devin. 'What's going on here? What's the matter?' he asked. The look on my face told him something dire, and he rushed to our son and kneeled down. 'Devin, honey. Are you okay?' he asked. When he reached out and touched him, he could feel his body was ice cold."

Jess was on the edge of her seat.

"Steve shook him and kept calling his name. When there was no response, he got up, wearing an expression of sheer terror, and faced me. 'Is he?' was all he could ask. I broke down sobbing again and nodded yes. Then I looked at my husband and said, 'I'm sorry.'"

"His eyes widened as he understood. 'What do you mean you're sorry?' he asked. But I didn't answer him. I couldn't say the words. I just turned away. 'What do you mean, Abigail?' he asked again as I ran from the room."

Abigail's voice cracked as she spoke.

"I could hear him break down. He was wailing, 'Nooo!

Not my boy! Oh, God, nooo! Not my son!' while I leaned against the wall in the master bedroom."

Abigail wiped her eyes. "That's when I realized I'd killed them both. The two people I loved more than anyone in the world. After that, I went numb. I remember hearing the police sirens, first in the distance and then getting louder. Two officers were cuffing me and talking, reading me my rights. I saw the ambulance arrive and watched from the back of the police car as they loaded my son onto a stretcher, his body covered with a white sheet. The last thing I saw was Steve. He glared at me right before we pulled away. The look in his eyes was pure hate."

Abigail looked up. She wore the expression of a dazed trauma patient. Jess was crying now. She couldn't help it.

"There was a funeral, of course. And I was in jail and wasn't allowed to go. My poor parents," Abigail said, shaking her head. "They were horrified and confused. But they jumped right in and hired an attorney. He didn't have much of a chance since I confessed to everything. His task basically boiled down to getting me life in prison versus the death penalty. So in the end, I guess he did what he was hired to do."

"And here I am," Abigail mocked. "I'm alive. Not that I deserve to be." She started laughing.

"You want to know the ridiculous part?" she asked. "Somehow, I'd gotten the crazy idea that if things were like they were before, when Devin wasn't around, without the constant pressure and insanity, that I could turn back time. I thought Steve would stop seeing his old flame and he'd love me the way he used to. I thought I could have the life I dreamed of having in my childhood. You know the one. The happy marriage. The house with the white picket fence. Every girl's dream."

Jess listened to everything Abigail said and then watched as she closed her eyes, exhausted from telling the tale. If Jess had the chance, she would give Abigail the life she dreamed of. She'd make it her mission to make every one of those dreams come true. Nothing would make her happier.

Jess grew excited, thinking about how she could do just that, then ran headlong into the realization it was all in vain. Abigail was serving a life sentence. She'd never be able to fulfill Abigail's wish. There was no point in even thinking about it. Frustrated, Jess ran her hands through her hair. "I love you," she said.

Looking tired beyond belief, Abigail opened her eyes and managed a small smile. "I love you too, Jess."

They didn't make love that night. And they didn't talk about the past. They just lay next to each other on the lower bunk, with Jess' arms wrapped around Abigail, providing comfort.

They had each other. And that was enough.

Chapter 27

Kristen gazed at her reflection in the bathroom mirror. Her blonde hair was gray in the front and on the sides. The wrinkles around her mouth and eyes had deepened. She'd accepted it, though. She'd even stopped obsessing over what Jeremy's girlfriend, Cindy, might look like. The divorce papers never came, so there was no reason to stay in a constant state of panic. It wasn't healthy.

Besides, it was Christmas. And although her parents never showed because they'd been too busy at Disney World, then got side-tracked sight-seeing in South Beach, she had a lot to be thankful for. There was breath in her lungs, all her limbs were still attached, and she had a future. Each year that passed, it came closer, and she'd been blessed with decent cellmates so far. There was much to be happy about.

A very pregnant Lakeisha had baked an assortment of cookies and brought them to be served with the holiday movie. This year they were showing the classic *It's a Wonderful Life*.

While Debbie and Kristen waited for the movie to start, Debbie said, "I used to watch this every year. I had a thing for Jimmy Stewart."

Kristen cracked up. "Really?"

"Yep. He's so sweet. I think of him as tall, dark, and sincere. I'm gonna find one like him when I get out."

Smiling, Kristen said, "I have no doubt you will."

"All right, ladies. Let's keep it down," one of the guards said. "The movie is about to start, and everyone wants to hear."

Kristen looked at Debbie and grinned.

As Kristen watched the film, she recalled that she also had seen it almost every year when she was free, but this time it seemed different. Certain scenes had new meaning for her. They jumped to the forefront. She'd heard it was similar with books. You could read one at age nineteen, reread it at thirty, and again at fifty, and your experience would be different each time. That made a lot of sense, she thought, as she took a bite of a chocolate chip cookie.

When Kristen got back to her cell, she lined up her Christmas cards on her section of the shelf. There was one from Olivia and Bob with their cat Cocoa dressed up in a Santa hat. There was one from her son Ryan and his wife, Valerie. Lupe had stayed in touch, too, sending a card that included a photo of the whole family. A great-looking bunch, Kristen thought.

And this year, she'd gotten one from Toby. The mystery woman on his arm at the wedding had been his new girlfriend, Erica. With his passion for music and the amount of time he devoted to it, Kristen had worried he might never find a girlfriend. But alas, hormones won out, and the young lady was both smart and beautiful, having moved from Russia to the United States with her family after graduating high school.

Olivia had filled her in on Erica in a previous letter. She was highly-educated and spoke three languages fluently. She also put a high priority on getting a college education, which according to Olivia, had motivated Toby. He hadn't been sure if he wanted to go to college, but she'd convinced him no matter what he did, he couldn't go wrong with a business degree, even for a career in music.

Kristen was glad things were looking up for both her sons. She wished they'd come back and visit because she missed them so much. She decided to be patient. That was all she could really do.

"Who did you get the card from?" Kristen asked Debbie.

"The man who's giving me the job at the restaurant. That was nice, don't you think?"

Kristen picked it up and read it. Happy Holidays, it said. We look forward to having you back on the team.

"That was very thoughtful," Kristen agreed, sounding a bit glum. She set the card down and faced Debbie. "I almost forgot. You'll be leaving us soon."

The mixed message was evident in Kristen's tone. She was both thrilled for her and sad to be losing her. They'd become good friends.

"True," Debbie said. "But you're invited to feast on one of my multi-course creations just as soon as you get out."

"You'll save me a seat?" Kristen asked.

"There will always be a table for you," Debbie said,

then reached out and gave Kristen a big hug. "Merry Christmas, sweetie."

Kristen hugged her tight, imagining what it would have been like to have a mother like Debbie. "Merry Christmas," she said back.

*****

"Do you remember *The Donna Reed Show*?" Abigail asked Jess once they'd come back from the movie.

"No. I don't think so."

"It was before our time, a TV series in the late fifties, early sixties. My parents and I used to watch old episodes on cable. Anyway, seeing her in the movie got me thinking of the show. They were the ideal American family. The husband was a doctor, and he and his wife got along great, and the children behaved. When I was growing up, my parents' friends compared our family to them."

Jess pulled the blanket down on her bunk. "I could see that."

Abigail took off her shoes and started to change into her pajamas. "Could you imagine what people think of us now?"

Jess shrugged. "Real life isn't like TV. People know that."

"I guess," Abigail said. She was quiet for a while, reflecting on her childhood, thinking hers had been very much like the show.

"Did I ever tell you my dad wanted to try the whole

Doctors Without Borders thing?" Abigail asked.

"What's that?"

"It's a medical program to help people in less developed countries."

"Oh, now I know what it is," Jess said. "I saw a movie like that."

Abigail lay in her bunk and thought about her dad. He was a good person. Always had been. And like her, he had unfulfilled dreams.

"I wish he'd go do it," she said.

Jess seemed to have lost track of the conversation. "Do what?" she asked.

"Take a job in another country, like he's always wanted."

"He's not going to do that, Ab. He'd miss you too much."

Abigail considered what she'd said. She was probably right, and she hated that she might be what was holding him back. It made her sad, and she let out a deep sigh.

Jess hopped off her bunk and took a seat on the edge of Abigail's. "Are we going to dwell on negative stuff tonight? On Christmas?" she asked, with a pleading look.

"I'm ruining your holiday. I'm sorry."

Jess reached out and took Abigail's hand. "You could never ruin my holiday. Being with you is all I want." Then she leaned in and kissed her.

*****

On the first day back at work after New Year's, Lakeisha

sat at her desk and found it difficult to get comfortable. Her abdomen was so large it kept getting in the way. She'd been through this before and didn't mind, though. She just hoped to give birth to a healthy child this time. And even though she suffered from wicked hormone swings, Lakeisha made a point of being kind to her co-workers. Their lives already stunk enough because of where they all worked. They didn't need any of her crap.

"So when are you going to find out the sex of the baby?" Laura asked.

"We're going the same route as before. We want to be surprised. Only this time, I've decided to do the epidural. As Megan said, God gave us the technology to feel less pain. Amen to that."

Laura smiled. "I'm praying everything goes smooth. You sure you couldn't use any extra help around here?"

Lakeisha shook her head. "Nope. I've got it under control." She had a feeling Laura would offer again, and if so, she planned to decline. She didn't like to appear weak.

"If you say so," Laura said, heading for the door.

Finding just the right angle to sit in her chair, Lakeisha got started with incoming mail. The holidays always brought plenty of unauthorized material. Boyfriends tended to get tipsy and thought it wise to include photos of their private parts. If she had a dollar for every picture of a penis she'd seen through the years, she could afford a Coach handbag, she mused.

Toward the bottom of the pile, she saw an envelope for Kristen from her son Ryan. Her interest piqued, Lakeisha opened it, performed her obligatory contraband check, and began reading.

Mom,

I hope you got our Christmas card and had a happy new year. We thought of you while listening to the countdown.

I have great news. Valerie's pregnant. You're going to be a grandmother!

Love,

Ryan

If Lakeisha weren't expecting herself, she would've jumped for joy. This was wonderful, and because she was so excited, she decided to break with protocol and do a special delivery for just this piece of mail. She'd have to expend precious energy reserves, but it was worth it.

Kristen was in her cell reading the latest book Olivia had sent. She looked up when she noticed her.

"Special delivery," Lakeisha said.

The look on Kristen's face brightened. She put her book down and walked to the cell door, one eyebrow raised.

"You're gonna like this one," Lakeisha assured her, then handed her the envelope.

Kristen took it and sat down. Debbie stood nearby, waiting to hear. Lakeisha lingered in the doorway, something she'd never done but couldn't help herself as this was too good to miss.

After ripping open the letter and reading it, Kristen shouted, "I'm going to be a grandma!"

Kristen's eyes were wide with delight, and she jumped up and down. Debbie high-fived her, equally thrilled.

Lakeisha made eye contact with Kristen. "Congratulations," she said.

The happiness that lit up Kristen's face made the trip worth it, and as she walked back down the hall listening to the jubilant commotion, Lakeisha smiled.

Her work here was done.

Chapter 28

Winter was still pretty hot in Florida, but for the natives, whose blood had thinned, some days seemed downright chilly. An afternoon in the mid-sixties felt like a deep freeze. Today was one of those days, sunny but breezy and mild.

Abigail rubbed her upper arms to get warm. "It's so cold," she complained to Kristen as she gathered her gardening tools. Her position as Kristen's assistant had become permanent, with a new, more muscular girl taking over the wheelbarrow and heavy lifting.

"I like it when it's cooler like this. It's the only break we get from the constant heat and humidity," Kristen said.

Working side by side, the two women had gotten to know each other better, but it was still on a superficial level. Abigail didn't dare discuss her intimate relationship with Jess or tell Kristen about her crime. And thankfully, she hadn't asked. Kristen never mentioned why she was in prison, either. All she had told Abigail was she had an estranged husband and two grown boys. Abigail thought she'd heard someone say she was in for white-collar crime.

"Hey. I've got some amazing news since I saw you

last," Kristen said.

"Yeah. What's that?" Abigail asked. It was noteworthy when someone mentioned something positive.

Kristen stopped digging. "I'm going to be a grandma," she proudly announced. "My oldest son, Ryan, and his wife are having a baby."

"How exciting!" Abigail said. Abigail swallowed hard, feeling her old pain for just a moment. But her joy was sincere. She really did love children.

Kristen continued as she sprinkled seeds into the just-dug furrows. "It is. And even though I won't be there when the baby is born, I still get to be a part of its life later on, when it's a toddler."

It was nice to see a woman get a second chance. But, of course, not everyone did.

"How about you? Do you have children?" Kristen asked.

Abigail's breath caught. She couldn't think up a quick enough response. There was an eerie silence.

"I had a son," Abigail said while averting her gaze.

No doubt Kristen noticed the past tense and that she didn't elaborate on what happened to him. Kristen rose, looking more than a little uncomfortable. "I'll be right back. I'm going to rinse off my hands and grab more seeds."

As she headed to the storage shed, Abigail wondered if Kristen had figured it out. She was in for life, after all. That was common knowledge. It didn't take a genius to put two and two together. Of course, Abigail would never tell her, but if she had surmised, she hoped Kristen didn't think she was a psycho like Tanya.

Then again, maybe she was. How else could a mother convince herself it was in the best interest of society to kill her own kid?

*****

Jess's mom had taught her daughter to smother her enemies with kindness. It was great in theory but didn't always work in real life, like when that enemy was sleeping with your girlfriend. But also when someone was just downright mean.

Shanice had grown more obnoxious by the day. It took every ounce of patience Jess had to put up with her, and no amount of Bible-thumping could make her love the woman as her fellow man. Moreover, Shanice had recently gotten into the annoying habit of quoting Bible passages to prove she was superior.

Jess pretended the comments didn't bother her and focused on the basketball game. She couldn't stomach Shanice but had continued observing her on the court and learned some of her moves.

Jess concentrated and then made a shot, releasing the ball at just the right arc before Shanice knocked her to the ground. The sound of the ball sliding through the net only pissed Shanice off more. Jess just smirked.

"What you smiling about? Your girlfriend's pussy?" Shanice taunted.

Jess got back up and grinned. "Maybe. Or your momma's."

Shanice charged her. "What'd you say, bitch?"

The first punch missed Jess' jaw as she ducked. She heard Abigail scream in the background and remembered her promise that she wouldn't get into trouble, then jumped back, just missing the second.

Two guards came running and pulled Shanice off Jess. As they hauled her away, Jess couldn't resist getting in the last word. "Thou shall not kill. Bible basics, asshole."

Looking infuriated, Shanice struggled against the officers and got clubbed in the process.

Jess laughed. She couldn't stand the prejudiced witch.

Abigail jogged over with a look of concern on her face. She crossed her arms in front of her chest. "What was that all about?" she demanded.

"The usual. Dumb skank doesn't practice what she preaches."

"And what about our agreement? You gave me your word," Abigail said.

Jess felt like she was being scolded. "I didn't break it. I didn't hit back."

Abigail gave her a cynical look. "She attacked you for no reason."

"I might've said something, but it was in response to her talking shit first," Jess said. She could tell Abigail was pissed.

Abigail shook her head and let out an exasperated sigh. Then it was time to go back in.

During dinner, Abigail was quiet and seemed to chew her food more than usual. And as Jess slurped at her pea soup, she felt Abigail's eyes bore into her.

"Sorry," Jess said. "I forgot you hate that."

Abigail was on edge again. Anxious. She'd been doing so much better lately, hardly ever having a flare-up, but stressful situations seemed to aggravate her.

"You still mad at me?" Jess asked.

"No," Abigail said. "I'm just thinking."

Jess wasn't sure that was a good thing. She turned back to her soup. If Abigail wanted to tell her what was troubling her, she could.

More silence followed that evening. Jess let it go, choosing to play cards by herself.

"What if something happened to you?" Abigail eventually blurted out.

Crap, Jess thought. She was going full circle, back to the beginning.

"It didn't."

"Yeah. But what if it did?"

Jess climbed down and took Abigail's hand in hers. "I wouldn't let anything happen to me. My job is to protect you. How can I do that if I'm hurt?"

Abigail shook her head, which confused Jess. "Your job isn't to protect me," she said. "Your job is to take care of yourself, so you get out of here someday in one piece."

That wasn't what Jess wanted to hear. Even a casual mention of Jess' eventual release aggravated her.

"I told you I don't want to talk about that," Jess said firmly.

She started kissing Abigail in a more forceful manner than usual and began tugging at her top. Abigail responded with high-pitched panting, and Jess took this as her cue to throw her down onto the bed and put an end to the matter.

*****

After finishing up for the day and clocking out, Lakeisha said goodbye to her co-workers. She'd gone past her due date, and the doctor had scheduled a time to induce labor the next morning.

"Remember: epidural," Megan said. "Don't be a hero."

Lakeisha laughed. "Don't worry. I've got it covered."

"We'll stop by later tomorrow to see how everything went," Laura said with a hopeful look on her face. "It will be fine. You'll see."

"I hope so," she said, then nodded and began to walk away.

"Lakeisha," Megan called out, causing her to turn back. "Good luck!"

When Megan and Laura stopped by the following night, Lakeisha was embarrassed about her appearance. Her hair wasn't done, and she had no makeup on. She knew she looked awful, like she'd done battle with fire-breathing dragons.

"It's a boy," she said, sounding excited and haggard at the same time. "We named him Tony, after my grandfather."

"Congratulations!" they said in unison. Megan handed her a small plush ivory-colored bear.

Lakeisha took it. "Thanks." She looked at Laura and smiled. "You did tell me things would be fine."

"I did. And you had both of us praying for you."

Lakeisha nodded. "I'm sure that helped."

Megan glanced around the room. "So where's the baby?" she asked.

"Nurses' area right now. They're bringing him back in a few if you want to wait."

No sooner than Lakeisha uttered those words, the nurse came in with Tony in her arms, and the women lit up and began making cooing sounds.

After they left, Lakeisha closed her eyes and smiled.

She had never been happier in her life.

Chapter 29

Abigail's parents had missed a few weeks of visitation in a row. They'd taken a trip to Thailand for their anniversary, something they'd always planned to do. Her mom wanted to soak in the sun on the beach, just like she'd seen in the Leonardo DiCaprio movie, and her dad wanted to visit the temples and historic sites. They had written saying they were home, that they'd had a blast, and would be coming this weekend.

"Hey!" Abigail shrieked, waving at them as she entered the visitation area. Realizing she was being too loud, she looked over at the guard and silently mouthed, "Sorry."

Abigail's parents waved back and came toward her. They both gave her a hug.

"Hey, honey," her mom said. "We missed you."

"I missed you guys too. You look great. You both got a lot of sun."

"It was impossible not to. We wore sunblock, but look at us. We're positively bronzed."

Abigail giggled. "So, tell me about your trip," she said as they sat down.

Her mom began talking, and Abigail zoned out. The sound of her voice was so relaxing. It soothed her spirit. Then she heard the word hospital.

"Hold on. Repeat that last part," Abigail said.

"Which part?"

"What you said about the hospital."

"Oh, that," she said. "Your dad met a fellow doctor at the resort. He was there visiting a relative from out of town. Anyway, they got to chatting over drinks, and he invited us to take a tour of the hospital. It was unbelievable. State of the art."

Abigail glanced at her dad. "You should get a job there."

"Funny you should mention that," he said. "I was offered one, but I turned it down."

He didn't have to tell her why. She knew.

"You should try it for a year or six months. It would be a lot of fun. An adventure."

"We wouldn't want to leave you, honey," her mom said.

And there it was. Out in the open.

"I'll still be here when you get back. Don't worry about me. I've got friends and a job in the garden. You could write, and we'd be in touch just like always."

Abigail could tell what she said fell on deaf ears. They both had that glazed-over look she knew all too well. They had already made their decision.

They weren't going anywhere.

*****

The time had come for Debbie to leave prison. They'd spent five years together. Kristen was overjoyed for her, but she'd be deeply missed. The two of them had stayed up late the night before and re-lived all the funny stories they'd experienced together, laughing until they almost peed their pants.

Kristen sat in her bunk and watched Debbie organize her small pile of possessions. This was how it always was, she thought. People came into her life, then left, each one of them significant in some way.

It was just so hard to say goodbye.

Kristen tried to fight the tears that filled her eyes but couldn't. She wiped them away and sniffed. "Look at me. I'm a blubbering mess!"

In a reassuring voice, Debbie smiled and said, "That's okay, sweetie. I'd expect nothing less. I'm going to miss you too." She came over, wrapped her arms around Kristen, and hugged her tightly.

"I want you to stay positive. Think only good thoughts, and whenever you find yourself dwelling on a bad one...stop. Do it for me, okay?"

Kristen nodded and wiped her eyes. "I will. Enjoy your new job at the restaurant. I'll make sure to visualize a Jimmy Stewart look-a-like stopping in for a meal and asking to meet the chef."

Debbie grinned. "Atta girl. Now you're thinking."

"Don't forget to write," Kristen added, embarrassed the second she said it. Of course, Debbie would write.

"I'd never forget to keep in touch. You can count on me."

The guard arrived to take Debbie, and the two hugged one last time. Then Debbie gathered her things and left.

Kristen pressed her face against the vertical bars so she could see her walk away.

And then she was gone.

Within a short time, Kristen had a bunch of gossip to share with Debbie. She'd written her a letter with all the latest but couldn't send it until Debbie wrote her first with the return address. When weeks passed without a single word from her, Kristen began feeling slightly disappointed. Then she decided Debbie must be really busy. There was a big world on the outside, filled with plenty of things to do. She'd promised to write, so Kristen continued to wait patiently.

When weeks turned into months, and there was still no word from Debbie, she found it disturbing. It seemed so out of character for her. It didn't make any sense. Lupe had kept in touch, which she hadn't expected. And Debbie, well, she had the feeling they would be friends for life.

Kristen concluded that she wasn't upset, though. She could understand someone wanting to forget their time in prison. Especially if their new life was busy and full of adventure. Debbie had been a positive force in her life, like a breath of fresh air, and she hoped whatever became of her, wherever she was, it was someplace good.

*****

Megan and Lakeisha had signed up for a gym membership together at a health club near work. Lakeisha wanted to burn the baby fat off, and Megan, already in fabulous shape, just went along to keep her company and decompress.

Huffing and puffing on the elliptical, Lakeisha asked Megan, "So, how's married life treating you? Everything good?"

Megan smiled, working at a faster pace and breathing easily. "Yep. The man is always busy, never a pain in the butt."

Lakeisha laughed.

"You two thinking of having kids?"

Megan wrinkled her nose. "I don't know. I think I'd like to, but if I did, I'd want to stay home with them."

Lakeisha looked surprised.

"So you might be leaving us one day then."

"I don't know. I don't think so. I'm not fond of walking out on my patients."

Megan realized she sounded ambivalent, but that didn't bother her. She was still young and had plenty of time to make up her mind.

After their workout, Lakeisha asked, "And how are our slew of crazies? Getting better?"

Only she could get away with calling the women crazy. Megan would've corrected anyone else. "Oh, you know. Some improve, or at least I think they do. They have fewer violations in their files, so at least they fight less."

"I gotta hand it to you, Meg. You've got to be a special person to do the kind of work you do."

Megan grinned at the compliment. "Not special, my dear. Nosy! I find there's nothing more fascinating than human behavior."

It was true. She often felt like a cryptographer trying to solve mysteries of the mind, unlocking her patients' secrets bit by bit, week by week.

Then there were patients like Abigail who wouldn't let her in at all. Megan found cases like hers the most interesting, mainly because she hadn't found a single key. That made her even more eager to try.

Human nature, she mused while running a brush through her hair.

Her favorite.

Chapter 30

Not hearing from Debbie had Kristen feeling down, but soon enough, the focus shifted to more important things. The birth of her grandchild. Olivia had been keeping her abreast of all the details, and things were going smoothly so far. She wished more than anything she could be there, but as the years passed, she'd gotten better at not beating herself up over things. It was best to think of the future.

Since Debbie left, Warden Laura hadn't transferred anyone new to Kristen's cell. And with her newfound alone time, she stepped up her mantra, repeating it under her breath many times per day instead of just before bedtime. If anyone had heard her doing it, they'd think she was nuts. And maybe she was.

It wasn't like there was much else to do. When she was on the outside, she always raced against time, trying to complete everything on her "to-do" list. She always went to bed tired but had trouble sleeping unless she'd had a few drinks. The stress of stealing was suffocating her. And the more she took, the more she had to knock back each night to fall asleep.

Olivia said Jeremy had originally put what they hadn't sold off in the estate sale into a storage locker. But as the years passed, they questioned paying a monthly fee to store clothing that would only go out of style by the time Kristen got out. In the end, they'd whittled her belongings down to important keepsakes, diminishing any evidence of items purchased through theft. What remained was small enough to put in a hallway closet.

When Kristen first heard the news, she was distraught. All she could think of was losing her things. But after counseling, the passage of time, and people coming and going in her life, she no longer cared. It was almost freeing to know it was all gone. Only what was important survived.

Kristen's birthday came, and she was excited to receive cards from Olivia and one from each of her sons. She missed Debbie, though. She had always gone out of her way to make her birthday special. Having access to the kitchen brought its own privileges, one of them being that she could sneak food back to their cell. Debbie used to sing Happy Birthday to her too, which was kind of goofy, but Kristen liked it. It reminded her of childhood, only better.

Sighing, Kristen hoped once again that Debbie was doing well. Then she delved into the newest book Olivia had sent and spent the rest of the afternoon reading.

*****

Jess' mom seemed especially cheerful this visit and wore a near-constant smile as she talked. "I've had your room repainted and bought all new bedding. I think you're going to like it. The look is eco-modern. Not too girly, because I know you don't care for that. Think Zen."

Her mom's voice sounded like it came from a faraway place. "Cool," was all she could bring herself to say.

Never in her wildest dreams did Jess think she'd not want to leave prison. Before meeting Abigail, all she could do was count down the days. Now the thought of going home felt like the most depressing thing in the world. She tried not to think of it, but each day the impending doom got closer. She wished she could make it stop.

"Or I could go with another look if you prefer," her mom said.

"No, Mom. The Zen thing is good. Let's stick with that."

Her mom smiled, but Jess couldn't find it in her heart to smile back.

Frowning, Jess' mom said, "Honey, I know you're happy with your friend here, but you're going to have to let that go."

Jess grew tense. "I don't want to talk about that. Okay?"

"We don't have to talk about it. I'm just saying—"

"Christ, Mom! I said I don't want to talk about it!"

Jess' mom looked down and folded her hands in her lap.

"I'm sorry, Mom. I didn't mean to upset you," Jess said. She wished she could reach out and take hold of her mom's hand, but it was against the rules. There could only be physical contact at the beginning and end of the visitation.

Jess's mom's chin started to quiver. She looked like

she was about to cry.

"I love the eco-modern thing. It sounds great," Jess said, trying to backpedal.

But it was too late. A stray tear had already escaped.

"Shit, Mom. I'm sorry. Aw…now you're…shit."

"I'm all right," she nodded. She looked across the table into her daughter's eyes. "I'm just worried about you."

*****

At dinnertime, Jess could sense Abigail studying her. They knew each other so well it was easy to tell when something was wrong.

After washing down a mouthful of mixed veggies with a glass of water, Abigail asked, "Is everything okay? You seem agitated."

Jess felt like she was about to spontaneously combust. "I'm fine," she answered in a clipped fashion.

"What is it? Bad news from home?"

Jess took a larger than usual bite of her dinner roll. It was either fill her face with food or let out a desperate scream. She was thankful Abigail didn't try to pry the issue out of her. She just wanted to be left alone with her thoughts.

Back in their cell, Jess grew moodier. She'd gone from feeling angry to being down in the dumps and sat on the ground sulking. Abigail stood and looked in both directions, checking that the guards were gone after the evening count, then began slowly running her fingers through her long red hair while provocatively swaying her hips from side to side.

Jess looked up, transfixed. She loved watching Abigail dance. Usually, it was ballet, but every once in a while, she'd treat Jess to an erotic show. She was really getting into it, with eyes closed, mouth half open, her body undulating like she had been hypnotized by a snake charmer.

Tears welled in Jess' eyes as she watched Abigail. She was the most beautiful creature that ever walked the Earth. Her personal goddess. And she was going to lose her.

Jess couldn't hold it together and began sobbing. The sound stopped Abigail in her tracks, and her eyes flitted open.

Kneeling, Abigail took Jess' hand. "Baby, what's the matter?"

Jess couldn't speak. She just kept crying. Abigail sat by and watched, looking helpless and confused. Jess felt bad she had ruined the moment but couldn't help herself.

Eventually, her sobs slowed to whimpers, and she wiped her face with the back of her arm. She inhaled a deep breath and let it out slowly. She beamed at Abigail. "You're amazing. Do you know that?"

Abigail looked perplexed. "I don't understand. Why are you crying?"

Jess fixed her with a tender gaze and said, "Because I love you. And when you do something incredible, like dance that way for me, I feel so lucky." She paused, then added, "And because I don't want to leave you, Ab.

You're everything to me."

"I love you too," Abigail cooed. "And where you claim to feel lucky, I'm bewildered, wondering how I could possibly deserve a wonderful person like you."

Jess could hardly believe the words that were coming out of Abigail's mouth. She started to speak, but Abigail put a finger over her lips, shushing her.

"Let me finish before I can't get it out, okay?"

Jess nodded, and Abigail sat back down.

"Because of my feelings for you, and because I know how truly special you are, I'm happy you're being released soon."

Jess blurted out, "What do you mean you're happy? How can you say that?"

Abigail frowned. "I don't mean to hurt your feelings. Let me try to explain." She paused, looked Jess directly in the eyes, and said, "I'm sad, of course, because I don't want to be without you, but the reality is we can't have a future together. You're going to be free, and I'm not. It's just not meant to be."

Jess began sobbing again.

"I want to see you leave here and be happy," she continued. "I want to see you start a new life and share that love with someone else someday."

Jess had no desire to share a life with anyone else. She couldn't picture it and was becoming increasingly upset.

"Put yourself in my shoes, Jess. Wouldn't you want the same for me?"

"No!" Jess snapped. "I wouldn't. I don't want a life without you. I want us to be together. Always."

Jess couldn't accept what Abigail had. And she couldn't take any more discussion of the matter. She was hurt that Abigail could let her go just like that.

Abigail leaned in and gave Jess a gentle kiss on the lips, then whispered in her ear, "All I want is the best for you."

Jess closed her eyes in an attempt to make it all go away. Watching Abigail dance made her feel more alive than she'd ever felt. She revisited the image, letting it awaken her every sense. Intoxicated, she pulled Abigail close and spent the rest of the night memorizing the surface of her skin, the scent of her hair.

She wished she could possess her very being.

In the wee hours of the morning, after Abigail was fast asleep in her own bunk, Jess lay awake, thinking. She decided there wasn't a chance in hell she was going to lose the woman she loved. She'd rather spend the rest of her life in prison than be free with anyone else.

Then, as if in answer to her prayers, a solution began to form in her mind.

Chapter 31

The news of Kristen's grandchild's birth came rushing in. She got a letter from Olivia and a card with a baby photo from Ryan. It was a girl, and they named her Melissa. The excitement was almost too much for Kristen. She jumped up and down in her cell by herself, with no one around to high-five or celebrate with, and for once, she couldn't care less. Nothing could bring her down from the incredible high.

Kristen had always wanted a girl. Granted, she loved her two boys, but if she'd had a third child, she'd hoped it would be a girl. She couldn't wait until she got out and could see her. It would only be a few more years. All she had to do was sit tight.

As Kristen stared at Melissa's picture, her heart doubled in size. Melissa's wrinkled pink face and fuzzy head might have looked like every other newborn baby to anyone else, but this wasn't any other baby. It was her granddaughter.

And she already loved her.

An odd thing happened as she sat gazing at Melissa's photo. She found she didn't feel angry at her husband anymore. She didn't hate Cindy or whomever Jeremy might be dating. She didn't even feel jealous. It was as if all that toxic emotion had fallen away.

For a split-second, she felt anxious, wondering why she didn't have the expected feelings. Then she realized there was no point in chasing after the past. A wise woman would let it go.

Kristen smirked. Was that what she'd become? Wise? She had no idea, but she felt good.

At peace.

She returned her attention to Melissa's picture and spent the rest of the afternoon visualizing all the fun things they'd do together. She continued floating on a cloud over the birth of her granddaughter. Her mood forecast was bright and sunny every single day.

*****

"Jess. Come here," Abigail called as she sat in the soil, working next to Kristen.

Jess reluctantly headed her way. She wished Abigail would stop attempting to involve her in their conversations when she wasn't interested.

"You'll never guess the news. Kristen's become a grandmother. Isn't that awesome?"

Jess wanted to reply that she didn't give a shit but thought better of it. "Wow," she said. "That's really great. Congratulations."

Kristen smiled. "Thanks, Jess. I really appreciate that."

Her response surprised Jess. It was so cordial,

easygoing even. They held each other's gaze for a moment, and in that time, signed an unspoken truce.

When Abigail and Jess were alone later, Abigail asked Jess, "I'm curious. Have you ever wanted kids?"

"Who me?"

"No," Abigail giggled. "The other girl in this cell. Of course, I mean you."

Jess was embarrassed. The question had taken her off guard. She sat down and rubbed her face with her hands. "I don't know. I guess I've never given it much thought."

"Well, you've got the equipment," Abigail teased.

Chuckling, Jess said, "It takes both pieces of equipment, if I'm not mistaken."

"What? You couldn't do it just for that?"

Jess made a sickened expression.

"You mean. You've never?"

"Been with a guy?" Jess answered. She shook her head no. She looked like she'd been grossed out.

"How do you know then?"

Jess was used to this question. It was a common one from straight people. "I've always known. It was never in question," she said.

Abigail looked to be digesting the information. Jess was thankful that by some sort of miracle she'd been able to have a relationship with her. Abigail hadn't even experimented with another woman in college, like some of Jess' other straight friends.

"I understand," Abigail said. "But if you ever change your mind, you could always go the artificial insemination route. You never know what the future holds."

That was the thing, though. Jess did know what the future held, and she wasn't going to be doing anything like that. Her reply was a simple shoulder shrug, a cue Abigail knew meant she didn't care to discuss a topic any longer.

*****

As the months passed, Kristen began to feel good about life. Her focus was on finishing her sentence and getting out to see Melissa. She'd received a few more photos, which she bore holes through, and had been informed of all the cute things the baby had done, her every move proving to be of great interest.

When Kristen thought about Jeremy, it was different than before. She still loved him, but it no longer mattered how he felt in return. She wasn't weighed down by the past, beating herself up over what went wrong. She didn't dwell on old memories, trying to analyze them for deeper meaning. She just loved him. It was like an expansive wave of warmth emanating from within, extending into the space around her. She had never experienced anything like it before.

Kristin stopped repeating her mantra too. It was no longer necessary. Things would work out however they were meant to, and that was okay. How these changes occurred within, she didn't know, but lately, she'd experienced zero stress. She could almost go so far as saying life was good.

If she was served with divorce papers, then she was

served with divorce papers. If her parents never visited and stopped sending money at Christmas, then so be it. To the outside world, it might appear she had stopped caring. Nothing could be further from the truth. She just stopped letting things bother her that she had no control over.

The joke that people on the outside sometimes made, that all prisoners do is eat, sleep, workout, and read books, that they haven't a care in the world, was finally true for her.

All due to a shift in attitude.

One day, Lakeisha stopped by to deliver a letter. She looked exhausted, like maybe working full time and having a child was becoming too much for her. Kristen used to think her job was kind of cool, like having a window into people's worlds. Now she realized it was probably a bummer. Lakeisha sure looked beat down today.

Kristen didn't recognize the sender. She'd never received mail from a stranger before, and like a kid in a candy store, she hopped onto her bunk, opened up the note, and read it.

Kristen,

I'm Debbie's old boss from the restaurant. I feel terrible I didn't handle this sooner. My sister, who Debbie was staying with, found your name and address after going through Debbie's things, and we thought you two might be friends.

Anyway, I'm so sorry to tell you this, but Debbie

passed away. It happened right after she got out. She was killed by a car that ran a red light while walking to work on her very first day back. We were so very saddened by the news, as she was a wonderful person. I considered her a friend.

Again, I apologize I didn't write earlier to inform you.

Sincerely,
Mark

Tears welled in Kristen's eyes as everything became clear. Poor Debbie, she thought while covering her mouth with her hand. Debbie was one of the sweetest ladies on the planet. She was always positive and full of encouragement.

Kristen sobbed. Life could be so unfair sometimes.

Kristen spent that night remembering Debbie. She thought about her past, all the terrible things she'd endured, and how she always looked toward the future. She remembered the treats she'd sneak from the kitchen, her passion for cooking, and the movies they watched every Christmas. She remembered her crush on Jimmy Stewart and how funny she thought it was until she realized he was the quintessential nice guy.

Sighing, Kristen thought about how there were no guarantees in life. One minute you were here, and the next, you were gone.

She was grateful she'd never had a bitter thought about her old friend.

After they'd lost touch, Kristen had continued to think of her often, hoping Debbie was in a better place.

Now she knew she was.

Chapter 32

Jess had one month left until being released. Abigail was sad, of course, but she didn't let it show, always wearing a brave face. She had meant what she said and wanted only the best for Jess. She was a rare, wonderful person, Abigail thought, and she wished she'd find someone much better to love, someone who might want to have kids and who could be a good parent. Jess had the rest of her life in front of her, and that made Abigail happy.

One night, after a mind-blowing lovemaking session, Abigail said, "I don't want you to get the idea I don't love you just because I want you to find happiness out there. I'm going to miss you, Jess. I really will."

Jess responded with silence.

Abigail was confused by her reaction. "You understand how I feel, right? You know I care."

"I don't think I'm going to leave," Jess answered in a low voice.

Abigail bolted upright. "What do you mean you don't think you're going to leave? You don't have a say in the matter."

"Don't I?" Jess asked.

Abigail raised an eyebrow. "What are you getting at? I don't like where this is going."

Jess sat up. "Don't worry yourself. I've got it all figured out. Just calm down."

Furious, Abigail jumped from the bunk. "You don't have it all figured out! And I don't like what you're insinuating. You'll leave here as scheduled and have a wonderful life. Understood?"

Jess giggled. "You're so adorable right now. I've never seen you this angry. It's kind of hot. Why don't you come back and give me a kiss?"

This only provoked Abigail's indignation. "Don't try and twist this into something cute. I'm really upset."

Abigail began pacing the small room, getting more worked up with each step. Jess sat in the bunk watching her, not seeming to take her seriously.

Abigail spun on her heel and faced Jess. "Whatever kind of plan you think you've hatched is a mistake. I won't allow it. Don't even consider anything like it."

Jess exhaled deeply. "It's my life, Ab. I can live it how I want. And I want to spend it with you."

"Ugh!" Abigail said, throwing her hands up in frustration. "Do you hear how crazy you sound?"

"What's so crazy about being in love with you? Tell me," Jess said, in a blatant attempt to try and turn the conversation around.

Abigail wasn't falling for it. Not for one second.

"Don't try and twist things," Abigail said, pointing her finger. "You're leaving here. End of discussion."

"Okay. Okay," Jess said. "I'll leave. Now, will you come back to bed?"

Abigail gave her a wary look, then padded back to the

bunk. Jess didn't like to be told what to do, especially by her girlfriend, but sometimes she just had to put her foot down. Like when she was right.

Once Jess snuggled up to her, Abigail asked, "Do you promise to leave?"

Jess held her and said she promised, but a feeling of trepidation came over Abigail.

*****

Kristen, Abigail, and the rest of the group were doing yoga when the commotion hit. Climbing back to her feet from a Downward Dog position, Abigail looked on in horror as she saw Jess on top of Shanice, beating her to a bloody pulp.

"Stop! Jess, stop!" she shrieked from across the field, but her cries went unanswered.

Guards came rushing in what looked like slow motion, their mouths barking commands. The two women ignored them, both visibly fueled with rage to finish each other off.

When Jess wouldn't stop bashing Shanice's head against the ground, a swirl of batons spun, clocking her from all angles. The officers tried to beat her into submission, but Jess wouldn't stop. Abigail saw that Jess was in the zone, releasing all the pent-up anger she'd held in for way too long. Jess glowed with exhilaration as her fists connected with Shanice's self-righteous face.

Alarms wailed in the distance. Tear gas came next. If they didn't respond to either of those or the rubber bullets, the tower guards were authorized to shoot for real. Only in the leg to stop them, but if they missed and someone died, well, there was one less asshole to deal with.

Every prisoner understood this possibility if they didn't adhere to the rules.

Luckily, the noxious fumes worked their magic, and both Shanice and Jess lay on the ground choking. When the smoke cleared, all Abigail could see was a bruised Jess being hauled off by two guards and a medic coming for Shanice, who lay unresponsive.

There was chaos on the yard as the remaining inmates were lined up and escorted back to their cells. Abigail was dazed. She couldn't believe Jess had broken her promise.

At dinnertime, Abigail wasn't hungry but went anyway to see if there was any word on Jess. As she waited in line, Kristen came up behind her.

"Hey," she said in a soothing voice.

"Hey," Abigail sulked.

"Someone heard an update on Jess, so I figured I'd pass it on," Kristen said.

Abigail perked up at the chance to hear news.

"Shanice is alive. She was just knocked out. And Jess is okay, but she has two broken ribs and a lot of bruises."

Abigail's voice shook, betraying the outward calm she tried to convey as she asked, "Where is she?"

A cafeteria worker dumped food onto Kristen's plate, and she slid her tray down. "Solitary. Not sure for how long."

A pain shot through Abigail's heart, and she accepted

what was slapped on her plate and followed Kristen to a table.

"What I can't figure out is why she'd attack Shanice now?" Kristen said. "Granted, Shanice is a massive bitch—no question—but Jess was getting out soon. All she had to do was play it cool." Kristen shook her head. "No offense, but I think that was a dumb move. She'll get more time for that stunt."

Abigail took a sip of her drink and nodded in agreement.

Indeed, she would.

*****

That night, Abigail lay alone in her cell. She was sad Jess had lied to her but understood the motivation behind her actions. Still, it was unacceptable. She couldn't allow Jess to ruin her life to stay with her. There was no way in hell she was going to let that happen.

As the hours ticked by, Abigail let herself be swept away by old memories. She remembered her childhood and how happy it had been. The first few times she rode her bike with her parents watching, making sure she didn't fall off, and them cheering her on in the background. The memory made her feel warm all over. It made her smile. She thought about the sugar cookies her mom used to make. No one could replicate her results. She'd been accused of adding a secret ingredient, to which she always laughed and said, "No. Really, I just follow the recipe." They tasted better because she made them. That was the special ingredient.

She remembered her ballet lessons and recitals. The shows were so much work, but it was her passion, and she loved it. The experience was made even more special because both her parents had never missed a single performance. They were always in the front row with their camcorder, smiling and cheering her on.

Abigail turned on her side and thought of her French teacher, Mrs. Lambert, one of the truly great educators at her high school. She'd made such an impact on her as a kid with stories of her visits to Paris and Cannes. Abigail's parents had taken her there on vacation, and they'd had a blast. They'd even managed to take in a ballet at the Paris Opera. The show was so beautiful that watching it was like stepping into a fairytale.

Life wasn't like in the storybooks, though. She'd learned that lesson.

When she was a child, she dreamed of having a future like her parents. A happy marriage. Children surrounding her and bringing her joy. Growing old with her husband, Steve. He had been a good spouse. He had always treated her like gold, and like her father, he called her his princess. What girl would have a problem with that, Abigail mused as she remembered his adulation.

Steve had only drifted away when the problems became too great. She used to feel despair and anger over it, thinking he was a coward, but she'd forgiven him. She realized that if the roles were reversed, she would have done the same thing.

Abigail still loved her ex-husband and always would.

Abigail's thoughts turned to Devin. The one she had loved the most.

There was no forgiveness for what she had done to him. And every single day, she was disgusted with herself for having gone through with it. He was just a child, a needy, defenseless child. She'd tried and failed miserably as his mother.

Usually, thinking about the past brought on a flood of tears. But today, she viewed all these memories as merely a series of events, like pages turning in a book. In the end, she was just a person who ruined people's lives. Everyone who loved her ended up hurt, dead, or immobilized. Steve. Devin. Her father.

Jess.

How many more people need to get hurt because of me? Abigail thought. Shanice could have died. What stunt would Jess pull next to remain by her side? Who else would get hurt?

Sighing, Abigail came to a conclusion, one she had been mulling over all day long. She had to take herself out of the equation. She had to make sure everyone she loved moved on.

She'd already done enough damage.

Just like that, Abigail made her decision. She stood up, squared her shoulders, and walked over to grab a pen and a piece of paper. She got down on one knee when she finished writing and said a silent prayer. Then she rose, pulled the sheets off her bed, and arranged them in a makeshift noose, attaching them to the top bunk in a way that would guarantee success.

Abigail's final thought as she left this world was of her beloved son, Devin.

Chapter 33

Laura approached the cell and took in the sight. "Damn it," she cursed.

There hadn't been a suicide in five years. Precautions were taken to prevent it, and if someone displayed depressive behavior, they were given meds and put on suicide watch. But Abigail had been a model prisoner, considering her crime. By all accounts—her work in the garden, her participation in the workout routines, even the way she interacted with other inmates—she had been doing fine.

"Take her down," Laura ordered.

As the guard fumbled to get the door open, Laura gazed at Abigail's tiny pale body. Suicide was a horrible thing, against her religious beliefs, and she wouldn't wish it on anyone. Yet there was a small part of her that felt, in this case, justice might have been served. Nothing sickened Laura more than a woman who could kill her own child. She would never share that opinion with anyone, of course, and she felt guilty for even having the thought, but there it was, a real feeling all the same.

While Abigail's body was being taken away, Laura saw the suicide note and scooped it up. She let the guards finish while she strode back to her office to handle one of the worst parts of her job, contacting the family.

She was not looking forward to that.

Laura propped her elbow onto the desk and used her hand to support her forehead. Then she began rubbing it in an attempt to ease the stab of an instant migraine brought on by stress. She couldn't remember the last one she had. All she knew was this one was intense.

She pulled her desk drawer open and rummaged through it, searching for medication. She didn't find any and let out an irritated sigh.

"Might as well get this over with," Laura said aloud, then opened her PC and searched for Abigail and her family's contact numbers.

When Laura saw Abigail's dad's name had Dr. in front of it, she cursed again. This wasn't going to go well. White-collar professionals asked a lot of questions. Especially doctors and lawyers.

She reached for the phone and dialed, and to her surprise, Abigail's father answered.

"Hi, this is Warden Laura Johnson calling. I'm afraid I have some terrible news to share."

"What kind of terrible news?"

"Sir, I'm sorry to inform you, but your daughter Abigail passed away last night. It was suicide."

There was no response from the other end.

"Doctor. Are you still there?"

"Yes," he finally answered in a shaky voice. "I'm here."

The rest of the conversation went fairly smoothly, and

when Laura hung up, she hoped Abigail's parents would focus on planning the funeral and saying goodbye to their daughter instead of placing blame on the institution she ran. They would meet when they came by to pick up her belongings, and she would once again offer her sincere condolences.

She hoped that would be enough.

*****

Jess sat in solitary confinement, trying to fall asleep. It was midday, and there was nothing else to do. She couldn't get comfortable because her ribs hurt, and the purplish bruises that covered her body were tender. She'd just about dozed off when a guard came to the door.

"Get up," she said, cuffing her without explanation.

As they walked toward Warden Laura's office, Jess inwardly smiled, satisfied her plan had worked. No doubt Laura was going to tell her she was in deep shit, that she'd have to go to court where a judge would charge her with battery, and she'd be given additional time.

She couldn't wait.

Warden Laura stood looking out the window with her back facing the door when Jess and the guard entered. After they walked in, she turned and said, "Have a seat," to Jess, sounding calm. Jess couldn't read Laura's mood. Usually, she glared at her with disgust, but not today.

Laura sat down at her desk and opened a large manila folder. "As you know, there will be consequences to your actions. It was a rather foolish move on your part."

Laura looked up from the file and made eye contact with Jess. "It's almost like you don't want to leave us," she said.

The expression on Laura's face made Jess uncomfortable.

"Here's the deal," Laura continued. "I'm going to add a charge of battery, and you'll have to go to court for the incident with Shanice. So it looks like you'll be staying with us a while longer."

Jess tried to contain her excitement and look tough. She was surprised at how easygoing Laura's demeanor was. She thought she would've been much harder on her.

Laura got up and nodded to the corrections officer, and then all three of them began walking back toward Jess' regular cell. Jess had no idea why Laura was coming along and grew fearful. Something definitely wasn't right.

When they arrived, the guard opened the door and uncuffed Jess. Then Warden Laura walked into the cell with her, and the officer stayed outside.

Jess began to panic.

Warden Laura reached into her pants pocket, pulled out a piece of paper, and handed it to Jess. "I believe this is for you," she said.

Jess took the note from Laura, unfolded it, and read what was written.

Jess,

I'm not going to let you ruin your life so you can stay here with me. I love you with all of my heart and want you to leave here and be happy. Promise me

you'll do that.
   Abigail

Jess felt her stomach drop. She looked up at Warden Laura, then around the room.

Abigail's things were gone.

Gripped by terror, Jess looked to Warden Laura for an explanation.

"I'm very sorry, Jess, but Abigail committed suicide last night. The guard found her hanging in her cell at morning check."

Laura nodded, and the officer standing outside opened the cell door, and she walked out. When the door shut, the sound was so final, so crushing, it killed every last bit of hope in Jess' heart, and she fell to her knees and wailed like she never had before.

Her life was officially over.

Jess wouldn't leave her cell for the rest of the day. Her broken ribs and bruises were the least of her pain, although constant crying had caused them to hurt even more. Jess lay on the lower bunk where Abigail used to sleep and sobbed. She hadn't seen this coming. She never could've imagined this.

"Oh, Ab," she sobbed. "How could you leave me? Why did you do this when I love you?"

Jess cried into the void expecting an answer, but all she got in return was a broken heart.

She lay in pain, remembering the first day she saw Abigail. She was a vision from Heaven. It had been love at first sight. And from that moment on, all she wanted to do was make her happy, even if it meant all they could ever be was friends. It was almost impossible to believe that her prayers had been answered. She used to feel she was the luckiest person alive.

Jess remembered Abigail's stiff neck and how she used to rub her shoulders, how she'd pace and bite her nails when she was stressed out. She thought of all the times they'd read aloud to each other. The adventures they went on right there in their cell. She almost smiled when she thought of Abigail's train wreck attempt to mimic a man's voice while reading that first time.

The memory of Abigail's provocative last dance surfaced, and Jess could still see every detail as clearly as when it happened. With eyes closed, she re-watched the sensual show, appreciating it all over again.

She thought of all the times she'd touched her, kissed her, every intimate moment they shared. She didn't want to forget any of them. Then she rolled over, buried her face in her pillow, and began sobbing harder. She couldn't accept reality, that Abigail was gone forever.

Jess couldn't fathom what it would be like to live in a world where she no longer existed. Abigail was everything to her.

Before lights out, Jess wiped her tears, dried her hands on her uniform, and read Abigail's note again. She read it several times in a row, hoping she'd obtain some message other than what was written.

She had killed herself so I wouldn't stay. How could she do such a thing? Jess wondered. How could she think she was doing it for me?

As darkness filled the room, Jess realized what she'd done with Shanice. Thinking she knew what was best for them had been a horrible mistake. Abigail had done the same thing. Only her decision made the matter final.

Jess remembered Abigail's words that night: "You're leaving here and living a happy life. End of discussion."

Jess had promised her she would.

Picturing her beautiful goddess hanging dead in the room horrified Jess. Abigail had sacrificed her very soul to make sure Jess moved on and lived a happy life. "Promise me you'll do that," she'd written.

But Jess knew she could never be happy again. She wouldn't be able to keep that final promise.

Chapter 34

Lakeisha, Laura, and Megan were eating lunch at the employee cafeteria when Megan said, "I think I might go to Abigail's funeral."

"Really? Why?" Laura asked.

"Personal reasons," she answered, looking pensive. "And I thought it might be nice if someone from here made an appearance. It would look good."

Lakeisha nodded. "That would be mighty kind. I'm sure her parents would appreciate that."

Laura seemed to be evaluating the pros and cons of the idea. "I think it's wise. I'll give you the time. No need to clock out or take a personal day."

"Okay. Thanks. I think I will then. I just feel like saying goodbye to her."

Without saying it, she'd said it all. Lakeisha knew how serious Megan was about her job. If she couldn't help someone, she took it personally. And Abigail had never been easy. She knew Megan had tried hard and hadn't made a dent.

After Megan cleared her tray and left for the restroom, Lakeisha said to Laura, "You know she feels responsible, right?"

"What? That's ridiculous," Laura said. "How could she feel responsible? Abigail hadn't been to a session in ages. Plus, she'd been acting fine. Not even on suicide watch."

"I agree, but you know how Megan is. She tried so hard to reach Abigail. She really wanted to help her."

"Hmmm," was all Laura said in response.

*****

Megan got the funeral information by contacting Abigail's father, Gary. Although clearly exhausted from grieving, he seemed thankful Megan would be attending. When she pulled into the parking lot, she could see why. There were hardly any cars. Not many people wanted to pay their final respects to a woman who had killed her child.

The place had dimmed lighting and smelled of fresh flowers. And as Megan walked in, she felt unease in the pit of her stomach. After seeing the trio of family members in the room, it was like she'd intruded on someone else's private world. Her reason for being there seemed trivial.

Abigail's parents rose when they saw her. They'd never met before, but it was probably easy to figure out who she might be. They came to meet her halfway.

"Hi, I'm Gary, and this is my wife Lois," Abigail's father said.

Megan put out her hand to shake theirs. "I'm Megan. We spoke on the phone. I'm so sorry for your loss."

The words caused visible pain on both their faces. And Megan's heart broke. She wished she could've done more for Abigail.

Abigail's parents introduced her to the gentleman sitting nearby, a little off to the side by himself. "This is Steve," Gary said. "Abigail's ex-husband."

"Nice to meet you," Megan said, studying him closely. He looked vacant, devoid of emotion.

Services hadn't yet begun, and it was customary to chat for a while. Instead, Megan found herself drawn to a pin-board of pictures displayed on a nearby table. There were photographs from all stages of Abigail's life. Baby pictures, childhood photos, some candid, and some while the family was on vacation. There were shots of her in ballet performances. A high school prom picture. And a wedding photo.

Abigail's ex-husband looked a whole lot older since that picture was taken. She couldn't imagine the toll of losing a child the way he did.

Then she saw photos of Abigail with a baby in her arms. The remaining ones were of the child, his parents, and the extended family throughout his short years, all smiling, looking like life was treating them just fine.

Megan knew better, though. It was never like that.

A priest walked in, and that was everyone's cue to take a seat. It would be just the four of them. As the priest began reading bible passages, asking them to pray along, Megan found herself tearing up. She listened to Abigail's parents sob one row in front of her, and it was all too easy to feed off their despair. Steve sat with his head down, silent.

"If anyone would like to speak on behalf of Abigail, I

invite them to do so now," the priest said afterward.

Abigail's dad rose, looked at his wife, who shook her head no, and then went up to the podium.

Gary cleared his throat and smoothed his jacket. "I'm here to talk about our daughter, Abigail. She was our only child, our beloved princess, and..." Then, losing composure and his voice cracking, he added, "and she always will be."

After pulling a hanky out of his pocket and wiping his nose, he continued. "She was a joy to be around and was loved dearly by everyone. She had lots of friends in her life, a husband, and a son, both of which I know she loved very much."

Steve sat expressionless as he listened.

"Our daughter wasn't perfect. She made many mistakes. Some of them larger than others. And still, we love her. Always."

As Abigail's dad stepped down, he wiped his eyes and looked at his wife, who shook her head no again.

There was a long silence, and then Abigail's dad turned and looked at Megan. She hadn't planned on saying anything, but under his gaze, she felt the weight of her guilt amplified tenfold, so she nodded yes.

Megan stood before them, unsure of what to say. "Abigail was one of my patients," she began. "I'll admit she was a bit of an enigma, one of the few I struggled to connect with, and now that she's gone, it makes me sad." She paused and considered walking back to her seat. What else was there to say? But then the words came to her. "Abigail was well-liked and had several good friends, especially Jess and Kristen. She'd taught some of the ladies ballet as a form of exercise and had done beautiful things in the prison garden. The flowers for my wedding came from the garden where she and the other women worked. They were beautiful flowers."

Megan stopped and nodded. "Truly beautiful," she added before returning to her seat.

The priest was about to walk back to the podium when Steve rose. Abigail's dad looked surprised.

Steve climbed the steps to the podium and cleared his throat. "My counselor and wife thought it was a good idea that I come today." There was a long pause, and when Steve spoke next, he was choking back tears. "They suggested I make my peace with Abigail."

Sniffling, and with tears rolling down his face, he said, "I loved Abigail once. She was my first wife and the mother of our son, Devin. And what I want to say is." Steve's voice cracked, and he couldn't get whatever he had to say out.

Everyone waited while he tried to pull it together.

"What I want to say is goodbye. And to tell you I forgive you."

Abigail's mother gasped and began sobbing. Her husband took her in his arms, and the priest went to the podium and put his arm around Steve, comforting him. Steve made his way back to his seat and waited while the priest said the final prayer.

When he finished, music began to play. Maurice Ravel's "Pavane for a Dead Princess." A solo piano piece that was hauntingly beautiful, befitting the woman whose life it was meant to commemorate.

Megan went up first, walking slowly to match the notes being played. Then, she kneeled down at the foot of the casket and prayed. In her mind, she said she was sorry she wasn't able to save Abigail and that she wished her happiness, wherever she may be. Then she rose and moved on.

Steve went next. He reached out and placed his hand on top of Abigail's. "Goodbye," he whispered.

Megan lingered in the doorway before leaving, and as the melody repeated and grew more powerful, she watched as Abigail's parents stood in front of the casket holding hands. They knelt in prayer, and Megan took a memorial prayer card from the basket, nodded to the priest, and left.

She was supposed to return to work for a half day but couldn't. She was too emotionally exhausted. So after getting into her car and pulling out of the parking lot, she called Warden Laura.

"Laura, I hope you don't mind, but I don't think I'm going to be able to make it back today. I'm spent. Would you mind if I take the rest of the day off?"

"No problem. That's no problem at all. Are you okay?"

Megan sighed. "I'm fine. It was just a lot to handle in one day. More than I bargained for."

There was silence on the other end of the line, and Laura said, "Understood. Thanks for going. That was over and above."

"No problem. I'll see you tomorrow."

Megan went home and lay down for a nap. When she woke later, she found she was still humming the piano piece.

Like Abigail, it was unforgettable.

Chapter 35

Kristen had heard the news of Abigail's suicide and was both shocked and saddened. She couldn't believe she'd lost two friends in such a short time. It just didn't make any sense.

What could have happened to make Abigail do such a thing?

Of course, there had been gossip. That Abigail had been depressed, that she'd snapped because she couldn't handle her life sentence. Others whispered it was because Jess was leaving, and she was heartbroken. Kristen didn't believe any of it, especially because half the crap was coming from people who didn't even know her. She'd find out soon enough, she thought, once she found Jess.

While working in the garden, Kristen felt lonely without Abigail at her side. She hadn't really known her all that well, but she was fun to talk to, and she seemed genuinely kind.

As Kristen snipped some dead branches, she sighed. Losing Abigail was so unexpected. Just like losing Debbie was. People were like tides that flowed in and out of her life.

*****

Warden Laura was nervous because Abigail's parents were on their way to pick up her belongings and had asked to speak to her. She didn't have a good feeling. And she wanted things to turn out well.

The phone rang, and she lunged for it. "This is Laura."

"Hi," the officer said. "They're here."

"I'll be right down."

Laura hung up, took a deep breath, and tried to calm herself. Not much made her tense, but losing a prisoner to suicide was just about as bad as things could get. It made her look incompetent. Plus, how was she to console the family? She never knew what to say.

A guard stood outside the meeting room and handed Warden Laura a bag containing Abigail's things.

Laura walked in and shook both their hands. "Gary, Lois," she said. "I'm so sorry for your loss."

The pair looked like they'd been depleted of all energy. They didn't seem like trouble at all.

The three of them sat down. "I guess we're still in shock. It's just so hard to take," Gary said.

Laura wore her most consolatory expression. "I can't imagine it," she said. "I have children of my own, and it's a terrible thing."

She was going to get down to business and turn over the personal items but noticed Abigail's mom was about to speak.

"We lost our grandchild, now our daughter," she said, her eyes tearing up.

Laura couldn't begin to comprehend the depths of their pain. She reached out and squeezed Lois' hand. Just a tiny bit to comfort her. An uncharacteristic act but one driven purely by instinct.

"You know what surprised us?" Abigail's dad said. "When the lady who works here, Megan, called and asked if she could come to Abby's funeral. And then how she got up and spoke about our daughter. That meant a lot to us."

"Megan was very upset over what happened to Abigail. She cares deeply for the inmates that have been her patients."

"She said Abby had friends here. She mentioned the names Kristen and Jess," Gary said.

Laura stiffened at the mention of Jess. Sexual relations between prisoners was against the rules. And a situation like theirs was a lawsuit in the making. As far as Laura was concerned, there never was a suicide note.

Playing it cool, she nodded and said, "Yes. Kristen and Abigail worked in the garden together. Jess was her cellmate and best friend."

They seemed to brighten a bit on hearing that, and Laura waited patiently, seeing if they wanted to talk more.

"Last time we saw our daughter, she seemed fine. We're just so stunned by all this. I mean, it's probably hard to live in a place like this, especially for life, but we didn't think…" Lois trailed off.

"We do our best to evaluate the women here. And you're right. Abigail seemed mentally stable. She was never involved in a fight. She followed all the rules. She was a model prisoner. No one was more surprised than me."

Abigail's mom began to cry, and her husband put his arm around her. "We should be going now," he said, nodding at Warden Laura.

Laura nodded back, slid the bag across the table, and asked him to sign the required forms.

"Again, I'm so very sorry," Laura said softly as she rose.

Gary nodded, too emotional to respond, and Laura watched as they left the room together.

Once it was verified they'd left the building, Laura went back to her office and shut the door. She didn't want to be disturbed for the rest of the day.

*****

Jess hadn't left her cell in days. She nibbled on candy, chips, and soda that she had in her locker but didn't have much of an appetite. The world had gone black, and she didn't care anymore. They could beat her, give her a life sentence, and put her back in solitary. She didn't give a shit. All she could do was think of Abigail and how much she missed her.

The sound of keys clanking caught her attention. Jess looked up and saw a guard.

"Time to get up. You have an appointment with Megan."

No surprise, Jess thought. She rose, walked over, and let the woman cuff her. On the way down to Megan's office, Jess squinted as the bright overhead lights seemed to penetrate the very core of her brain.

After they got to the office, Megan said, "You can uncuff her."

Jess sat down and sighed.

"You've had a horrible week," Megan said.

Megan didn't understand. She couldn't. But Jess knew the routine. She'd go through the motions.

"Horrible is putting it mildly," Jess mumbled while staring at the floor.

"I was very sad to hear of Abigail's passing," Megan said. She paused and added, "She was my patient, too. For a while, anyway."

Jess already knew that. She'd said therapy wasn't for her.

"I went to Abigail's funeral."

Jess' head snapped up. "You did?"

Megan had her attention now.

"How did it go?" Jess asked.

Megan sat up straighter in her chair. "It was a small gathering. Only four people. Abigail's parents, me, and her ex-husband."

Steve showed. She couldn't believe it.

"No one else came? No other relatives or friends?"

Megan shook her head no. "Her parents were distraught, as expected, and they'd put up a nice little display of photos showing Abigail at all ages of her life. There was a baby picture. Kid pictures in ballet costumes. Group family photos. Wedding pictures."

Jess got teary-eyed. "That's nice." She tried to wipe the

tears away, but they were falling too quickly. "I wish I could've gone."

"I know, Jess. I'm sure she would have wanted you there."

Megan handed a box of tissues to Jess.

Reaching for one with a shaky hand, Jess said, "I still can't believe she's gone. I'm devastated. She was…"

Megan sat listening, waiting.

"I loved her," Jess admitted.

Sighing, Megan said, "It's so hard to lose someone you love. I know what that's like, too."

Jess studied her, wondering what that was all about. She'd never say, of course, because therapists don't talk about their personal lives. Still, she was human too. Maybe she did understand.

"Will you tell me more about the funeral?"

"Sure," Megan said in a soft voice. "Her dad got up and made a speech, saying how much he and her mother loved their daughter and that they missed her, and I said a little something."

"You did? What did you say?" Jess asked. She was still sniffling but talking to Megan was helping. She had something new to focus on.

"I can't remember the exact words. Just that Abigail was a patient, one that I would have liked to have better helped. I mentioned she worked in the garden and had been involved in creating my wedding bouquet. I said she had friends here: you and Kristen."

"You mentioned me?"

"Of course," Megan said.

Jess smiled for the first time in days. Just a tiny one, but a smile nonetheless.

"Her ex-husband made the most touching speech of all."

She couldn't imagine what he'd said, and she waited for Megan to continue.

"He said he loved Abigail once and that he forgave her."

Jess' jaw hung open. Knowing what she knew and how he must have felt. That took a lot.

"That would have made Abigail very happy," Jess said.

Megan nodded. "I thought so. I could see it affected her parents deeply too."

Jess could picture them there and felt sad. She couldn't imagine what their life was like, how much they must be suffering.

"Oh, and they played the most beautiful music as we said our goodbyes. I'd never heard it before. I think it's on the prayer card. Let me check in my purse."

Megan reached for her bag and dug it out. On one side was a picture of Abigail, and on the other side was the prayer and chosen music with the date and location of the funeral.

"May I see that?" Jess asked.

Megan handed her the card, and Jess held it in her hand, admiring Abigail's photo.

God...she was as beautiful as ever, Jess thought. Her goddess. She didn't even have a picture of her.

"Pavane for a Dead Princess," Jess said, choking up. "I know this piece. I can't think of anything more fitting."

Megan smiled. "Why don't you keep that?"

Sobbing over her kind gesture, all Jess could manage to get out was a "Thanks."

"How about you come back next week?" Megan suggested.

Jess smiled through her tears and nodded yes.

Chapter 36

Okay, Kristen thought. Don't freak out. Stay calm.

She had a new cellmate. Someone she could never have imagined.

"Hey," Jess said. She put her things down. "I'm used to the top bunk so…"

Kristen nodded. "Cool. Have at it."

While Jess got settled in, Kristen felt uncomfortable. They hadn't spoken beyond the garden truce. Kristen knew Jess was madly in love with Abigail, and she thought Abigail cared for Jess too. All things considered, she felt it was best to leave her to her thoughts and not ask questions.

Lying in her bunk, Jess broke the silence within the first hour.

"I'm sure you know about Abigail's death," she said.

Kristen was pretending to read a letter. She set it down. "Yes. I heard. I was devastated."

"Me too," Jess said. "I can't believe she's gone."

Kristen couldn't imagine losing a loved one. Losing her spouse.

"I'm sorry you're hurting," Kristen offered.

Jess sat up and glanced down. "Thanks."

After another uncomfortable stretch of silence, Kristen spoke again. "I was so shocked by the news. I didn't know Abigail like you did, but she seemed okay. As okay as a person can be in this place, I mean."

"She had some issues, like we all do. Plus, she was a lifer. There's nothing good about that."

Kristen sensed there was more to the story but didn't want to push. "Well, I liked having her around. She was a lot of fun. That ballet shit was hard."

"She was fun," Jess agreed in a softer voice.

"How about how she learned to handle that wheelbarrow?"

"The thing was bigger than her." Jess smiled faintly. "She was in so much pain the first few days, but she got it. I knew she would."

"The ladies on the yard were in a world of hurt after she taught us ballet too. It looks so easy until you try it."

Jess' smile faded, and she looked down. "I wouldn't know. I never gave it a shot. She seemed to love it, though. She'd done it all her life."

Jess' voice cracked on the word life, and Kristen stiffened.

"I sure am going to miss her," Kristen said.

Jess' reply was a wave of tears.

Kristen didn't know what to do. She wasn't used to having Jess around or seeing her act like a normal person. Were it not for their history, she would have freely offered a hug. She was at a loss.

"I'm so sorry, Jess. I know you and Abigail were...close."

Jess was sobbing hard now. "I loved her," she admitted.

Nervous, Kristen got up. "I wish I knew what to say."

Jess wiped her tears. "There's nothing anyone can say. It just hurts so much."

Jess climbed down to grab some tissues. Kristen awkwardly put a hand on her shoulder to try and comfort her. It seemed like the right thing to do, and contrary to Kristen's expectations, Jess didn't pull back. She just nodded and then began blowing her nose.

After dinner, the two of them spent the rest of the night talking. Kristen mostly. She told Jess the reason she'd been sent to prison. She discussed a little bit about her childhood and her parents. She told Jess about her sons, the new grandchild, and the situation with her husband. She thought it might help Jess to take her mind off her problems and think of something else for a while.

"Kristen," Jess said later as they lay in their own bunks. "I want to apologize for the past. I can't believe I ever treated you that way. I'm so embarrassed by what I did. If I could go back in time, I'd undo it."

Sighing, Kristen said, "I think we all feel that way about things we've done in life."

She couldn't believe Jess had apologized. But her own response surprised her even more.

"That's nice of you to say," said Jess. "But still, there was no excuse. I'm truly sorry."

"Apology accepted," Kristen said.

And that quickly, the matter that had caused so much grief for so many years was officially closed.

*****

Visitation was not going to be fun this time around.

Jess didn't bother telling her mom about the broken ribs. What was the point in making it worse?

"Hi, honey," Jess' mom said.

She gave her a big hug, and Jess winced.

"What's the matter?"

"Oh, nothing. Just a little sore."

Jess' mom gave her a look of disapproval. "Maybe if you didn't fight with people, you wouldn't be sore. I see the faded bruises."

There was no way Jess was going to argue. She knew better. "You're right, Mom. I shouldn't have gotten into trouble. I'm sorry."

After Jess agreed with her, she seemed to soften. "So, sweetie. How are you? I've been so worried about you after what happened to your friend."

Jess let out an exhale. "It's hard, Mom. Like I said in my letter, I'm hurting like I've never hurt before."

Her mom sat opposite her looking helpless, and that made Jess hurt even more.

"I'm so sad you're not coming home soon. I was looking forward to it," she said. "And now, with what you're going through. I wish I could be there for you."

"I know, Mom. I wish I could be home with you too."

And she meant it. Had she known Abigail would commit suicide, she wouldn't have fought Shanice. She would've left when she was supposed to and continued to visit. She would've found some kind of life with Abigail, even if it wasn't the one she wanted. Now she had nothing. More than ever, she needed her mom and wished she could go home.

"Well, honey. We can't change the past," Jess' mom said. "All we can do is look toward the future. We'll be together soon enough, I guess. Two years isn't forever."

Jess nodded. Time went by faster as she got older. But now that Abigail was gone, time seemed to stand still. Like her life, it seemed to be going nowhere.

*****

Kristen had suggested Jess come back out onto the yard. Not to exercise or play ball but just to get some fresh air. Knowing she couldn't stay inside forever and that she'd eventually have to face Shanice again, Jess decided now would be as good a time as any. Might as well get it over with.

As Jess headed outside with her group, she felt eyes on her. She was a person of interest. Not only had she been absent from outdoor activities since the fight, but she had also been the cellmate of a suicide victim. Too drained from grief to care or feel nervous, Jess found a spot off to the side and sat down by herself. She alternated her focus between watching the ladies in the aerobics group and staring into her lap.

What's the worst thing that could happen? Jess mused. Shanice and her crew could jump her, and she'd get shanked?

They'd be doing her a favor. She was dead inside anyway.

But no one came to kill her, and in the end, the brief visit outdoors had done Jess good. Seeing the sun and the clouds in the sky made her think of Abigail. Would she be in Heaven? She'd read about the subject in her religious education classes years ago. Suicides don't go to Heaven.

Screw it, Jess thought. This time she wouldn't go with what was written. She'd go with what she believed in her heart.

Jess gazed at the sky and smiled.

"I know you're up there."

Chapter 37

Within a few months, Kristen and Jess became friends. Jess continued seeing Megan for help with the grieving process and kept her distance from Shanice. She'd stopped playing basketball and had taken up walking around the track instead.

Lakeisha stopped by with mail for Kristen. It was from Olivia.

"Probably more pictures of Melissa," Jess said with a smile.

Kristen perked up at the promise of an update on her granddaughter. She ripped the envelope open.

Kristen,

I'm afraid this letter is bad news. I've been putting off writing until I knew more, but now that I have all the facts, I'm letting you know.

Jeremy had a stroke. He's alive, but half his body is paralyzed. It happened a few weeks ago. He was treated and released, but without insurance, well, you know how it is. Also, I never told you this in the past because I didn't want to hurt you, but Jeremy had a girlfriend. She was around for a few years, but now she's gone. She'd gotten tired of waiting for him to get a divorce, but I think the stroke just put her over the edge. I mean, he's a burden to her now. I liked her okay, mostly because Jeremy did. But not so much anymore. The people that really matter don't run away when things get tough.

I apologize I never told you about her. I just didn't think it would be helpful for you to know. I hope you understand. Anyway, Ryan and Valerie are busy working and raising Melissa, so they can only help so much. Toby has been doing the majority of the work since he's still living at home. Between him and his girlfriend Erica, they've been putting in a lot of effort.

I went down to see Jeremy recently. He hasn't been able to work, so I helped him get signed up for disability. They were renting an apartment but just moved into a foreclosed home our parents bought for him. Thank God for all their help. Toby has gotten a part-time job while going to community college too, so the extra money comes in handy. I swear, it's such a disaster right now. It was tough seeing him that way— my big brother. I never expected things to turn out like this. I wish you were out and could take care of him. We could really use your help right now.

Love,
Olivia

Kristen sat down slowly, holding the letter in her hand. "It's my husband," she said. "He had a stroke."

"Holy shit!" Jess said. "Is he?"

"He's alive," Kristen finished. "But he's paralyzed on one side."

Kristen didn't break down crying. Instead, she began trembling. "My husband needs me right now, and I'm fucking stuck in here," she cursed.

Jess stood opposite her looking nervous.

"He needs someone, and the stupid bitch he'd been dating left him," Kristen said. She tossed the letter aside. "Can you believe it?"

Jess' jaw hung half open. "Maybe that's a good thing. Maybe you and your husband might still have a chance."

"I don't know. I'm not even thinking of that right now. I'm just thinking of all the nights I lay awake in my bunk, picturing her with my husband, spending time with my children. She was living my life, and I managed to let it go, you know. I accepted her. And now that he really needs her, the chick is gone."

Kristen threw her hands in the air in exasperation.

"Well, you don't have much time left, right?" Jess asked. "You can still help when you get out."

"Meanwhile, I have to sit in my cell while my youngest son takes care of my husband instead of focusing on starting his own life. What the hell was wrong with that lady? Why the heck didn't she care?" Kristen was so angry with her that she forgot to see the positive, that Jess could be right. She might actually have another chance with Jeremy.

Later on, after she'd calmed down and was lying in bed, she let herself wonder if that might be true. Who else could really want him and love him the way she did?

She stopped analyzing the situation. She'd done plenty of that over the years. Whatever happened, happened. That night, before she fell asleep, she said a prayer for Jeremy, asking God to give him improved health.

The following day, Kristen woke feeling her life had purpose. She reached for a sheet of notebook paper and wrote a letter to Olivia.

Olivia,

Thank you for letting me know what happened to Jeremy. It's awful. I'm so heartbroken. I wish I could be there to help. Please tell him when I get out, I'll be there for him, whether he wants me as his wife or just as a friend. I love him the same.

Has he quit smoking?

In regards to the girlfriend, I already knew about her. When the boys visited that one time, Toby slipped up and said something. Don't worry. It wasn't your place to tell me anyway. That would have put you in an uncomfortable spot.

I want you to know I appreciate all the times you've written and all the books you've sent. It has helped me more than you know.

Please take care of your health too. We're all getting older. It's scary.

Love,
Kristen

*****

Lakeisha smiled as she read Kristen's outgoing mail. She had changed through the years. A lot had. With Debbie's death and Abigail's suicide came sadness, but there had been plenty of joy. She'd had a child. Megan had gotten married. Lupe had left and started a family.

She only followed two stories now. Jess and Kristen's. The rest of the mail had become just mail. Maybe it was because her own family had given her so much. She wasn't sure. But she knew one thing. Her life was happy and full.

Warden Laura stopped by on her way out. She was carrying a stack of colorful brochures.

"What do you have there?" Lakeisha asked. It looked a bit more exciting than what she was working on.

"Stuff from the travel agent. We're planning a trip for my retirement. I know it's early, but we want to do it right. Plus, with a big family, you have to plan way in advance."

Lakeisha giggled. "You don't have to explain to me. If I were leaving, I'd be excited and planning way in advance too. So where are you thinking of going?"

Laura shrugged. "We haven't been out of the country yet, so the world is our oyster, as they say. We're thinking of Europe. We're looking into a tour so we don't have to learn how to drive on the wrong side of the road."

"Good idea. That way you can relax. It's coming up soon enough. Only a few more years, right?"

"Two more. Then I'm free," Laura joked. "Listen to me. I act like I'm incarcerated."

Lakeisha smiled politely. The truth was they kind of

were. Even though they got to leave at the end of the day, they still spent a large part of their life in prison. It took its toll emotionally and physically.

*****

After a long day of hard work out in the garden, Kristen and Jess lay on their bunks, exhausted.

"You ever gonna tell me what you're in here for?" Kristen asked Jess.

"I didn't tell you that yet?"

"Nope."

"Huh. I thought I did. Brace yourself because it's going to come as quite a shock."

Kristen waited.

"I beat the crap out of a woman I found having sex with my girlfriend. I almost killed her."

Laughter erupted from the lower bunk where Kristen sat.

"What's so funny? Too predictable?"

"No," Kristen said while giggling. "It was just how you prepped me and the way you said it. Okay, I admit it. I'm not shocked. I figured it was something along those lines."

Jess hopped down and sat on the floor. She smirked. "So far, you're the only one who found it amusing. The judge wasn't pleased, nor was my ex-girlfriend."

Kristen sat up. "I'll bet she wasn't. You know what? My husband has a temper like that. He's gotten into several big fights throughout his life. When I was sent to prison, he couldn't believe it. He had said if anyone was ever to go, he thought it would have been him. But he always managed to escape the law. Either the person would make up with him and not press charges, or he'd drive off and never see them again. You know, like after a traffic altercation. Stuff like that."

"Wow. That's lucky. The man has a shamrock shoved up his ass."

Kristen sighed and looked down. "Not anymore. He's not so tough now."

"Oh, shit," Jess said. "I didn't mean. I forgot. I was just saying—"

With a wave of her hand, Kristen shushed Jess. "Don't worry. I know what you meant. He was lucky. He really was."

Jess nodded, then got up and grabbed a book. "Hey, do you like to read out loud?" she asked Kristen.

"Not really. Why?"

Jess shrugged. "No reason. Abigail and I used to do it, that's all. I'd read a chapter, and she'd read a chapter."

Kristen thought about it. She wasn't much into that kind of thing, preferring to get lost in the inner landscape of her own mind while reading. It was a private thing for her.

"I miss Abigail," Kristen said. "She was a sweet person."

"I miss her every day. I wish things didn't turn out the way they did. I had hoped to stay here with her."

Kristen eyed Jess, and everything began to make sense. The fight with Shanice was a ploy—a way to get more time with Abigail.

Jess must have realized she'd slipped because afterward, she said she wanted to turn in early and call it a night.

Chapter 38

Olivia had been keeping Kristen abreast of all the news on Jeremy and Melissa. The baby was doing fine and couldn't be cuter, but Jeremy was still struggling. Not just physically, but emotionally. He wasn't used to needing anyone for anything, having always been pretty much a badass all his life. He was the one who stepped in and took care of problems. Not the other way around.

Kristen obsessed over one thing Olivia had mentioned in her most recent letter. She said Toby had asked his dad if he was looking forward to her release, and he had nodded his head yes.

She wondered what she was coming home to, what kind of relationship they would have. Would he regain the use of his arm and hand? Was he still angry? Maybe he just wanted her to be his nurse. If so, that was fine.

Kristen had run all these ideas by Jess.

"Man. I'll tell you. I know women overthink things a lot, and I know I am one, but I'm glad I don't suffer from that particular affliction," she joked.

"What do you mean? You don't think about stuff?"

"Of course I do," Jess said. "Just not like that. I don't let a bunch of worries swirl around my head at the same time. I tend to focus on just one thing."

She really was like a man, Kristen thought. Maybe it was hormones.

"I guess I've got too much time on my hands," Kristen said, hoping she wasn't annoying Jess. If she was, she didn't mean to.

"Why don't you just take it easy and see what happens? No matter what, it will be an improvement on sitting around here, right?"

"True," Kristen agreed. She had a point. "So, how about you? You're getting closer to leaving, huh?"

Jess nodded. "Yep. Time flies when you're having fun. No offense."

"None taken. Seriously though. I doubt you'll miss this place."

Jess looked conflicted. "All I'll miss are the good times. I guess like any other part of the past. That's all we end up missing."

Kristen thought about it. There had been some good times through the years.

"How are you doing?" Kristen asked. "I mean, with the counseling and with what happened before?"

Jess sighed. "I'm depressed, but I'm hanging in there. I'm actually about to go see Megan in a little bit."

"Cool," Kristen replied.

That afternoon, after Jess had gone to her appointment, Kristen was looking for one of her old books. She couldn't find it in her stack and decided to dig around. It had to be somewhere. It was a small room, after all. It couldn't just disappear.

After searching everywhere, the book was nowhere to

be found, but she'd stumbled on one of Jess' that she hadn't read. She picked it up, figuring Jess wouldn't mind. She climbed onto her bunk and got comfortable. Then, as Kristen opened it to the first page, a piece of paper fell from the center of the book. A note.

Jess,

I'm not going to let you ruin your life so you can stay here with me. I love you with all of my heart and want you to leave here and be happy. Promise me you'll do that.

Abigail

Kristen stared at the letter in disbelief, then recognition hit.

"Oh, my God," she whispered. Then, with shaky hands, she refolded it and put it back in its place before hurrying to return the book to where she'd found it.

"Christ," she said. She climbed into her bunk and tried to appear sleepy. Jess would be coming back soon, and she felt awful. She hadn't meant to snoop.

After five minutes, it was no good. She was too nervous. She got up and grabbed one of her own novels off the shelf, and then got situated and set the book aside. She'd pick it up and pretend to be reading once Jess returned.

In the meantime, her head spun. Poor Abigail, Kristen thought. How terrible and sad.

A chill ran down Kristen's spine, like she'd uncovered something she wasn't supposed to know. "Don't worry," she whispered aloud. "This secret stays with me."

Kristen heard footsteps coming. She lunged for her book and held it up to her face, trying to act casual.

She wanted to ask Jess how her visit with Megan went. She usually did or initiated some form of conversation, but not today. Instead, she found herself hyper-aware of Jess' presence.

Kristen let out a breath she didn't realize she'd been holding, and as she hid behind her novel, she let herself digest what Jess was going through, what she and Abigail had been through together.

It was like a star-crossed love story, she thought. So heartbreaking. And here she was, hitting Jess up with all kinds of mundane questions.

Kristen set her book down and asked, "How did your visit go?"

Jess let out a deep breath. "Good, I guess. The shit is just exhausting sometimes."

"I agree."

"You know how you asked if I like to read books out loud, and I said no? Well, I've been thinking. Maybe I'm missing out on something."

Jess managed a weary smile. "You never know until you give it a shot."

"You up for it now?" Kristen asked. "I could read from the beginning of this book today, and then if you like it, you can pick up where we left off tomorrow."

"Sure. Why not," Jess said.

"Okay," Kristen replied in an upbeat tone.

For the next hour, Kristen did her best to read out

loud in the hopes of cheering Jess up. She wasn't sure how she was doing as a narrator, but Jess' spirits appeared to lift as she listened to the tale. And for that, Kristen was grateful.

*****

Fall came, and with it, hurricane season. It wreaked havoc in the garden, and Kristen and Jess had a lot of extra work to do. Some plants needed to be covered, and others secured with sticks. Jess was getting ready to leave soon, and Kristen only had one year left on her sentence. Warden Laura had taken some time off for good behavior since she'd never been in trouble or broken any rules.

One cloudy day, Jess and Kristen walked the track together out on the yard. It looked like it was about to rain, and even though it was cooler, they were still drenched in sweat.

"Your mom must be happy you'll be home for the holidays this year," Kristen said.

"Yeah. She's psyched. I'm pretty excited too."

A clap of thunder sounded overhead, and Jess and Kristen eyed each other.

"We better run for it," Jess suggested.

The two of them sprinted back to the entrance, where they both leaned over, trying to catch their breath. A moment later, the rain came down heavy.

Kristen sighed. "I'm gonna miss you, Jess. I want you to know that."

Jess smiled. "I'm gonna miss you too."

*****

Megan reviewed her notes before Jess came for her final visit. Their recent sessions had proved therapeutic to her as much as they had to Jess. Megan had always wanted to know Abigail. She was the unsolved mystery, and now she seemed a little less cryptic. As far as Megan was concerned, the case on Abigail was closed. And she felt she'd made great progress with Jess.

After Jess was brought in and un-cuffed, she took a seat.

"Looks like we've come to the end of the road," Megan said. "At least our road together, that is. Yours is just beginning."

Jess smiled half-heartedly. "I guess it is."

"You've grown and learned more than most of my patients. And for that, I'm glad. I just hope you take all that knowledge and run with it. Live a happy life."

Megan and Jess held each other's gaze, and Jess's eyes began to tear. "Like Abigail wanted, right? For me to keep my promise?"

Megan couldn't help it. She got emotional too. "Yes. I think she would like that."

Jess sighed. "I'll do the best I can."

Megan smiled. "That's all anyone can ever ask from you."

*****

Kristen was sad as she watched Jess pack her things. She knew the drill. She'd gone through it all before.

"Your mom waiting out there for you?"

"Yes, she is," Jess said. "Going home."

"You're gonna write, right?"

"Of course. I'm a person of few words, though. Not prone to long letters. But I will for sure keep in touch."

Kristen had something on her mind. Something she'd wanted to ask Jess for a long time but never did.

"You never told me what Abigail was in here for."

Smiling a warm smile, Jess said, "No. I never did. But I think she'd prefer that be kept a secret."

Nodding, Kristen smiled back. "Understood."

And she did understand. Jess was a true friend and confidant. She loved and respected Abigail and protected her even in death.

Kristen stepped forward and wrapped her arms around Jess. "Take care," she said, giving her a bone-crushing hug. The only hug she and Jess ever shared.

Jess squeezed her tight. "You take care too."

*****

When Jess stepped outside, she noted it was cooler today, windy. As she began walking toward the car, her mom caught sight of her and got out. She jumped up and down like a kid in a candy store, and once they reached each other, they hugged each other tightly.

Afterward, Jess' mom grabbed her bag and shoved it into the trunk. She closed the hatch and glanced back at her daughter, and they exchanged a look. Then her mom got into the car, and Jess paused before climbing into the passenger seat.

Jess looked one last time at the prison building. She could never have imagined she'd think a faded brick enclosure surrounded by barbed wire could be a beautiful place.

But it was.

And she would miss it. The good times she'd had with her friends. The memories they made.

Most of all, she'd miss her one and only true love, Abigail.

Chapter 39

The holidays were lonely for Kristen. She hadn't gotten a new cellmate, and everyone she knew and liked was gone. Her parents still deposited the Christmas money, which was nice. She realized that despite all their faults, this was a way of saying they still thought of her. And she'd gotten a card from Lupe. She was doing great, and everyone in her family was healthy. She was still loving Las Vegas.

Jess had sent her a book and a card. In it, she'd written that she and her mom were remodeling the kitchen and that she was still trying to readjust to life on the outside. She was looking for a job so she could save some money but still hadn't found one. She said it wasn't always easy but that she was doing well. "I'm learning how to hope again," she'd written.

Kristen smiled after she read the note. She had no doubt in her mind Jess would figure things out. And she told her so in her return letter, thanking her for the book.

Ryan and Valerie sent a card, and they'd included the latest picture of Melissa. Ryan wrote, "Can't wait 'til next Christmas, Mom. We'll be spending it together."

Kristen couldn't wait, either.

She'd also gotten a card from Toby. He and his girlfriend had broken up, and he was devastated, which made Kristen sad. She knew how much pressure he was under taking care of his dad, and now this. She wished she could hug him and tell him everything would be all right, but he'd have to learn that on his own. Like she did. That always seemed to be the best way.

Olivia had sent a book, a card, and a letter. Kristen had so enjoyed the letter she sat down to read it again.

Kristen,

I hope you're doing okay this Christmas. Last one there, thank God. I'll bet you miss your friend Jess. I'm glad you two were able to mend things and end up on a positive note.

Now for the holiday gossip. It's cool that you know about Cindy so I can share this with you. Anyway, you know how she left when Jeremy got paralyzed? Well, she recently came back. She wanted to make up with him and said she was sorry, but he wasn't having it. He may have trouble speaking now, and it sounds slurred, but he still has a way with words, if you know what I mean. I guess he asked her to leave and said he didn't want to see her again. He said he couldn't count on her. Toby said she cried and made quite a scene.

Bob said hello. He said we'll see you next year at Christmas. Happy Holidays!

Love ya,
Olivia

Kristen thought of Cindy and, for the first time, felt sad for her. Maybe she wasn't a bitch after all. Most likely, she was a nice person who had just gotten overwhelmed and made a mistake. It happened. She knew she'd made a few mistakes herself. In fact, at this point, she probably held a PhD in fucking shit up.

Kristen laughed at the idea even though it wasn't funny. She was fond of saying if you couldn't find humor in things, you'd go insane. There were murderers who had gotten less time than her, but she'd stopped trying to figure that out or appeal her sentence. She just served her time the best she could. And now here she was, leaving pretty soon. Maybe it was good she was alone this Christmas. Next year, she wouldn't have anyone to miss or say goodbye to.

The months passed quickly and without incident. No one got shanked, no one committed suicide, and a sense of monotony seemed to have set in. But in a good way.

All Kristen had to do was sit and wait.

And think of the surprise Olivia had in store for her. Olivia said she would be the one to pick her up when she got out and that she'd take her home after they went somewhere together first. One more day wouldn't change things, she'd said. Only she wouldn't say where they were going. She had left Kristen hanging in suspense.

There had been some good news in the last month too. Toby had scoured the internet and watched YouTube physical therapy videos. With the information he'd gained, he worked with his dad, and to everyone's surprise, there was a mild improvement. Jeremy was slowly regaining movement in his hand. Kristen was amazed at what could be found online now.

A month before Kristen was set to leave prison, she got a letter from Jess.

Kristen,

Bet you're excited as heck to leave. I wish you luck, although you're not going to need it. I'm sure everything will turn out great. You'll see.

Things are going better for me. I finally found a job at a school as a maintenance person. You know how I like to fix stuff. It pays decent and has benefits.

Oh, there's one other thing. I met someone. She's a teacher here, and she's really nice.

Jess

Kristen smiled after she finished reading.

Abigail would like that, she thought.

*****

The day had finally come for Kristen to leave prison. She had dreamed what it would be like. Wondered where she'd go and what she'd do. Now all those questions would be answered. She didn't know what the future held, but she knew where to start.

A guard stopped by, and she looked up. "You have an appointment with Megan," she said.

"That's odd," she said aloud. She hadn't set one up.

When she arrived in Megan's office, the guard uncuffed her, and she sat down.

"Didn't think I'd let you leave without saying goodbye,

did you?" Megan asked.

Kristen smiled. "That was nice of you. I would've made an appointment, but I don't like to take up your time. I know how busy you are."

"Never too busy for important patients," Megan said. "So, how are you doing? Are you good? Is there anything on your mind you'd like to discuss before you go?"

Sighing, Kristen said, "I guess I am pretty nervous. I've been gone a long time. I don't know what to expect. Part of me wants them to jump for joy and would love a big party with balloons and streamers, but part of me wants it to be low-key."

"Your family is probably just as nervous as you, just as unsure how to welcome you back. How about this: when you get there, try to go with whatever they've planned. Don't have any expectations."

"I'll do that. I want them to be comfortable, even if I'm not. I'm worried about seeing Jeremy, though. It's been such a long time." Kristen hadn't told Megan of the stroke, so she didn't bring it up now.

"Take it day by day. That's all you can do," Megan said. She paused and added, "And how do you feel about drinking? Any thoughts?"

Kristen shook her head. "I don't think about it much. But I'm not sure how I'll do when I have access to it. I want to think I'll never touch it again. That's what I hope."

"Don't forget, there are support groups. You can find one just about anywhere. But you already know this. I know you'll do well."

"Thanks, Megan. I really appreciate everything you've done for me."

The session ended, and Megan stood and reached out to shake Kristen's hand. "Good luck," she said.

"Thanks," Kristen said, letting her hand go. "Thanks for everything."

The next morning, Kristen filled out all her paperwork, changed out of her uniform, and was handed a small bag of her belongings. After stepping outside, she spotted Olivia, and they ran toward each other. They hugged and laughed and squealed like teenagers.

"Hop in," Olivia said, throwing Kristen's bag in the back seat.

Kristen opened the door and climbed in, and after slamming it shut, they sped away, the interior of the vehicle filled with the sound of bubbly, girly chatter.

Kristen never looked back. She'd already said goodbye to everyone she cared about and was ready to move on.

"Holy shit, you're buff!" Olivia said. "You look awesome!"

"Thanks. I've had plenty of free time to work out."

"You never had a problem with weight."

Kristen giggled. "One of the few things I didn't have a problem with."

"You want some gum?"

"Sure."

Olivia handled the steering wheel with one hand while rummaging through her purse with the other. "Here you go," she said, handing her a piece.

After popping it into her mouth, Kristen asked, "So

are you going to tell me where we're going?"

Olivia grinned. "You'll see soon enough. Trust me."

They continued their easy conversation like they'd only just seen each other last week and were catching up. Within a half hour, they pulled into the parking lot of a fancy hotel.

"What's all this?" Kristen asked.

"Just a little treat. I figured you might like a nice meal, a good night's sleep, and some pampering."

Kristen was overwhelmed and started to get teary-eyed. "Oh, my God. You've really outdone yourself. I had no idea."

"That's why it's called a surprise," she said. "Now, let's head in. There's more."

The two checked in and went to their room. It was a junior suite decorated to the hilt with crisp white linens, white roses, sheer white floaty drapes, and a massive jetted tub.

"I figured you'd like to get cleaned up in private, maybe take a bath and chillax," Olivia said. She walked to the side of one of the queen beds and pulled out a shopping bag. "I got you a few new outfits too."

Tears spilled from Kristen's eyes. She was overjoyed.

Olivia handed her the bag. "Take your time. There's no rush. We have dinner reservations at six. You still like filet mignon?"

Kristen nodded yes and smiled brightly. She hugged Olivia. "Thanks for this," she said, then skipped to the bathroom with her bag.

Once inside, Kristen slipped off her worn and out of

style old street clothes. She picked up the hotel shampoo that was displayed on the side of the tub. She took off the cap and inhaled the delicious fragrance, a combination of floral and a spice she couldn't place. A whole lot better than the bar of soap she'd been given to wash her hair with in prison or the generic shampoo she could buy at Canteen.

Kristen filled the tub with water and turned on the jets. When she climbed in, she let out a satisfied sigh. That was more like it, she thought. No one sitting on the toilet nearby. Some privacy. Finally.

After soaking so long she'd pruned, Kristen decided she should probably get out. She didn't want to, but there was the steak dinner still, and she was equally excited about that. So she forced herself up, reached for a fluffy towel, and then wrapped it around her head and put on the robe they'd so kindly hung on the door.

Kristen heard a light knock.

"Come in," she said.

Olivia poked her head in. "I forgot to give you this." She handed her a bag from Sephora.

Kristen pulled the contents out. Some makeup, hair products, and a mini perfume.

"That's from Cocoa," Olivia said before Kristen could put a sentence together.

"Cocoa shops at Sephora?" Kristen teased.

"Of course. Only the best for that cat!"

Kristen shook her head. "I'm blown away. Thanks so much. This is amazing."

Olivia smiled. "Don't worry about it. Enjoy. I'm going

to watch TV while you're doing your thing."

A half hour later, Kristen emerged from the bathroom wearing one of her new outfits. When Olivia saw her, she sat up and smiled. "That's the sister-in-law I know and love. Now let's eat. I'm starved."

Once seated at the upscale steak house, the waiter arrived to take their drink order. "Here's the wine list," he said, handing it to Kristen.

There was an uncomfortable moment, but Kristen diffused it. "None for me, thanks. But I think Olivia might want a glass."

Olivia hesitated.

"Please," Kristen said. "Order whatever you usually get. Don't worry."

Olivia took Kristen's suggestion and went with a glass of Pinot noir. Kristen chose a Coke. When the drinks arrived, Kristen found the scent of the glass of wine still appealed to her and remembered Megan's advice to join a support group. She would definitely do that, she thought. Soon.

After chatting for what seemed like only a moment, the steaks arrived. Kristen cut into hers and took a bite. The sound she made was almost indecent.

"It's good. No?" Olivia asked.

Kristen was still chewing. "I think it's the best steak I've ever eaten."

*****

After an incredible night's sleep, it was time to check out.

Kristen thought they were on their way to Jeremy's place, but Olivia had told her not yet.

"You mean there's more?"

Olivia grinned. "One more stop. Then you'll be ready to go home."

They drove to an upscale hair salon, and Olivia parked the car.

"We have to do something about your hair and nails. I'll be honest. They're awful."

They hadn't had the best haircuts in prison, and styles had definitely changed. Kristen nodded. "You're right. I really do need help with this," she said while flipping her hair and making a disgusted face. "How can I ever repay you?"

Olivia waved her hand in front of Kristen, shushing her. "C'mon," she said. "You've got an appointment."

Two hours later, Kristen looked like a beautiful woman again. She already had the figure, she just lacked the necessary polishing. Now she was back in business, with blonde, shoulder-length hair, freshly polished nails, and wearing one of her new outfits.

Kristen looked in the mirror and nearly cried because she almost didn't recognize herself. Or maybe it was that she finally did.

"You ready to go home?" Olivia asked her.

Standing straighter but feeling nervous, Kristen replied, "I sure am."

Chapter 40

Kristen had prepared for this day thousands of times. She knew it would be overwhelmingly emotional for her, and probably for her family too, but she didn't want it to be. She wanted to play the role of a calm, happy mother, one that could just be returning home from a trip to the grocery store. That might make it easier, she thought. She wasn't sure she'd be able to pull it off but having the new outfit and hairdo helped build her confidence a little. Fake it until you make it, or so the saying went.

Olivia pulled up to the house. It looked similar to the one they had before, the one they had lost.

A knot formed in Kristen's stomach, and her chest grew tight.

Relax, she thought. You have nothing to fear.

Kristen took a few deep breaths that she knew Olivia could hear. Luckily, Olivia pretended not to notice. Maybe she was on the same page. Make this a simple thing, low-key. Kristen opened the car door, and her hands were visibly shaking. She felt the tears coming but willed them back through sheer force. She wouldn't ruin her beautiful makeup for anything. Not today.

"I'll get your bags from the trunk," Olivia said softly.

Kristen couldn't find her voice, so she nodded.

An all-out panic attack gripped Kristen as they got closer to the door. It opened before they knocked, and Toby stood there, looking all grown up.

"Hey, Mom!" he cried out before giving her a big hug.

Kristen wrapped her arms around him and squeezed him tight. She hadn't seen him in years. She loved him so much that she never wanted to let go.

"Ow! I can't breathe," he said. His comment made the three of them laugh, bringing a bit of relief from the tension.

"Sorry, honey," Kristen said as she smiled. "I just love you so much."

Toby looked into his mom's eyes, more serious now. "Love you too, Mom. Let's go in. Everyone's waiting."

Kristen nodded and then followed him into the house. When she stepped into the foyer, she saw a very grown-up Ryan. He looked like a man now. Next to him stood Valerie, and wobbling to her side was Melissa.

The three of them came toward her, all smiling.

"Mom. This is my wife, Valerie," Ryan said.

Kristen extended a hand. "Nice to meet you."

"Don't even," she said, giving Kristen a big hug and kiss. Then, when she pulled away, she added, "We're family now. No need to be formal."

Kristen smiled brighter. She was trying her best not to cry. So far, she was succeeding.

"I always wanted a daughter," Kristen admitted. "No offense," she said to Ryan.

Ryan giggled. "I knew that. But now look who you've got to spoil," he said, lifting Melissa.

Kristen's heart swelled so large it almost burst from her chest. "Hello," she said in a baby voice. "So nice to meet you."

Melissa looked unsure and hid her face in Ryan's chest.

"Ah, don't worry. She's just shy. Once she spends some time with you, the two of you will be inseparable."

That was music to Kristen's ears. She could think of nothing she'd like more.

"Would you like something to drink?" Valerie asked. "We have soda, water, tea, lemonade."

"Lemonade. Thanks," Kristen replied.

As she walked away, Olivia took Kristen's bags and set them down next to the sofa. Kristen did a quick scan for Jeremy and didn't see him. Then Ryan stepped forward and hugged her tight.

"I missed you, Mom," he whispered. "Glad to have you back."

"Missed you too," Kristen replied. This time her voice cracked a bit.

Valerie returned with an ice-cold glass of lemonade, and Kristen took a sip. It tasted amazing. She had taken such simple things for granted before. No more. She would savor everything she ate, drank, or did from now on. Unless one had been imprisoned, they could never understand.

"Let me go get Dad," Toby said. "He was just resting after his medication."

"I'm up," a slurred voice said from behind them.

Everyone turned to look at Jeremy. He'd started

walking more and more but still had trouble with his arm, his hand, and the side of his face.

Kristen's heart stopped beating, and she froze. She was rooted in place. Jeremy walked up to her slowly and said, "Hi."

"Hi," she replied.

There was an awkward silence, and he added, "Your hair looks nice."

Olivia seemed to swell with the pride of her own genius.

Kristen blushed and said, "Thank you."

There was a moment when she didn't know what to do next. Should she hug him? Wait for him to hug her? She was filled with confusion and anxiety.

"Who's hungry?" Olivia asked. "I was gonna order pizza."

A flood of "I am's" filled the air, and Kristen relaxed her shoulder muscles a fraction of an inch. She was still so nervous.

"Mom. Let me show you your room," Toby said.

Kristen had assumed she'd be sleeping on the sofa. She hadn't expected her own room. When Toby opened the door, a few tears managed to escape. They'd taken some of her old things and decorated the room so it looked like her bedroom from before. They'd painted the walls a warm tone and hung her framed prints throughout. Her favorite Pier 1 lamp sat on a nightstand. The bedspread looked new, yet it coordinated perfectly. Kristen had a gut feeling this might be Olivia's doing.

"You like it?" Toby asked.

"Do I like it?" Kristen sighed. "I love it. I'm so happy. You have no idea."

"Cool," Toby said as he looked around the room. "Aunt Olivia did this a few days ago."

Kristen smiled. "I had a feeling."

The doorbell rang, and a teenage boy with droopy jeans stood holding three pizza boxes. Olivia paid him, and shortly afterward, everyone was seated around the table, munching contentedly. Kristen felt like she'd died and gone to heaven. The spicy flavor of pepperoni danced on her tongue.

"I imagine that's tasting pretty good right now," Jeremy said, eyeing Kristen.

She nodded. "Like the best pizza I've ever eaten."

Jeremy smiled and took a sip of his Coke.

The rest of the evening, Kristen caught up on family news. She listened intently, preferring not to share much of her own story unless asked. Olivia sat with Jeremy on the sofa, and eventually, Melissa warmed up to her grandma.

As the night drew to a close, Olivia announced her flight would be leaving soon. Ryan and Valerie had offered to take her to the airport.

Olivia pulled Kristen aside. "How are you doing? You okay?"

"I think so."

Olivia grinned. "Well, you look fabulous while trying to seem calm."

"You think they can tell?"

"Nah. They don't have a clue."

"I've rehearsed this one a few times."

Olivia smiled. "Call me. Text me or email me. Toby will show you all the latest gadgetry."

"I wish you didn't have to go," Kristen said.

Olivia pouted. "I know, but I have to. I'll be back at Christmas. Besides, my work here is done."

Kristen hugged her goodbye. "You're the best sister-in-law ever."

"I know," she joked.

Kristen thought Olivia looked a little teary-eyed too, but she didn't let on that she noticed. If she wanted to appear calm, Kristen thought it best to let her leave that way.

"Later, chica. Love ya."

"Love you too," Kristen said.

*****

Months passed, and Kristen learned to settle into her new life. She'd taken a load off Toby, and he was thrilled. He hadn't said it, as he wasn't the complaining type, but she could see how happy he was. He'd found a new girlfriend and practiced his guitar more while going to college and working. His plate was full now but not overflowing.

Two days per week, Kristen babysat Melissa. One day so Ryan and Valerie could have time alone, and one day so Valerie could work. Kristen had also applied for a part-time job at a health club teaching a fitness class and was waiting to hear back. She continued sleeping in her own room while helping Jeremy. She hadn't gone into the situation expecting anything more, so she wasn't disappointed. She'd gotten into a routine: cooking, cleaning, babysitting, and helping her husband. It was quite a bit more domestic than her old routine, she thought, remembering her scandalous past.

It felt nice.

The holidays were approaching, and Kristen bustled about setting up the tree. She strung lights and added ornaments in just the right pattern to create balance. She lit an evergreen candle on the kitchen table to add to the holiday mood.

As she hurried back and forth like an elf, she felt Jeremy's eyes watching her. She ignored him and continued with her work.

"It looks nice," he said, his voice still slurred but improving.

Kristen stopped what she was doing and looked up. "You like it? I wasn't sure if I'd done too many of the oblong ornaments. I was thinking of moving some."

Jeremy smiled. "Come here," he said.

Kristen walked over to him.

He looked at her, and she felt her skin prickle.

"It looks perfect. Just like before. You always knew how to do the holidays right."

The compliment made Kristen beam. She was about to say thank you, but he chimed in before she could.

"I've been meaning to tell you something," he said, looking serious.

Kristen waited. There was a pause that felt like eternity.

Jeremy's eyes got glassy, and he continued. "I've been meaning to tell you I never stopped loving you all this time. I was just angry. Do you understand?"

Kristen's eyes filled with tears as she nodded her head yes.

Jeremy leaned in to kiss her, and when their lips met, it was like old times. Kristen felt like she was floating.

Later that evening, with the family room bathed in colorful blinking Christmas lights and the house smelling like a pine forest, Kristen climbed up on a step stool and added the gold star on top of the tree. As she climbed down, she had a satisfying thought:

There was a difference between hoping for a second chance at life and actually getting one. And that tiny distinction made all the difference in the world.

Chapter 41

Lakeisha got situated at her desk to start the day. She was pregnant again, and this time it just happened without even trying. She had all her Christmas shopping done and wrapped a month prior. With prison mail growing by the day, it took all the energy she had just to complete her job.

After opening a few letters, scanning for contraband, and resealing each with a single piece of tape, she saw something odd. A card addressed to her.

It was from Kristen.

Curious, Lakeisha opened it. It was a Christmas card with a note inside.

Lakeisha,

I've been thinking about you lately and how you read the mail all those years. I never got a chance to say goodbye.

I just wanted to say things are going great for me. I've reunited with my husband and have been spending my days with my family. I hope your holidays are wonderful too.

Kristen

Lakeisha set the letter down, and a satisfied smile crossed her face.

There was nothing she liked more than when one of her stories had a happy ending.

Thanks for reading *On the Inside*.

I hope you enjoyed it.

Your FREE book is waiting.

The Rescue is the heartwarming story of the dog that cheated death and transformed a woman's life.

Get your free copy at the link below.

Send My Free Book!

To get your free copy, just join my readers' group here:

kimcano.com/the-rescue-giveaway-lp

Books by Kim Cano

Novels:

A Widow Redefined

On the Inside

Eighty and Out

His Secret Life

When the Time Is Right

Novelette:

The Rescue

Short Story Collection:

For Animal Lovers

About the Author

Kim Cano is the author of five women's fiction novels: *A Widow Redefined, On the Inside, Eighty and Out, His Secret Life,* and *When the Time Is Right.* Kim has also written a short story collection called *For Animal Lovers.* 10% of the sale price of that book is donated to the ASPCA® to help homeless pets.

Kim wrote a contemporary romance called *My Dream Man* under the pen name Marie Solka.

Kim lives in the Chicago suburbs with her husband and cat.

Find Kim Online:

Website: www.kimcano.com

On Twitter: @KimCano2

Facebook Fan Page:
facebook.com/pages/Kim-Cano/401511463198088

Goodreads:
goodreads.com/author/show/5895829.Kim_Cano

Made in United States
Troutdale, OR
10/30/2024

24290823R00179